Where the Black Line Ends

Where the Black Line Ends

MEAGAN WILLIAMSON

For Abby

*And for anyone who intimately knows the meaning behind a
reason, a season, or a lifetime.*

Dear Reader,

I started writing this book back in February and typed "the end" before the summer even began. I imagined myself in June, July, and August sitting on my patio as the sun set while I edited these pages. But that's not what happened. Instead, I glanced out the window from my second-story desk, gazing at an endless haze of smoky sky.

Summer of 2024 has been a devastating season for Idaho fires. To the forest service crews who have tirelessly fought to keep this beautiful state from burning, thank you. I hope my admiration for the people who work in this industry translates on the page.

As a work of fiction, liberties were taken with situations and experiences that may not otherwise occur in a job like this one.

Where the Black Line Ends contains sensitive topics including forest fires, parental loss and abandonment, accidental death, (side character) cheating, and on-page intimacy. If you prefer closed-door modifications, you can skip the second half of chapters 25, 34, and 41.

Thank you for reading Reed and Hailey's story!

Meagan

A wildfire can change in a second.

A gust of wind.
A clap of thunder.
A rain shower.

It sweeps the ground, creeping up trunks and crawling through tree crowns. One moment it's insignificant and the next, an inferno of blazing light. In the hottest season, in the densest backcountry, it feeds off oxygen, adopting a life of its own. Only surrendering to the perfect combination of nature and nurture.

They told me to be ready for anything. Prepared me for the worst-case scenario. But they didn't tell me my life wouldn't be the same. They never said the fire would change *me*.

PROLOGUE

Reed

12 years old

"So, do you love it?"

My mother towers over me, her hand pressed to my shoulder as I cradle the wooden handle of a switchblade. A Diamondback mountain bike, a VR headset, six packs of football cards, and a pair of Nike Air Force 1s form a U-shape among a pile of wrapping paper scraps surrounding me.

I run my thumb down the dark walnut, studying the smooth texture and brushing over initials carved near the butt of the handle—*SM*.

I lift my gaze and find my father watching me from across the living room, his shoulder tipped against the arched entrance. A smile stretches across his face—something resembling pride— as he pushes off the wall and strides toward me.

"Yeah, son. What do you think?"

By the way he's looking at me, I think it must mean something to him. I stare down at my gift, and my eyebrows sink into a deep V.

"SM?" I say as he stops in front of me.

"Samuel Morgan. It was your grandfather's."

I look up again and find him smiling at the pocketknife.

Do I ask him about it? We don't talk about personal things like this, but I'm curious. Grandpa Morgan is a man I never met. At least not that I can remember. He died of a heart attack when I was three.

How old was Grandpa Morgan when he got it?

Did he carve his own initials into the handle?

When did he gift it to my dad?

Dozens of questions swirl in my mind, but I get stuck on one: *Why did my dad gift it to me?* I'm not even the oldest.

With the sun spilling through the front windows, the sliver of metal wedged between the wooden exterior glints. I press the release button, deploying the blade. The sight of it takes me back to the beginning of the summer when I met my best friend, Miles. We spent nearly every day fishing off the dock between our cabins. Whenever a line snagged on the bottom of the lake, he'd use the razor edge of his pocketknife to cut it free.

I smile at the memory.

"I think that's a yes," she says, pointing to my face.

"Oh." I startle, my daydream turning to smoke. "I do."

"That's good because I have one last surprise," he adds.

By anyone else's standards, getting showered with gifts on your birthday is something to celebrate. For me, it feels like an ordinary day. A new video game left on the counter on a Friday night with a note that says *Have fun.* An automatic pitcher because my dad isn't around to play catch. An Apple Watch to reach us if they need anything. My parents use material possessions to cover up the fact that they work all the time.

They own a family practice law firm with our neighbors, the Browns, and have made it their life's mission to help other people through their problems. Yet somehow, they miss the ones right under their roof. Like the fact that I've spent most of my life feeling invisible to them. I could do what's expected of me or say the right thing and it's not until I do something reckless that they pay attention.

But today is different.

Today I think things are destined to change.

Because today, they surprise me with the kind of attention I never expected.

"You and I are going camping this weekend!" Dad thrusts his arms out wide with his announcement.

I fumble the open pocketknife but steady it before it clatters to my bare feet.

Camping? We've never been camping before.

My parents bought a cabin in Bear Lake at the beginning of the summer. It was the closest thing to ever come to that, but it had cell service. They could still work there. Camping's different. No phones, no distractions.

"Just the two of us?" I gape at him, trying to imagine it... No Rex, no Ronny.

"Yep. Just me and you, kid." He claps a hand on my back, and I jump up to hug him. Of all the gifts that have ever made their way into this three-story house, this is the best one I've ever been given.

"Woah!" He backs away from the open blade that's swinging near his face.

"Sorry." I cringe. I disengage the lock with my thumb and fold the sharp edge back into its safety position.

My dad's voice remains playful, but his expression slips into a semi-stern glare. "Don't make me regret trusting you with that."

"Yes, sir." I salute him. "I promise; I won't."

"Good. Well, we better start packing. We need to be on the road in an hour if we want our tent set up by nightfall."

I shove the switchblade in the front pocket of my basketball shorts and leap from the couch cushion toward my bedroom.

I picture it. A whole weekend away, just me and him. His undivided attention. Time to tell him about all the things that I love.

It's going to be the best weekend of my life.

A camping trip I'll never forget.

CHAPTER ONE

REED

Present Day

Beep. Beep. Beep.

"Sir, I'm going to have to ask you to remove your shoes."

A woman in a crisply pressed security uniform points to my boots. There's an edge to her tone that suggests uptight but no bite, so I'm not at all surprised when I look up at her and she blushes under my eye contact.

Airport security is the last place you'd find an adrenaline junkie like me. But I wasn't the one who booked this flight. That man is the whiner behind me lacking his typical TSA PreCheck privileges. The same one who was so bent out of shape that he confronted what had to be the burliest security officer Salt Lake City Airport has ever employed—a guy with little tolerance for sob stories, even from an attorney at Morgan & Brown with frequent flier miles.

It may make me a heartless son, but I get a kick out of watching him squirm. Which is exactly what Emmett Morgan did when said officer pointed us in the same direction as the other 95 percent of the population flying out of this airport today. *High five, airport security, for the comic relief.*

But that was thirty minutes ago. And after listening to him relentlessly drone on, I flung my canvas duffle bag on top of the conveyor belt and cleared the metal detector in a single stride.

At the sound of that beep, maybe I should have taken my time.

"My bad," I say, flashing the officer the cheeky grin women tend to swoon over and backing up through the archway.

Even if she looks a decade older than me, her reaction is a familiar one. Getting women to notice me has never been my problem. It's getting them to stick around that I struggle with. But I'm not worried about that right now. All I need to do is to keep this lady happy enough so I can be on my merry way.

It takes a minute to loosen the laces on my new Whites, the premium leather manacled to my ankles and feet. Of all the items that came recommended by my recruiter, these all-terrain boots were at the top of the list, and I can see why. Once they're on, they fit like a second skin.

She watches me jerk the rubber wedge heels and toss them on the rolling bars before plunging through the opening a second time.

Beep. Beep. Beep.

The sharp ringing stuns me. Not in a hit-to-my-confidence sort of way—even if I wasn't expecting it—but more like *What the hell could I have possibly missed?*

"Your, um"—she fumbles over her words and nods to my lap—"belt. Sir."

I don't have to look down to remember the leather band I strung through the loops of my khaki denim this morning. I simply hold her stare and unbuckle it, watching her eyes heat and then blink a handful of times in the ten seconds it takes me to pull it off.

I have to admit, I enjoy this part of flustering women. The amount of control I feel. It's a hit of adrenaline I haven't found a replacement for. The exact opposite of that feeling slaps me across the face when I clear this machine a third time.

Beep. Beep. Beep.

This time she looks embarrassed. Like she feels bad for me. As if she's taking pity on some kid who can't read the signs plastered all over the walls—no sharp objects, handbag restrictions, 100 ml rule. Gigantic signs, with bright yellow borders and bold red letters. Impossible to miss unless you're someone who is distracted because the girl you love broke up with you less than seventy-two hours ago and you need to get the hell out of town.

I startle at a firm tap.

"Sir, I'm going to need you to follow me," demands a sturdy security officer.

That's when it hits me—the switchblade in my back pocket. I found it in the top drawer of my nightstand when I was packing my bags this morning. It seemed like a smart thing for a hand crew recruit to bring at the time. Only, I didn't anticipate forgetting to transfer it into my checked bag.

"Listen, man." I chuckle. "It's not what it looks like."

"Arms in the air," he barks, and I extend them up like the limbs of a tree, adding a good two feet to my already six-foot frame.

He begins at the top of my right arm, waving a wand down the front of my body and up the other side before swirling it in front of me in a gesture to turn around. I do what he asks, and the wand reacts ten seconds later when it hovers over the back pocket of my pants. The officer pats my ass.

"Like what you feel?" I say as his hand dives into my pocket and fishes out the object.

Whether or not the blade is extended is irrelevant as he jabs it in the air and pins me with a glare.

He reacts quickly, gripping me by the arm like I'm a common criminal. His other hand closes in on his gun holster.

"Looks like a concealed weapon to me," he scolds, jerking me in the direction of a nearby door. Ten strides later, he pushes it open and reveals an interrogation room. It's dermatologist white. Empty, minus a round camera attached to the far corner and a single foldout chair and table. A long beam of light stretches overhead.

I glance behind me, my dad gaping from the other side before I'm shoved into the opening. He mouths, *What the hell*, as the heavy metal seals shut.

"What are you doing with a concealed weapon?" The officer circles my body like a starved vulture.

"Well, it's not concealed anymore, is it?" I wink at him. By his beady eyes and scowl, that was the last thing I should have said.

He shoves me down onto the metal seat and continues his pacing in slow, even strides.

"What's your name, kid?"

I let my gaze follow his dance.

"Reed Morgan."

He grabs a clipboard from the table. Jots something down—I'm assuming my name—then tucks it under his arm. He stops in front of me, bending at a forty-five-degree angle to look me in the eye.

"Why do you have a knife on you, Mr. Morgan?"

If he's trying to scare me, it's not working.

"Used to," I remind him.

"Excuse me?" he spits.

It's entertaining how personal he's making this encounter. Mad at a complete stranger for not following his trusty rules.

I smirk at his hand. "I *used to* have a knife on me."

He tracks my gaze and squints. Then a sly smirk twists across his lips.

"Is that how you get everything you want in life, Mr. Morgan? Attention?"

I don't know, if I were to flag that female security officer over here, would I be able to get out of this situation?

"Pretty much," I say.

He inches closer to my face, his stare drilling a hole through my forehead.

"I was kidding." I hold my arms in a goal post.

Jeez this guy is uptight. This is exactly what happens to people in a job like this. Like the one my father has. They forget that life shouldn't be taken so seriously all the time. They forget to have fun! I refuse to get like that—in a dead-end job doing the same shit every day. It's not me. I need stimulation. Adventure. A challenge.

"The way I see it, you have two options, Mr. Morgan. You can either cooperate and answer my questions, or I can go ahead and slap you with a civil penalty and you can forget about your flight today. There are rules for transporting weapons. I know I don't have to tell you that knives are prohibited on an airplane. Or maybe I *do* since you seem to act like the rules don't apply to you."

I roll my eyes. "I forgot it was in there, okay? I got a last-minute job out of McCall. I'm looking at a six-week camping trip and thought it would come in handy. I never meant to leave it in my pocket."

He blows out a gust of air. "What job requires you to camp?"

"Wildland firefighting."

His smirk settles, and he straightens. "Consider this your verbal warning then. Don't expect to go through an airport checkpoint without anticipating that every part of you will be checked. Understand?"

I nod.

"You can go." He motions for the door and the metal feet of the chair drag against the cement floor, the sound echoing off the walls like a prison cell.

"And my knife?" I ask.

I doubt that I'm getting it back at this point, but it belonged to my dad. Add it to the long list of ways in which I disappoint him.

"You should have checked your pocket, kid," he says.

Thought so.

He tugs on the exit door, propping it open with the toe of his boot. I meet the eyes of the next obstacle in my journey on the other side.

"Keep it real, officer." I salute the guy.

Was that a chuckle?

Regardless of the consequences, it makes me feel like I won. Like I might've made this guy's day a little less dull.

"What the hell, Reed?" The door isn't even shut before he's closing in.

"What?"

"Your pocketknife? Are you *insane?*"

A wicked smile lances my face. "Thought we could do a little sparring on the flight like those old Indiana Jones movies you love so much."

"You mean the plane we almost *missed* because of your little stunt?"

"First of all, it was an accident. And second, I'm still getting on it, aren't I? It's not like I said screw it and bailed. I just had a hang up." I shrug.

"A hang up that cost you a family heirloom!" he shouts.

I sigh. That part I feel bad about.

"I know. And I'm sorry."

"Dammit, Reed. It's not just that it was sentimental. It's that you never take anything seriously. There are consequences for your aloof behavior."

"Wait—" I hold out a hand, stopping him. "I'm sorry, aloof behavior? I spent the better part of last year preparing for this. Getting my red card, training to be in the best shape of my life and applying to every open slot on the western coast that usajobs.com listed. Then yeah, I didn't get hired at the start of the season. It wasn't my fault that every position got filled with someone other than a rookie."

I think back to how different my summer would have turned out. I'd planned to be fighting wildfires, not going back to the small town in Bear Lake where I'd see *her* all of the time.

"I get that, but it didn't stop you from getting distracted all summer either."

He's talking about Teddy. I know he is. But I'm not about to hash out my feelings for my ex-girlfriend with him right now. And it pisses me off that he can never seem to notice or acknowledge any of the good things I do.

"You mean the summer I spent working doubles at your new restaurant?" I argue.

He glares at me. "I didn't know guaranteeing you a paycheck was such a trial. I didn't see your brothers complaining."

I shake my head. *Unbelievable.*

"You'd like that wouldn't you? Rex, the strait-laced, rule-abiding son with the aspiring law degree, or Ronny, the baby of the family who, despite wanting to spend a summer back-packing around Europe, can do no wrong."

I want to add *I'm not just your middle child but your middle finger. The one you want to flip the bird to the world for. To pretend I didn't happen.* But I bite it back.

"Reed, I didn't mean—"

"No, I think it's pretty obvious what you meant. Well, don't worry. I won't be the thorn in your side for much longer." I start to walk away from him, then stop. "But just for the record, you're making it sound like I sat around freeloading off you all summer, which is simply not true."

I pick up my pace, passing a community restroom, several gift shops, and a Cinnabon before he stops me in front of an illuminated Starbucks sign with a sigh. A long, heavy, weighted one. Deep enough to drop the conversation.

"We have ten minutes," he says. Another way of reminding me how ill-equipped I am at keeping track of time. He motions inside the coffee shop. "Do you want anything?"

What I *want* is to get to this job in my own way—without him in tow. But now we've got two booked flights, and we're way past our usual banter.

I shake my head. "No thanks. I'll just meet you at the gate."

The fact that I'm turning down a pastry should be enough to show him my commitment to this. That I'm not screwing around with this opportunity the way I did my first semester at Idaho State.

I partied. Skipped classes whenever I was hungover. I didn't understand why Teddy wouldn't message me back after her car accident. I thought it was because I didn't stay. I visited her in the hospital the night it happened, but my parents were worried I was getting in the way. I knew she was healing from a traumatic brain injury, but she didn't wake up for seven days. It was the end of summer, and I had to make a decision for my future. I committed to going to Idaho State. Paid tuition with the hope that she'd eventually join me there. I didn't know she'd need an entire year off the grid to recover, or that she wouldn't even remember I existed.

The memory loss was not something I saw coming.

By the second semester, I got my act together and tried to move on. Drove forty miles one way to the Downey Volunteer Fire Department every Tuesday night for eight weeks. I took a two-hour wildland fire course there. Not to mention the hours I logged training: pull-ups, push-ups, chin-ups, trail runs, all for what's on the other side of this flight.

Besides a raspberry milkshake from LaBeau's this summer, eating as clean as possible was a choice I made a long time ago. A commitment to myself to be ready for this. I'm not about to blow that streak on a sugar-induced coma from a whipped cream–covered Frappuccino and a chocolate croissant.

He drops his gaze to the leather band fastened around his wrist and mine follows. The shorthand is clinging to six a.m., which means he'd better hurry.

"I'll meet you at the gate in five minutes then," he says, jogging over to the line that snakes outside the confines of the store. The one that screams *You're gonna be late.*

I push forward, passing gates ten and eleven before double-checking my boarding pass.

Gate 16.

It's another quarter-mile walk before I sink into the nearest empty chair and drop my head in my hands. The length of my trimmed hair between my fingertips feels foreign. The sandy brown ends no longer curl up over my ears after the haircut I got on a whim last night. It was necessary though. Where I'm going, there'll be no barber of any kind for a while.

The terminal starts to quiet with my head dipped low. Here I was thinking I'd breathe a sigh of relief the first moment I had to myself. But now that it's finally here, I'm in the middle of a crowded space as lines from a letter I wrote just forty-eight hours earlier replay inside my mind, suffocating me.

CHAPTER TWO

REED

12 years old

Two hours later, I'm waiting in the hallway outside of my dad's office with a backpack sagging the shoulder it's slung over. The zipper bulges in sections, and there's a gaping hole that won't close on one side. I made sure to slip the pocketknife in the one on the back.

Through my paned-glass-door view of my dad's office, I watch him scuff his loafers in a jovial gate against the carpet. He circles his desk. Loud laughter seeps through the crack in the door.

"I'm so glad you can come. It's been a long time," he says to the person on the other end.

Who is he talking to?

I drop an irritated glance at the Swiss Army watch fastened around my wrist. We should have left an hour ago.

"Sounds good. See you soon." He hangs up the phone and plants his palms on the edge of the desk, leaning over his computer. He squints at the screen as he pulls at the top drawer, taking out a pair of cheater glasses.

"Dad, are we leaving soon?" I holler into the room, not moving from behind the door's entrance.

He stops what he's doing and looks up at me through the lenses that have slipped to the bridge of his nose.

"Oh, hey. Just finishing up some work stuff. But..." He pounds on the keyboard for a few seconds and then hits the power button. "There. All done."

Finally.

"You ready for McCall?" he asks.

With a backpack carrying everything but the kitchen sink and a lifetime of waiting for this moment, I'm ready for anything. I've never heard of McCall, but I don't care where it is we're going as long as the Avalanche's tires leave the garage.

"Born ready," I say, leading the way.

Five minutes later, my mom perches her palms over the driver's-side window.

"Did he say yes?" she asks.

"He did."

"You boys have a good time then." She leans through the frame and kisses him on the mouth. "And tell Jack I say hi."

Jack?

"We will," he says.

He punches our destination into the LCD screen on the truck's dashboard.

The GPS system configures the route: a squiggly line about six inches long that ends with a dot labeled *Lower Payette Campground.*

He backs out of the driveway onto our street, and ten minutes later, we're cruising down the interstate.

This is it. Our time to get to know each other. I better use it wisely.

"Hey, Dad, have you ever heard of Silverwood?"

He grips the steering wheel at ten and two. "Isn't that the

new coffee shop they just opened up by Sundance Mountain Resort?"

"That's Wood River Brewing."

"Oh. That's right. Then no. I've got nothing."

I drag the zipper open on the front pocket of my backpack. It catches three quarters of the way across, and I have to pry it open with both hands. Rolled up with a rubber band is the brochure I found at All Caught Up. Miles's dad's fishing shop has a rack of pamphlets next to the checkout desk, and this one has a wooden roller-coaster on the cover. Every seat is filled with people of all ages, their hands in the air.

"It's a theme park near Coeur d'Alene." I show him the image, and he steals his eyes from the road to glance at it.

"That's your idea of fun?" He cringes.

Should it not be? I stare at the truck's dashboard until it blurs into a mirage of the ride. I feel the rush of the wind on my face as I crest the highest peak. The plummet in my stomach as I tip over the edge. The thrill of the speed and the twist I never see coming near the end.

"Yeah," I say, a grin on my face. "It is."

My dad brushes off the idea with, "Coeur d'Alene is a long way from home."

I study the map on the screen. The city name is even further than our current destination. Four hours to be exact.

I guess it is, I realize. But his response still feels more like an excuse than a legitimate reason.

Will it always be like this? The two of us so different? Miles and his dad have fishing. Maybe camping will be what we have in common.

We stop once to refuel but then push through the long trek until we're pulling onto a gravel road. A carved wooden sign welcomes us to the campground. He traverses a winding gravel road until he pulls up next to another truck, and I squint at the silver exterior.

"Are you sure this is it? Looks like the spot has already been taken."

"I invited my friend Jack to meet us for the weekend," he says.

Jack, I repeat inside my head. I wrap my arms around my waist.

He brought someone else?

"Jack's an old client and a good friend of ours. He lost his wife a long time ago, and, well, he's been through a lot, him and his daughter. I thought he could use a guys' weekend."

It's always the same story with him. Someone else who's been through a lot. *What about me?* I want to scream. *I'm going through a lot too. Do you know what it's like struggling with algebraic expressions and not having a parent to help you through your homework at night?*

"But you said..." That it would be just the two of us, my memory fills in. He did say that, right? I freeze, sifting through this morning's conversation.

"Just the two of us?"

"Just you and me, kid."

The exchange I overheard from his office doorway replays next, and it stuns me the moment I recognize that he changed his mind.

My dad turns off the ignition and faces the passenger seat. "Come on, champ. You'll like this guy. It'll be fun. You'll see."

Fun? What's fun about feeling like the leftovers you eat in your fridge for the fourth day in a row because no one's been around to cook anything new?

I can't believe I let myself hope that this time would be different.

Present Day

Dear Miles and Teddy, I hope when the two of you find this one day, you're stupid happy. The kind that makes getting out of bed in the morning the best part of your day, knowing you get to spend it with your favorite person.

I thought sitting at that booth at the Bear Shore where I worked with her all summer, putting pen to paper while staring out at the lake one last time, would provide closure. But like some form of twisted torture, my brain memorized the damn thing. It repeats the lines like I need to remember *why* I'm happy for them, *why* I was willing to walk away, that I meant what I said.

"Good morning, Delta passengers flying Salt Lake City to Boise. We're now boarding Zones A and B."

I scan the ticket resting in my lap.

Of course he bought first class.

I stand up and make my way to the growing line of passengers. There's an elderly woman in front of me wrestling with the handle of a flimsy straw bag. She's dragging a rolling suitcase with a broken wheel too, her carry-ons stealing her attention.

She shuffles a few steps when the line scoots forward and loses control of one of the straps on the floppy bag. Half the contents spill onto the floor.

I do not have time for this.

She pivots to the side to assess the mess her worthless bag made and shows off her profile. Silvery permed locks serpent around her blue eyes and sweat beads above her wrinkled brow as she stares at the pile of her spilled belongings, like she's a magician able to will them back where they belong. Either that or she's questioning how important the contents are to her. I wouldn't be surprised if she's contemplating leaving them behind entirely.

As much as I want to board this plane—like, yesterday—I can't do that with her blocking the entrance. My dad and his overpriced beverage might miss it, but I won't.

I drop to a squat next to her things. "Mind if I help?"

At first she flashes me an irritated glance. I don't blame her when I'm just another stumbling block in the mountain of obstacles trapping her attention. But when she registers my question, all of that frustration melts away.

"Oh, that would be a delight, young man. This old frame isn't what it once was. If I were to bend as low as you right now, I'd never get back up." The deep grooves in her face crinkle even more with her warm smile.

"I'll be there one day myself I'm sure, so I have to lend a hand while I still can." I wink.

My hand sweeps across the floor, gathering a travel-sized bottle of Cetaphil lotion, an unopened package of Kleenex, a tube of lip balm, and a notebook with— I freeze. The pencil tucked in the binding transports me somewhere else, and another fragment of that letter comes back to me.

For as many summers as I can remember, you both were that for me. I gave this letter to your parents, Teddy, and told them to tuck it someplace meaningful, so that when you found it, it would feel more like coming home than saying goodbye.

"Oh dear! It's happening younger and younger these days. Must be the pesticides in our food," the old woman says as I gather my wandering thoughts and stuff them back and in their proverbial box.

With the objects collected in the palms of my hands I look back up at her.

What was that she said? Something about pesticides?

"I didn't think it would happen to such a muscular fellow like yourself. Look at you!" She gawks at my biceps before sweeping her gaze toward the desk two feet ahead of us.

"But don't you worry! Security will be here in a jiffy. Don't ask me how I know that." She points her index finger at me and winks.

I blink a handful of times, trying to recall what I'm doing crouched on the floor at this woman's feet, when she shuffles her white tennis shoes across the swirl of blue-and-gray patterned carpet, her suitcase catching air every time it tips on the side with the functioning wheel.

The waiting attendant reaches out her hand. "Ma'am, I'll take your ticket."

"Oh, no," she starts to say, but then leans in close and whispers something in the gate employee's ear, who flashes an amused grin my way.

"I'll get right on that, Dolores," she says.

Only then do I straighten and quickly close the gap in the line.

This Dolores character looks up at me with a start, and I drop her items back into her bag.

"Oh good! You're okay!" She grins.

Okay would have been a guy not stunned silent at the sight of a notebook, but I don't tell her that. As sweet as her demeanor is, she's a stranger. She doesn't need to know that one of her belongings catapulted me back to the moment I had to walk over to Teddy's front door one last time to hand-deliver a goodbye I hoped would never come.

I smile at Dolores instead. "Yes. I'm sorry. You've caught me on an off day."

"Oh boy... traveling on an off day is never good. Those are the kind when you forget your passport."

"Or a knife in your back pocket," I mumble to myself.

"What was that?" she hollers, the pitch of her voice fighting to keep up with the ambient noise of the terminal.

I clear my throat. "It's nothing. Why don't I carry those onto the plane for you?"

She grins, letting the bag slip down her arm and bundle at her feet. "If you say so." She abandons her suitcase handle without hesitation and shuffles her way down the jetway.

When I turn back to the attendant, she's sizing me up like a Marvel character with his shirt off.

"That was really sweet of you," she croons, her bright yellow ponytail swishing as she reaches for my ticket, brushing our hands together in the process.

It has the opposite effect she intended—an unfortunate prickling down my arm. I took this job in part for the new adventure, but mostly because it's miles away from the opposite gender.

"Thanks," I get out.

She finally looks down at her hand, and her panicked gaze flits toward the empty jet bridge. "Her boarding pass..."

I grab her arm and stop her. "It's okay, I'll take it to her."

Her eyebrows pinch together and she chews on her bottom lip. "I could lose my job for this."

What is she going to do... make the poor woman hobble back out here? Abandon this long line of people and take it there herself? No. Neither option is worth it.

"I won't tell anyone if you don't." I wink at her.

Her gaze drags down my face to my outstretched ticket, hiding her blush. "Thanks. Looks like you're in row two. Window seat." Her fake eyelashes flutter up and down.

I nod, needing to tug the two tickets out of her hand to get her to let them go. I feed Dolores's straw tote over the handle of her dilapidated suitcase and lift it off the ground.

The walkway is already empty by the time I board, and I glance over my shoulder one last time but still don't see my dad.

I hope he misses this flight.

I'm met with the stuffy smell of recycled air as I cross the plane's threshold and exchange a greeting with the flight attendant manning the door. When I turn the corner, I find Dolores, fixed in the middle of the aisle. The poor woman slides on spectacles that hang around her neck by a strand of glass beads and scours the floor.

"It's got to be here somewhere," she mumbles to herself, trying her best to rotate clockwise in the cramped space.

I squeeze down the aisle with her straw bag slung at my side—a terrible decision as it clunks into a sweater-covered shoulder on my left.

"I'm so sorry," I say to the passenger—a woman whose face is hidden by a layer of brunette bangs. She's distracted by her phone, and I'm past her before she ever meets my eyes, holding out the boarding pass beneath Dolores's glasses.

"Looking for this?"

CHAPTER THREE

HAILEY

It takes a full-on elbow hit to drag my attention away from the unopened text on my screen. That's what I get for booking this flight last night and getting stuck with an aisle seat. I never fly.

Travel has not been on my list of to-dos the last few years, unlike being close to home.

Even on my best day here, McCall, with its small-town cozy cabins and endless blue sky, is always on the forefront of my mind.

But who am I kidding. The landscape has nothing to do with why I quit my job on a whim this week. An EMT position opened up on Iron Summit, and I put in my notice with the University of Utah Hospital before even applying for the position.

Who *does* that? Someone desperate enough, I guess.

If I'm being honest with myself, I'm moving back there to be close to *him*. And I'm sure that overstuffed bag from the aisle won't be my last wakeup call reminding me how pathetic it is to leave everything at the drop of a hat for someone who doesn't want me around.

A frustrated huff echoes behind me, and I abandon my phone in my lap to see what all the fuss is about. A man with carry-ons stacked on his forearms like bracelets towers over a senior lady with a petite frame. His right arm locks at the elbow as he extends a flimsy piece of paper in front of her face.

"There it is!" she exclaims, grabbing it by the corner. It shakes beneath her unsteady fingertips as she studies it inches from her nose.

"Oh, for cripes' sake," she complains, moving it back and forth like it's under the seat of a microscope. "Do they always use twelve-point font on these things?"

He cranes his neck, surveying the rows of seats near the front of the plane, and I sink a little lower.

The sight of... *something* causes him to smirk, and a dimple the size of a crater sinks into his right cheek. My heart dips at the sight. He is window-display good-looking. In fact, I bet he's modeled for a Lululemon swim line with a tan like that.

"Good news!" he exclaims. "You're in row two!"

The lady studies her ticket with a confused stare. "Isn't that first class? I can't afford to be in the front."

"Well..." He lifts her off the ground like a statue and pivots her 180 degrees, bags tilt-a-whirling at his sides. He ushers her along in an impatient push. "It looks like today is your lucky day."

Why is this guy in such a hurry? In fact, his eyes are flitting around the cabin in the world's most nervous dance. I've memorized this look. It's the same one every first date I've ever been on gives right after they feed me the famous line. The one about how their dog's been stuck inside their apartment all day and needs a bathroom break. They scan the restaurant, flagging the nearest waiter for the check. Then they hightail it home to troll their dating apps in search of a person who will actually put out in the same evening. Yep, that's the one.

I, on the other hand, take things slow. And I won't apologize for it. Too many shady characters out there, and this guy is giving that vibe. I bet he's been on the giving end of enough one-night stands to sink a ship.

The elderly woman grabs his arm to get his attention and points at her boarding pass.

"Does it happen to be a window seat?"

He beams. "Dolores. Dolores. Dolores." One of his bags knocks against a lucky downturned head as he wraps his arm around her shoulders. "Is it ever!"

I stifle a giggle. If he thinks they're going to work their way toward the front of this plane with ease, he's got another thing coming. A linebacker with some of the broadest shoulders I've ever seen does not stand a chance in this pencil-thin walkway. At least he's offering an apology to every person they squeeze by.

I have to hang halfway into the aisle to continue watching their adorable sitcom after they've passed me. But it's a happy distraction from the reality waiting in my lap. Even if it might guarantee me another shoulder collision.

"May I?" he asks from her new seat assignment, gesturing to the mangled-looking suitcase under his right bicep. A bicep that's barely contained under the sleeve of his T-shirt.

She nods and he hoists it into the empty overhead bin one-handed. The hem of his crewneck rises an inch, exposing a sliver of bronzed skin along his belt line. It's August. Skin that pigmented is not surprising. But the guy looks like he spends all of his time outside with a shirt off.

I fan my face. Good grief, is it hot in here? The only other time I've ever been on an airplane I got cold. Hence the cowl-neck sweater in the prime of summer. But I reach for the nozzle above my head anyway, twisting it and finding relief from the draft of musty air that fans my bangs.

I hear the latch of the overhead compartment click shut and peek at them one last time, unable to help myself. Her glasses have slipped down the bridge of her nose, hanging on for dear life at the turned-up tip. She fumbles with her seat belt. Her uneasy steward bobbles his head between her struggling hands and the open door next to the cockpit.

He snatches both sides of the belt in a hurried grasp. "Let me help you with that."

My heart does another little nosedive in my chest watching him shackle them together for her.

Even if he's acting like a frantic mess, he's not leaving until she's completely settled. That gesture alone says a lot about a person. I would know. It's the one thing every man who has ever stepped into my life has lacked. There's always a "good reason" why they can't stick around.

By the time he gets her all situated, she asks him, "Who's the lucky lady?"

"I'm sorry?"

"The girl, honey. The one you're waiting for." She chortles at his ignorance, and the corners of his mouth droop. He checks the boarding bridge for the millionth time.

Is that it? Is he getting stood up?

"I better get to my seat. Enjoy that window." He pats her arm.

When he dodges into the flow of traffic, I launch at the flight manual in the seat pocket in front of me, stuffing my phone between my knees. I'd rather him not notice my gawking if I can help it.

I open the tri-fold card. *Life vest operation. Emergency exit locations. Securing an oxygen mask.* Bold text with black lettering jumps off the page and tattoos itself across my retinas. The concept that this plane could go down in a body of water at any point terrifies me. A knot tightens in the pit of my stomach.

The second sign that my anxiety is creeping in. The first is that unread text message I'm avoiding. If I don't get this feeling under control, I could really embarrass myself on this flight.

"Excuse me."

The laminated card flops toward my chest as rock-hard shins brush past my knees, filing in toward the window. I don't have to see his face to recognize that deep voice. The hot guy from the aisle is officially my new seatmate.

CHAPTER FOUR

REED

Finally.

I sink into the worn leather, sighing in relief.

I can't believe that actually worked. My father's navy-blue dress pants and penny loafers closed in on that boarding bridge and I threw myself into the aisle, just missing him. It's a good thing I read Dolores's seat number before giving back her ticket. Row seven has never felt better.

I tip my head back and close my eyes. A sudden explosion of air blasts across my face, and I revel in the current. Folding my arms across my chest, I accidentally knock into the plastic shield covering the window. It unfurls with a whoosh, and I unwind my arms and scoot back into the rigid seat as far as it will allow.

The arched plexiglass exposes some grass and an empty stretch of runway, not all that exciting of a view yet, so I notice something else. Like the fact that my kneecaps forge a war with the seat in front of me. My shins could take on the hex imprint from the pocket stitches during this flight, and I could care less. This cramped space is freedom. *Quiet* freedom and it dawns on me that I've yet to pay attention to the person seated beside me.

When I look toward the aisle, I'm met with laminated card-stock. *Emergency protocols*, the front cover reads.

"Do people really use those things?" I mutter to myself.

A yelp sounds as the person on the other side fumbles the booklet. It topples over twice before the woman catches the corner and straightens in her seat, pretending it wasn't about to drop to the floor.

I smirk.

A pair of chocolate-brown eyes settle on me. I get caught up in the gold flecks that warm her irises before I notice she's frowning. *No. Glaring?* Either way, it's hardly a menacing look with those rosy cheeks and plump lips.

"Some people like to feel prepared," she argues.

I take it my lack of interest in safety regulations offended her.

"Do they though?" I question. "Where's the adventure in that?" My eyebrow cocks of its own accord. The opposite of what hers are doing, which is drawing together in the center.

I'm not trying to be smug, but are any of those procedures really necessary? I guess I'm not one to comment. I cliff jump without much consideration for the hidden rocks beneath the water's surface.

"I wouldn't call nosediving to your impending death an adventure," she contends.

So, she *is* one of those people who would use it.

"There's a better way you'd like to go out then?" I tease her.

Am I really asking a nervous flier how she'd like to die?

"There is," she fires back. "Old age."

She can't be much older than me. I scan her body to be sure when my eyes zero in on her sweater. Wait a minute... is that the same one I knocked into earlier? Did it have those brown speckles in it? I can't remember. Then again—I glance around the few rows touching ours—no one else is sporting wool this time of year.

I grin. "I can picture it."

She chokes out a cough. "You're picturing me... *dying?*"

Wait... that's not what I meant. I can fix this.

"No, I can picture you in old age. Soft lines framing those pretty brown eyes, silver whisps to those bangs, a homebody who knits on her porch swing. Maybe a little grumpy from time to time."

She fights against the makings of a smile with the back of her hand. "You know nothing about me."

"You're right. So, tell me something," I say, in need of a distraction.

She squares her shoulders. "I think guys like you are notorious for acting intrigued by women like me. You strike up a conversation. Get to know them. It's playful at first. Until you realize you aren't getting any action at the end of it, and then you lose interest."

Wow. How many worthless guys has this girl dated? Apparently one too many with the way she crosses her arms like a shield to protect herself.

"So, you're saying if I act *uninterested* in you, then you'll believe me when I say I have no intention of ever trying to get into your pants?"

I thought my response was what she wanted to hear. But she winces when I emphasize the words *no* and *ever*. I'm not sure what this woman wants from me at this point, so I don't even bother giving her the chance to answer. I'm happy to give her uninterested.

I yank the brochure from her hands, tip my head back against the headrest, and pretend to ignore her. From my periphery, she's still gaping at me.

Point made.

Her face blooms into a deep rose color. I don't know if it's out of anger or embarrassment, but she has to believe that I'm not noticing it otherwise she'd hide that blush from me like the rest of the women I've talked to today.

I flip through the booklet, pretending to scan the pages, when she interrupts me.

"What I meant to say," she goes on, "is that I think it's best if you and I sit in silence for this flight."

I look at her and nod back. The way her eyes flit between her lost reading material in my hand and my self-satisfied face is just as entertaining as our verbal sparring.

She finally gives up, settling back into her seat. And I'm left in the same predicament I was in before—boredom. I need music.

Something crinkles when I shuffle through the side pocket of my duffle bag for a pair of headphones. I reach for it instead. A package with a bright-red bow surfaces—surprise trail mix. Mom must have packed it for me. The small gesture thaws a frozen edge from the ice box I tend to keep my feelings for my parents in.

I tear the corner off with my teeth and dump the contents into my palm. The nut to M&M ratio is paltry, but I pick out the colorful candy anyway and dump anything remaining into my mouth.

"Are you going to eat those?"

I *think* I heard her say that, but I don't dare assume after she was the one who initiated our vow of silence.

"Well?" she asks as her eyes flirt with the sugar in my hand.

I extend my palm. "They're all yours," I say, and she reaches for them, but before she can snatch them up, I trap them beneath my fingertips. "But I want it on record that you cracked first, not me."

She rolls her eyes and pries my fingers open. "Fine."

I watch her plop two red M&Ms in her mouth, followed by an orange, then four yellow and two green.

"What?" she says when she catches me staring.

"Nothing. I've just... never seen someone actually 'taste the rainbow' before. It's cute."

Does a comment like that count as flirting? Because I should *not* be flirting with her. For a whole host of reasons, but the biggest being that I'm about to prove her opinion of guys to be true. At the end of this flight, we'll part ways and never speak again. I'd rather not be another tally mark on the list of men with ill intentions toward her.

"Isn't that the slogan for Skittles?" she asks.

"Still applies, don't you think?"

"I guess it does, yeah." She blushes again, this time with me looking right at her. "It's a habit I picked up from my aunt."

Impending goodbye or not, I'm still bound to prove her wrong. Change her mind about me. Convince her that there are some guys in the world who truly care about getting to know someone. Some men who would do anything to keep the woman they're interested in.

"Can I ask you a personal question, or will you keep me in the same camp as those self-centered guys you speak so fondly of?"

She rolls her eyes. "I don't know, are you going to tell me your name first?"

I should have started with that.

"Reed Morgan."

"Hailey Hart," she says, offering her hand in a formal greeting.

Her eyes drop to the crease next to my smile as I shake it.

"Are you close with this aunt of yours?"

"Yeah. She's like a mom to me."

With the way her eyes cast down, I fear it's the most

personal question I could have picked. I don't press any further, just bump into her with my knee instead. "Well, your aunt has great taste in candy."

Her lips stretch into a smile. "My turn. Were you waiting for someone to get on this flight with you?"

Her question catches me off guard. How would she know that unless...

The apples of her cheeks darken.

"Were you watching me, Red?"

The nickname just slipped out. But... women don't generally blush under my stare and still look at me the way she is right now. Like she isn't afraid for me to see the way I affect her. It feels like a compliment, and it deserved to be noticed.

"Everyone was watching you," she argues. "You were blocking the whole aisle for a good seven minutes."

I chuckle and then sober. "Yes. I was waiting for someone."

There's an awkward pause, as if she's hoping I elaborate. I don't like talking about my family. But who am I to deny her an answer when my goal was to get her to realize not all men have one-track minds.

"Let me put it this way... I needed some space from that person, so I gave up my seat. But if it makes you uncomfortable, I can switch back."

She jolts her hand out. "No! It's fine."

But what's not fine is the way she white-knuckles her armrest seconds later.

CHAPTER FIVE

HAILEY

1 4 years old

A truck door swings shut outside my bedroom window. I'm sprawled on top of my plaid comforter. Aunt Karen's cackle echoes from the living room where she's been watching *Friends* reruns for the last three hours. Which means... No.

It's the end of August and the middle of fire season. There's no way it's him.

I convince myself to get up and look anyway.

Jack doesn't come home, even on his rest and recovery days. But when I pull back the gauzy curtains, I see him. He's dressed in casual clothes, popping open the tailgate of his Toyota Tundra.

Between the slight slump of his shoulders and the weathered lines on his face, he looks older than my friends' dads. Like he's lived a thousand lifetimes in the span of my fourteen years.

What is he doing?

He trudges through a blanket of pine needles that make up the landscape of our backyard and squats when he reaches the shed door. There's a rock the size of an orange, large enough to hide a key beneath it but small enough to blend in with the others. He palms the top, unearthing the silver object, and returns the rock to the same spot. The door swings wide with the latch undone. He disappears for a moment before stepping back out with a heap of fabric and an armful of long poles.

I should go talk to him. Find out where he's going.

I push away from the window and pad down the hallway. Aunt Karen is too engrossed in the TV to even notice me slip outside.

I stop on the last plank that meets the steps of the front porch and say, "Hi," with enough volume to make sure he good-and-well hears me.

He drops his first load of camping equipment in the bed of his truck, then pauses. "Hey, Hayes. Where's Karen?"

I pretend it doesn't bother me that he still calls me by my nickname. It's the one used by the closest people in my life, of which he is not.

I hoist my thumb behind me. "She's inside. Got hooked on an old series with a love triangle situation. The guy forgot to use oven mitts and pulled a pan of tater tots from the stove with his bare hands." I chuckle. Even repeating it back sounds funny. But it must not be his kind of humor. He doesn't return my smile.

I stuff my hands in the back pockets of my jean shorts. They fidget if I leave them at my sides.

"Going somewhere?"

He eyes his packed belongings. "Yeah." His back is my view as he ducks inside the shed. "I'm going camping with some friends this weekend."

I perk up. Camping's something I wouldn't hate doing with him, but he's never had the time.

"That sounds fun," I say.

I wait for him to invite me. To show a small sign that he'd

like to spend time together on his days off. But he just says, "Yeah. It should be."

He retrieves a fishing pole and cookstove to add to his pile while I just stand there.

I've learned by now if it means enough to me, I have to fight for it. And while I feel vulnerable putting myself out there, it's the only way I'll know my answer.

"I could come along. Help give you an extra hand with that tent?"

What am I even saying? The man doesn't need help. He *lives* out of a tent!

He slams the tailgate shut and dusts his palms together.

"It's okay. You don't need to come. I don't know how much fun you'd have anyway."

Gah, he's making this as painful as possible.

"I know I don't *need* to come. I... want to."

His expression twists. "Oh."

Did he really think I was offering because I feel bad for him? The only way we'll ever have a relationship is if we spend time together.

I slowly back away. "But if it's a guys' trip, it's fine."

"How about we take a rain check," he offers.

Not "I'd love to have you there," just "another time." I'm some scheduling obligation he's resigned himself to.

I'll admit, it doesn't feel good. I'm used to needing to be the bigger person to keep this relationship afloat. I try not to let it bother me and think of the positives instead.

He didn't say *no*, just *later*. Which means, deep down, there is a world where he doesn't find me repulsive to be around.

I convince myself that there's still hope for us.

Present Day

This is my nightmare.

The Boeing's tires grind over rough gravel with their sudden rotation, and I'm trapped in a human pinball machine with nowhere to go. Not even my armrests act as reliable support. They rattle with the motion of the cabin. I squeeze my eyes shut.

"Are you okay?" Reed says, and covers my hand with his. The hot center of his palm sends an electric current up my arm. I jump at his touch.

"I'm fine."

I lie to him for the second time in a few minutes. The first was telling him that I'm okay with him remaining in the seat next to me. I think Dolores might be more sympathetic about my fear. I have a feeling he's more likely to skydive from this plane than know how to secure my oxygen mask if I can't do it myself.

As if I weren't already a stressed-out mess, my iPhone chimes. I forgot that I left it wedged between my knees. When I flip it over, the text reminder flashes on the screen. What compels me to open it now of all times, I have no idea.

You don't need to come, it reads.

I messaged him late last night. But instead of telling him I took the job, I said I'd visit him on R&R. That was his reply.

I pinch my eyes shut.

It stings just as much as the first time he said it nine years ago. Can't he see that I *want* to come? That I don't particularly love going a solid year without seeing him in person, let alone four?

I planned to respond to him before we took off. But that doesn't seem to matter now that we're barreling down the runway. It's not like I'm turning back.

I hold the side button, powering down the device. The intercom dings, and a woman with a Delta branded vest and curls piled on top of her head pulls out a radio from the wall next to her. Her knuckles are nowhere near the same shade as mine when she presses it against her lips.

"Ladies and Gentlemen, welcome aboard Delta Airlines flight 3994 bound for Boise, Idaho. All carry-on items should be stowed securely in an overhead bin or beneath the seat in front of you."

I sacrifice my safety for a split second to stuff my phone into the front pocket of my JanSport backpack.

"All electronic devices should be turned off at this time. If you're seated in an emergency exit, please review the responsibilities for emergency exit seating on the back of the safety information card located in the pocket of the seat in front of you."

The nose of the plane careens forward as she wraps up her speech and takes a seat. My chest constricts with every pull of air into my lungs. My vision tunnels and my ears ring.

After all these years, it's clear I haven't learned my lesson.

Do you really think he'll talk to you? Finally ask you what it is that you love in life? my overactive imagination taunts.

You think he cares what you've accomplished while he was away? That he'd be excited you became an EMT like her?

My thoughts continue to mock me. The answers to those questions loom over me. But it's my final thought before this plane lifts off the ground that really does me in.

He hasn't missed me.

It surfaces now, my anxiety.

Claws at my insides like the raging beast that it is.

It eats its way up my esophagus from the place it's lied dormant, waiting to strangle me.

And I berate myself. Because I let this all-consuming feeling come back for a man who doesn't even care that I exist in the world.

CHAPTER SIX

REED

1 2 years old

"Reed, this is Jack."

A rugged man with lean features takes my hand in his for a shake.

"Nice to meet you," he says.

I have to tilt my chin to meet the steel gray of his eyes. "You too."

His smile warms behind the salt and pepper of his beard. But it isn't until he drops his grip and takes a step back that I relax. He looks far less intimidating with a couple feet between us.

"You picked a good one," Jack says, gesturing to the shade of navy blue that flickers between the pine branches. "It's closest to the lake."

I spin in a slow circle, taking in my first campsite. It's smaller than I thought it would be—no longer than a football's toss across. It seems a little too tight to fit two tents. Especially when Jack's is already staked to the ground and taking up more than half the space.

My dad pops the tailgate open and drags the green canvas and pile of poles to the edge of his truck bed. "Would you mind helping Reed set up the tent while I unload the coolers?"

"Sure thing," he says, and grabs the poles.

"Sarah made sure we'd all be well fed," my dad adds.

Jack nods but dodges his eye contact. "She's a good woman."

I'd feel disappointed that my father is already pawning me off on someone else if I wasn't busy studying their interaction. I almost miss the way my dad's smile slips at Jack's response.

What exactly happened to his wife?

A soft amber glow settles around us with the sun dipping beneath the skyline. I'd rather explore this place with the small window of light we have left, but I'm not given the chance. It seems they both have a knack for prioritizing work.

Dad ushers me over to where he's standing and pushes the fabric toward my chest. It takes an aggressive amount of kneading to gather the slick material in my arms without it trailing in a tripping hazard at my feet. How big *is* this tent? I can barely make out Jack's gray hair over the wad of canvas.

I follow the crunch of sticks and pinecones until he comes to a stop a few feet from his own tent. The poles clank as he drops them in a heap. He clears his throat as he approaches me.

"So, uh, Reed... you're twelve, right?"

He grabs an edge of the canopy I'm holding and backs up until we've stretched it wide enough to send it parachuting to the ground.

I answer when I can finally see him. "Yeah. Today, actually."

"Happy birthday," he says, handing me one of the poles.

"Thanks."

He points to the small hole to feed it through before finding his own. "Do you know what you want to be when you grow up?"

I haven't been asked that question since kindergarten. But to be fair, I don't know what to ask him either.

My pole snags on a section of fabric halfway through the center arch, and I bite my lip.

The last thing I need is to look incapable in front of my dad. With some aggressive wiggling, it breaks free and finds a home on the other side.

"Not really, no." I barely think past lunch, much less years into the future.

Jack grunts. "Yeah. I guess you'd be a little young yet."

He's threaded three poles in the span of time it's taken me to do one, so we work on the last one together as the tent takes shape.

"What do you do?" I ask. It's the only question I can come up with.

"I fight fires," he says.

"That actually sounds like something I would like," I say. Waaay better than my dad's job.

He circles the tent and stakes each corner into the ground. "Maybe you'd want to help me start the fire then?" he asks.

"Sure!" For the first time since we arrived, I feel excited.

I follow his lead to the west end of the campsite.

"You want dry fuel... dead branches, small sticks, fallen leaves, pine needles. Not hard to find this time of year," he says, wiping the sweat off his forehead.

Anything he misses from that list, I pick up. Except the flat piece of driftwood. He stops when he sees it, long and smooth. It sticks up from the ground like a sign. From the lake, I guess. He tugs it from the packed dirt and tucks it under his arm instead of adding it to his pile like the rest.

With arms full, we approach an empty steel rim charred black with ash. He dumps his bundle into the hollow pit, and I toss mine on top. He pulls a matchbox from his pocket and strikes the tip across the sandpapered side. As soon as it lights, he holds his arm toward me.

"Why don't you do the honors."

I reach for it. The heat of the tip singes the hair on the back of my pointer finger with the transfer. I pinch it steady and hold it in front of my eyes. The little flame on the end dances in the open air. It's mesmerizing to watch. I let it eat away the distance, nearly touching my skin, before I let go.

"You have no fear, do you?" Jack asks. But I'm too distracted to respond. Hypnotized by the flame that nests beneath two branches. The way it creeps under sticks and spreads over pinecones. Eats clean through crumpled leaves like they never existed at all. In just a few minutes, the flicker of a flame has swelled to almost ten times its original size.

"It's fun to look at," he says.

I'm certain I'm staring as if I've never seen fire before. But that's not it. There's something electric about how out of control it is, nothing stopping it from doing exactly what it wants to.

"I think I could watch it all night," I say.

"Good job on that tent." The sound of my dad's voice pulls me from the spell I was under.

"He made the fire too," Jack adds.

My dad wraps his arm around my shoulders, and I feel heat spread through my body in the same way that fire is right now—inside out. Maybe having Jack here isn't the worst part of this camping trip after all.

Present Day

I thought my worst-case scenario for this flight was being stuck in a seat next to my father. But then I met Hailey. Impossibly beautiful, endearing, and crippled with travel anxiety,

Hailey. After swearing off women, I don't know why I care so much about how she's feeling.

Maybe it's that my idea of a decent human being is someone who makes sure everyone around them is okay. So, when I catch the tremor of her fingertips on her thighs and her breath scraping past her lips, I want to help her. Regardless of whether or not I let myself experience similar feelings. I move fast through life on purpose. It drowns out the noise. Which gives me an idea...

"Electric boobs, below her shoes." I sing off-key into the open air, voice bellowing over the tops of the seats.

The gust of air she pulls into her lungs at the sound of my voice holds on a gasp. Her eyes dart around the cabin to see if anyone else heard me. Then she leans over and whisper-shouts, "What are you doing?"

The edges of my mouth tick up in a smile. "I'm sorry. Is this embarrassing you?" I peek past her down the aisle. As I suspected, my dad is wearing his gray noise-canceling head-phones. His head is not one of the many that turn my way.

Her big brown eyes gape up at me. "Stop!" she begs, tugging on my arm.

But I can't. Her hands are still shaking, and my job here is not done yet.

Positioned pretty close to the middle of the plane, I karaoke the next line of "Bennie and the Jets" through the entire cabin. "You know I read it in a wagon seat..." My voice pitches on that last word like the first syllable a donkey makes, and a deep crimson explodes across her cheeks.

She giggles. The most lighthearted sound. And I don't know what the hell she read on her phone a minute ago, but the way she's looking at me now—like Katherine Heigl looked at James Marsden in 27 *Dresses* when this song came on—tells me she has long since forgotten it.

"Did I not tell you I'm a rom-com lover? I can go all day," I tell her. And I mean it.

If it guarantees that she'll look at me the way she is right now, face flushed, eyes dancing. Letting me see all of her. I like it a little too much. In fact, I want to *keep* focusing on our intoxicating exchange, but it's difficult to do when she smells like a summer candle—something citrusy grounded in vanilla.

I continue with the chorus when a high-pitched humming sound competes with my voice.

The plane rises and dips like the drop in a roller-coaster as the wheels lift off the ground.

Her eyes flit to the eighteen-inch window, watching as we climb toward the sky. I press against the back of my seat so she has a good view. She watches the city dwarf into a patchwork quilt of earthy tones. The push and pull of her breath steadies as we drift away into a sea of translucent cotton balls.

When she finally drags her eyes away from the window, she whispers, "Thank you for that."

I shrug. "For what?"

She tilts her head and smiles knowingly. "Listen, I don't want to be rude... especially after what you did for me just now. But I got like three hours of sleep last night."

"No. I'm terrible company. I get it."

She grips my forearm, and I catch myself wondering what it would feel like if her fingertips slid down my wrist and across my palm. It's been a long time since I held a woman's hand.

"It's not like that, I promise!" She notices my smirk, and her palm falls away. "You're joking."

I nod, wondering if she's usually this easy to rile up.

She huffs and relaxes into her seat. Her head tips back, rocking from side to side until she finds a comfortable position against the headrest. Three minutes later, she's fast asleep. Right about the time I realize I miss her company.

You wanted this. A seventy-five-minute plane ride without anyone breathing down my neck.

I fish around for those headphones one more time, only to remember last seeing them in a coiled heap on my dresser. Right where I should have left that pocketknife.

Without someone to talk to or music to listen to, with nowhere to go and nothing to do to drown out the thoughts in my head, the words in that letter come crawling to the surface.

The truth is, as much as I joked that Miles wasn't any good at them, I've never been great at goodbyes either. The thought of never seeing either one of you again hurts too much. It was easier just to pack my bags early and move forward with what comes next.

And that's exactly what I'm doing, I remind myself.

Three days ago, a recruiter called me with an opening on a hand crew out of the Payette National Forest. They lost a member mid-season to a leg injury and needed an immediate replacement. I had twenty-four hours to decide and even less time to leave Bear Lake to pack my bags. It was *almost* the most difficult decision I had to make.

Letting Teddy Fletcher go was the worst of them all. I was falling in love with her all over again—the girl with the constellation of freckles I thought mapped my future. The one I spent five perfect summers with.

She was dancing in my arms at my parents' end of summer soiree one minute and walking away the next. And the sad thing is, I would have stayed for her... changed the trajectory of my life. But she decided for me. She picked Miles.

I hope you are off on wild adventures together, I wrote. *You deserve it.*

And I meant it. I still do. But that left only one other place in the world for me. So, I called the recruiter back, purchased the list of gear he forwarded, and that was that.

"Preparing for landing." The captain's voice sounds over the intercom.

Somehow an hour slipped by in what felt like minutes.

There's pressure on my right side that wasn't there before. Brown locks drape my neck in a scarf. I can't see her face but feel the rise and fall of her breath.

She's still sleeping.

The fasten seat belt signs chime on, and she jolts to an upright position. There must be some kind of product in her hair, because it's fixed in a giant wave on one side. A line runs across her cheek from a wrinkle in my T-shirt. Her lashes fan with each rapid blink as she takes in the scene. Then she covers them with her hands and groans.

"I fell asleep on you."

"Now what would make you think that?"

"Because you were... and I..." Her hands mime the way each of us were sitting until she freezes.

She mats her hair down with her palms as the plane floats into a dense pocket of clouds.

The turbulence bumps everyone forward and on instinct, my arm swings out wide.

The moment I touch her, my brain registers how much better off I'd have been letting her head find a home against the seat in front of her rather than her breast in the palm of my hand. I yank it away like it caught fire.

I did *not* just graze her boob. What has happened to me on this flight?

Her head swings my direction and she glares at me.

She thinks I did it on purpose.

I don't know what it would take to convince this woman I'm not like that. But the fact that this plane is landing... I'm out of time to plead my case.

"I'm sorry," I say anyway.

The second the seat belt sign turns off she reaches for her phone. I've got a few inches on her, so it's not hard to see when the screen lights up. I'm trying not to be nosy, but there's no mistaking a guy's name on that text banner.

She must be seeing someone.

Someone who doesn't want to be seeing her.

CHAPTER SEVEN

HAILEY

14 years old

The screen door slams. I meant to catch it with my hand but I'm too frustrated to slow my pace. I made stupid small talk while he finished loading his truck and then, like the sad case I am, I watched him pull away on his little adventure without me. The sting of that reality burns under my skin.

Aunt Karen flinches at the sound and sits up on the couch. She freezes the screen on Phoebe Buffay's scrunched-up face as she's hitting the chorus of "Smelly Cat."

"Is everything okay?" she asks.

No! I want to scream. Everything is not okay. I don't know where I belong in this world anymore.

How do you explain wanting to give someone the kind of energy they don't deserve?

"I'm fine," I mumble, pushing my way down the hall as fast as possible.

I flop on my bed, my arms splayed out wide, and try to catch the uneven breaths forcing their way out of my chest.

I close my eyes. If I could just focus on something else...

Aunt Karen raps her knuckles against the open door.

"You want to talk about it?"

I peel one eye open and wish I hadn't. I hate seeing the sympathy in hers.

"It'll never get better, will it?" It's a rhetorical question more than anything.

She drops onto the edge of my bed, the mattress dipping with our combined weight.

Wrapping an arm around my shoulder, she says, "I'd like to say that it will. But I don't know. Loss changes people. His was so big that ever since, he hasn't been able to see more than two feet ahead of him."

"This isn't easy for me either," I argue to the one person who I know won't disagree with me. "I wanted her to be here too. Get to grow up with a mom who taught me how to braid my hair instead of having to learn it from YouTube. But I'm here. You're here. Why can't he see what he still has?"

A tear drifts down my face and she tightens her grip, giving her support in a squeeze.

"He loves you, Hayes. He's just not great at showing it."

When she registers that her words don't make me feel any better, she changes the subject.

"It's Friday! You know what that means?"

Grenaldough's. A place filled with families on the weekend, and our Friday night ritual.

"Actually, do you think you could just pick it up this time? I'd like to invite Dean over."

She bows. "I'll be right back."

Present Day

"Forget about him."

A soft voice pulls me from the trench I've been trapped in since I powered on my phone.

Jack's message was only five words long, but somehow they mirrored the effect of a steel-toed boot connecting with my chest and collapsing my windpipe.

I blink at Reed and shield my phone from him. "Were you reading my texts?"

"It's a little hard not to when you've got it frozen in the air like that."

I clutch it to my chest.

"For the record," he continues, "that girl who fell asleep on my shoulder, the one who smiled at my ridiculous song... any guy would be lucky to spend time with her. This Jack guy doesn't sound like he deserves you."

If only he knew it was my *father* who sent it.

"I can't argue with that," I say.

A silence settles in the space between us as we watch the rows ahead empty out.

"So, where are you headed next?" he asks.

I tug the strap of my backpack, freeing it from the floor. When the aisle clears, I stand and look down at him.

"You know, we don't have to do this."

He stands too fast and smacks his head on the overhead compartment.

I gasp and reach for him. "Are you all right?"

He rubs the spot that took the blow and ignores my question. "We don't have to do what, exactly?" he says.

In a crouch, he shuffles three steps, and I move forward so that he can fit in the aisle behind me.

I try not to stutter. "Pretend that this was anything more than two strangers sharing a seat on an airplane. You can go your way, and I'll go mine. We don't have to do the whole drawn-out goodbye."

I make my point by silently turning away from him and traversing the long stretch of sage-green carpet to the front of the plane. My sweater and jeans plaster to my skin on the muggy jet bridge. Either Boise is humid today or I could benefit from slowing my Olympic speed walk. It's a welcome relief when a blast of air greets me at the terminal gate.

Why I peek at him one last time after my ridiculous speech is beyond me. I'm not the least bit surprised to find he's not looking back. My lips still press into a fine line.

Take your own advice, Hailey. He likes danger and you prefer to ride a bike with a helmet. And what kind of person doesn't eat the M&Ms in their trail mix anyway?

You have nothing in common with him.

I duck away as quickly as possible, saving myself from further humiliation. The signs blur until I slow at the sight of a royal blue one marking the restrooms. I slink inside and close the nearest stall to relieve my bladder.

"You're going to be fine. This was the right decision," I mutter to the empty stalls. I do my business and button my jeans, then jimmy the lock back open. If those same stalls could respond, they'd say *Not with the way that veil of toilet paper clings to the bottom of your velvet Mary Janes.*

The flapping of my foot does nothing to dispel it either. I have to reach down and peel the soggy end from my rubber sole. It dangles between my fingertips like a wet noodle until I can feed it into the nearest garbage can. Turning to the sinks, I scrub my hands until they're raw and grimace at my reflection.

"You're not going to regret a thing," I add to my earlier pep talk. Only this time, I sound far less confident.

With a swipe of drugstore lip gloss and the flick of my fingertips, my lips and bangs no longer look disturbed from that flight. I round my shoulders—*confidence*—and part from the bathroom mirror.

Compared to what Salt Lake has to offer, Boise is the hyphen of airports. Blink and you'll miss baggage claim.

Four dozen people circle the luggage carousel, the red indicator light still dim in the center. With nothing to occupy my attention but the people around me, I spot Reed from several yards away.

I groan.

I forgot I might see him here too.

His back is to another guy, but judging by the slight curl to their sandy-brown hair, I'd say they're related. Was it his dad he was avoiding? The man is sporting a dress coat and slacks. He could take a business meeting any second with the way he's glued to his phone.

Reed's lighthearted smile has given way to anxious pacing, and for the first time, I feel bad for him. Maybe we have more in common than I thought.

A red flash of light draws my attention back to the carousel. It begins spinning in a counterclockwise rotation, feeding an endless stream of luggage down a ramp. My hard-shelled suitcase is the third one to drop, but it travels in the opposite direction. I spend the next thirty seconds debating whether or not it's worth chasing before finally giving in.

When I sweep my bag from the belt and straighten, Reed is a few feet from me, drinking me in.

What do you say to someone you'll probably never see again? I decide on, "It was nice meeting you."

A grin splits across his face as he watches me walk away.

There's a bus waiting for me on the other side of those automatic doors, and I can't miss it.

The doors slide open.

"Remember me, Red," he shouts in my direction.

There it is. That nickname again. I feel it warming me from the inside out.

I turn around to face him one last time, the corner of my lips cracking into a subtle smirk and shaking my head.

He winks back at me, sending goose bumps skittering down my spine.

The automatic doors shut between us. A final reminder that I'll never get to ask him about that nickname. Or the hundred other unanswered questions my brain baits me with. I have somewhere else I need to be.

The Greyhound bus hugs the end of the sidewalk. A gentleman in a navy tracksuit leans against the side. He's balanced on a single Reebok sneaker, with his back covering a sliver of the canine logo on the metallic wrap. When I get closer, I make out a small badge clipped to his zipper. *Carl*, it says, printed on shiny plastic.

With an upward swing, I muscle my suitcase into the under-storage compartment. The sound of the wheels rattling against the metal frame does nothing to draw the driver's attention from his phone. A familiar ditty plays as I approach the stairs.

Candy Crush. Aunt Karen's pick-me-up game at the end of a long day.

I tried it once. All it taught me is that she is the queen of competition.

My own phone vibrates in my back pocket, and I slip it out. Speak of the devil...

"Hi," I say to her, but really intend it for Carl's ears. Because now he's blocking the doorway.

I shuffle back and forth, looking for an opening as he triple-taps the screen with his index finger. It chimes again.

"Take that, sucker!" he bellows, and I squint.

What is it with people and that game?

"Hayes? Did you make it okay?" I clutch my phone tighter.

"Yeah, my flight landed about thirty minutes ago."

I wave my hand near Carl's face. Nothing.

"How was it?" she asks.

"It was—" I picture Reed flashing me that dimple. Serenading the entire plane with his mixed-up lyrics. Distracting me from my crippling anxiety. Telling me to remember him.

"Unforgettable," I finish.

Did that come out breathy? I clear my throat.

"Uh-huh… and who's the guy?" she asks between smacks of her gum.

I tap Carl on the shoulder and he doesn't even flinch. It's like he's made of stone. Or existing in an alternate reality.

"What guy?" I grunt.

"Hayes, come oooon," she draws out. "You don't have an unforgettable flight unless there's a guy."

"It was unforgettable because I got a nap in," I bark, hoping the sound will startle the bus driver.

"Are you sure you napped?" she teases.

"Yeah, sorry. I'm just"—I huff, hoisting my bag over my shoulder—"TRYING TO GET ON THE BUS!" I shout it this time, clapping in his face.

"Woah! More like trying to get your hearing back. Did you chew *any* of that gum I stuffed in your backpack? I told you it would help during take-off and landing."

No. I ate a handful of M&Ms.

I scan the sidewalk. There's a family not far from me, but the dad is focused on loading their luggage in the back end of an SUV while the mom is buckling their toddler into a booster seat. No one is watching.

"Excuse me." I knock into Carl. Hard. He nearly drops his phone.

"Huh?" he says, acknowledging me with a blank stare.

I curtsy. *Curtsy.* Like he's the Duke of Westminster, and I am indebted to his service.

He peers at me through confused eyes.

I shoot up straight. "Sorry."

"Oh. Yeah. No problem," he says, scooting two steps to the side and resuming his game like nothing ever happened.

"I SAID—" Aunt Karen's voice booms through the speakers as I climb the steps, and I have to rip the phone from my ear.

"I'm sorry. The bus driver is a little... distracted."

"Maybe you should have worn something other than that cowl neck sweater. That would have gotten his attention."

I sink into the farthest seat I can find. The blue microfiber hugs my thighs, and I sigh as I look out the window. A handful of guys are loading their suitcases now, and Carl has dropped his phone to gape as they bend over.

"Yeah, I don't think I'm his type," I say.

She changes the subject. "Have you heard from him yet?"

"Once."

"And you think he doesn't care," she argues.

"He said, and I quote, 'you don't need to come.'"

She sucks air between her teeth. "Yeah, I'll admit, that sounds bad. But you have to trust me on this one. He means well."

"Please tell me I'm not making a mistake," I beg. "You know me! I'm not impulsive."

"Switzerland would be impulsive, Hayes. You're going *home*."

"So you *do* think I'm making the right decision?" I ask.

She hums. "I think I've watched you miss him for years. I think you're doing exactly what you need to do to find peace."

"I miss you already," I admit. I have no idea how often I'll have cell service when I'm not at the barracks. "How will I survive not talking to you every day?"

"You'll be fine, and I'll be busy." She giggles. "Besides, you'll have Dean if you need someone."

The mention of my former best friend's name sends the hair

on my arms standing. A lot has changed in four years. But that's the least of my worries right now.

"Let me guess... Tinder matched you with a new round of Utah singles."

"Ten!" She squeals. "I told you I'd set you up with a profile if you'd ever give me the go ahead."

"Never," I say.

I can't think of anything worse.

She sighs. "That's what I thought."

The bifold doors slap closed. With the high back chairs, all I can see of Carl now is a conductor hat in the same shade as his baggy outfit.

"I think we're about to hit the road, so I better go. I'll call you when I make it, okay?"

"I'm holding you to it," she says, and the call abruptly ends.

With the frequent rock and dip of the bus, my body eventually relaxes.

Even if I still have a two-hour-and-thirty-six-minute ride ahead of me, it feels a little late to respond to that text now.

I fix a pair of headphones in my ears and open Pandora. My favorite stations fill my collection page—Yuruma, Michael Bublé, The Piano Guys—I'm sure they'd all do the trick.

But instead, I get a sudden urge for Elton John.

CHAPTER EIGHT

REED

12 years old

Jack chuckles at the sound of heavy grunting behind us.

"I'm gonna go help your old man with those fishing poles."

I nod, watching him walk away.

My first impression of him was all wrong. After my dad's tent compliment, he got right back to work. But not Jack. He sat across from me—him in his camp chair and me on the seat of a soggy picnic bench—just observing the fire.

A broken branch hanging limply from a pine tree catches my eye. It hooks near the end like a walking cane, and I move closer to inspect it. The branch is just high enough that I have to press up on my toes to reach the torn section. Bits of bark flake off as I grab on to it and give it a tug. It doesn't budge.

I jog over to the truck for my backpack. The guys are too busy untangling some fishing line to even notice I've left my spot by the fire. I pull my birthday present free, excited I've found a reason to use it.

When I make it back to the tree, I use the blade to saw at the branch until it snaps free. I fold the sharp end of the pocketknife back into the handle and tuck it in my pants, then make my way toward the firepit. With the raw end of the stick exposed to the flames, I jab into the kindling. Ashes sputter a couple feet off the ground and then float down to die inside the steel circle.

"Reed, don't play with the fire," Dad warns.

A glow outlines their bodies in the shadows where they set up camp chairs on the opposite side of the fire.

He couldn't have brought them ten feet closer?

I acknowledge his warning with a single nod, but he turns back to Jack so quickly I'm not sure he saw. It pisses me off.

I jab the tip of the branch through the hot embers, sending a bigger log at the bottom tipping over. Sparks lift toward the sky and then fizzle out.

"Reed!" he barks again before reaching for a beer and tossing one to Jack. He pops the top open in his lap and takes a long, lazy pull from the can. He turns to his friend to tell him something else, and they both start laughing.

Why the hell did he bring me here?

If fire was an emotion, it would take the form of my anger.

I fight to control it as my chest pumps up and down. I glare at them both through the flickering haze, completely missing the moment my stick catches fire. The flames creep up the shaft and lick at my skin before I fling it out of my hands and onto a bed of pine needles.

In seconds, the whole campsite is burning.

Present Day

"You want to tell me why I spent an hour and fifteen minutes sitting next to an old woman instead of my son?"

My father trails behind me as I haul our luggage away from baggage claim.

He can't see it, but I smirk at his disgruntled voice. "You met Dolores."

He grips me by the arm to get me to look at him. "No, no. *Met* would have been 'Hi, how are you?'"

He extends his hand as if reenacting the formal way in which he wanted that greeting to go. This time I let him witness my amusement. Unpretentious, nonchalant, spontaneous—all words I'd use to describe the woman who ditched her baggage with a stranger and left behind her ticket. But *formal* is not one of them.

"Instead, I got Betty White on steroids," he vents. "I was the kind Samaritan who volunteered to play the piano at her nursing home and ended up listening to her hip replacement saga and how much it affected her sex life."

I chuckle at his made-up scenario. "Sounds like her."

We clear the double doors and my steps slow. Even though it's been at least ten minutes since we parted ways, I find myself searching for chestnut-brown hair.

My dad stops beside me. "Who's the girl?"

I stare at an empty sidewalk, imagining her gallivanting around the city in her fuzzy sweater rather than meeting up with the asshole who didn't want to see her.

"My version of Betty White."

My dad makes a grumbling sound, jolting me from my daydream. His scowl does an irritated dance between the open Uber app on his phone and the rusty Honda Civic that's backing up against the curb next to us.

"What the *hell*."

Here we go again.

A guy not much older than me with six inches of boxers hanging out of the waist of his cargos steps out of the front seat. Chains clank and swing against his thigh as he saunters toward the—*What happened to his trunk?* It's caved in on one side and requires a WWE wrestling move to open it. It pops a few inches and he pries it the rest of the way with clawed fingers. I'd load our own stuff but he's blocking the opening as he uses the shrouded hunk of metal for support.

"I think there's been some kind of mistake. I booked a—"

I interrupt my dad with a hand to his shoulder. "It's fine. We don't need an SUV for a duffel and two suitcases."

"Sorry, bro. Jimmy's main man, Ricky, needed the rig today. Got a wicked deal on a pool table for the crib. Facebook Marketplace is dope." He leaves his high-five hand hanging in the air as he chuckles to himself. When neither of us claps it, he swipes the underside of his nose with his thumb, and my dad squints.

I think he just spoke about himself in the third person.

"Jimmy, is it?" I ask. "I'm Reed. This is Emmett." I confirm our names just to be sure we have the right driver. When he doesn't deny it, I turn my dad by the shoulders, escorting him to the back seat. "We appreciate the ride."

The driver shows off a full grill. He has to fist the waist of his pants to keep them from dropping to his ankles.

When I climb into the car, I'm impressed by how clean the interior is. And by clean I mean lacking the pile of trash I expected to have to swim through. There's still a musty odor of stale fast food that clings to the fabric of the seats, and my dad holds the stiffest posture known to mankind, like he's trying to save his precious suit from needing a dry clean.

Whether we wanted to talk or not, there's no chance with the base booming the way that it is. While Dad uses our silent ride to leave Jimmy a scathing review, I make the mistake of opening Instagram.

A selfie of Miles and Teddy is the first thing to grace my screen. His arm is snaked around her waist and *damn* if she doesn't look beautiful in that black bikini. Spots flash in my vision and the muscles in my jaw tick. That same awful feeling that ate me alive all summer whenever I saw them together courses through me now. I know I shouldn't expect to be over it after a few days, but I want to be. I swipe the app closed and vow never to open it again.

Twelve minutes of Limp Bizkit later, we arrive at the Lithia Ford Lincoln of Boise dealership. We both choke out a cough as Jimmy peels out of the parking lot, leaving a cloud of exhaust as a parting gift.

"We could've avoided all of this had we just driven my truck," I remind him.

He stiffens.

"It's not just sitting around. Ronny will use it," he says.

I take that as my cue to drop the conversation and follow him. Rows and rows of vehicles with price tags painted on the windshields greet us. We don't make it more than ten feet before a salesman in a tight black polo makes a beeline to the row of F-150s we're looking at.

"Can I help you gentlemen find what you're looking for today?" He hugs a clipboard to his side. One of those *Hello, my name is* stickers clings to his pocket with the name *Waylon* scribbled in barely legible Sharpie.

Dad nods to the line of pickups. "We're interested in your 2024 model."

Waylon readies his clipboard. "Right this way."

"I don't need a new model," I whisper as we follow. "There's a good chance it'll just sit there for the next two months or get beat up in the mountains."

"I don't care what happens to the truck, Reed. You need a vehicle, and I'm not about to buy a piece of shit that could break down forty-five minutes down the highway."

I sigh. There's nothing I could say or do to change his mind at this point. My dad likes nice things. And the fact that both my parents are successful attorneys in Park City means they've never taken the practical road when it comes to financial deci-sions. I know when to pick my battles with him, and this isn't one.

The salesman stops in front of an olive-green Raptor.

"That's the sticker price. But I can knock it down to seventy-seven K for you."

My dad circles the truck like a predator stalking its prey. He inspects who knows what while I follow a few steps behind him, pretending to do the same.

I think it's about time to ruffle some feathers.

"Hey, Waylon! Do you think there's enough space for picking up a Facebook Marketplace find? Because there's this rad foosball table—"

"Reed," my dad grunts, and turns to the impatient auto salesman. "We'll take it."

Thirty minutes later, I'm pulling out of the parking lot in an overpriced hunk of metal.

We fight rush hour traffic that rivals Utah on its worst day just to get back to where we started—the airport.

"What are you going to do with that six-hour layover?" I ask. It sounds ridiculous even saying it out loud.

"Take some phone calls."

I could have guessed that.

Why did he fly all this way? Does he think I'm just chasing the next best thing? I won't be the guy to dress up in a fancy business suit, sit at a mahogany desk, and answer a phone all day. I'm not like him.

I twist my torso and snag his duffle bag from the back seat, then I drop it in his lap. "I'll see you in a couple months, Dad."

He sighs and climbs out of the truck. "Let me know when you make it. Happy twenty-first birthday, son."

My eyes flick to the display screen on the dash. August 21, it reads.

A truck for my golden birthday, go figure.

I reach over and pull the door shut myself. The tires crunch as I navigate out of the departure zone. I refuse to look back when all I'll see is a disappointed frown melting away in my rearview mirror.

To be honest, I don't mind the stretch of red lights across the city now that I'm alone. But the drive becomes ten times better when State Highway 55 reaches Horseshoe Bend. With my right wrist cradling the steering wheel, I take in the valley of dense pine trees like a staircase to the sky.

I fumble with the dashboard buttons until the radio turns on.

"Meteorologist Mike Stanza informed us this morning that temperatures in the Treasure Valley will be heating up this week. Residents will face triple digits by Tuesday with a high of a hundred and five holding strong the next couple of weeks. Get ready, Idaho. It's going to be a hot one."

Yeah, get ready for some fire, I think to myself as a ball of sagebrush tumbles across the highway. I jerk the wheel just enough to dodge the spiny plant as it sails past the lack of guardrail, over a strip of yellowed wheatgrass, and down a rocky ravine where the south fork of the Payette River rushes through. I correct the wheel just as a bus with a ten-man raft pulls off near an access point called Hells Canyon.

Always chasing the next best thing, yeah right.

Memories of Bear Lake threaten to invade—of long summer days boating, fishing with Miles and my brothers, chasing the sun—so I jack the radio even louder, as though my thoughts have a voice I can drown out with the sound.

I roll down the window as endless road stretches in front of me like a welcome mat.

It's here, under the desert sun, that I start over.

CHAPTER NINE

REED

$\mathbf{M}$*cCall Ranger Station, Payette National Forest,* reads the wooden sign.

I made it.

A few miles off the main road at the edge of town sits a big building with yellowed siding and a green roof. I follow a grove of pine trees twisting around the property until I can park my truck next to the five other brown vehicles with *Forest Service* logos stamped on the sides.

My new home.

I pull my phone from the center console, taking note of the single white line in the top corner. It's more cell service than I expected for a remote mountain town, but I doubt that'll be the case when I venture into the brush. Sounds nice.

I open the text thread with my parents' names on it and type, *Made it. See you in eight weeks.* I hit send and power off my phone, stuffing it in my duffel. I don't bother locking up.

"You must be the new recruit." A brawny guy with a full beard and a bag of mixed nuts clutched in his fist jogs toward me. He tips the contents into his mouth, then throws it in the trash can beside the front door. A jovial look spreads across his whole face when he stops in front of me.

"What gave it away?" I ask.

"You look like that," he says, pointing to the product in my hair.

I rake my fingers through the pomade. "Last shower for a while."

Judging by the layer of soot on every inch of his exposed skin, I gather he either tumbled off the edge of a cliff or hasn't showered in several days.

"Not the only reality check that comes with this job." He holds out his hand to me.

"Logan Murphy."

We exchange a firm grip.

"Reed Morgan."

I shadow him as he pulls open the door to the old building.

"Welcome to Iron Summit, rookie. Sixteen-hour shifts, shitty pay, no benefits."

All things I probably should have covered when I spoke to the HR recruiter. But I barely had enough time to get here, asking about money wasn't really on my mind.

"We eat, sleep, and breathe fire," he continues. "You won't find a crew stronger or better than this one."

We take a left turn down a hallway.

"I'll give you the grand barracks tour." The passage is so narrow and his voice so deep that it rattles the frames lining the tan walls. Pictures of crews and years of service fill the two cut-out spots in every frame.

Logan turns the gold handle on a glass-paned door at the end. It creaks as it swings inward, exposing a spacious weight room.

"You won't use this room much because we're rarely here, but if you need to let out some pent-up frustration, here's where you do it." He winks at me, and the right side of his ducktail beard lifts with it.

"Good to know," I say, memorizing the location. I'll be back here later.

I follow him down another hallway that stretches the back side of the building. An endless row of doors stack like dominos before me.

"Living quarters. Most of the time in the summer months you have to bunk up."

He stops at the one on the very end and kicks the cracked door open with his boot.

"This one's yours. You'll be with McCafferty." He slaps a hand on my shoulder and laughs. "Good luck, man."

What is *that* supposed to mean? But he doesn't give me time to ask. He points to a door at the end of the hall next.

"EMT wing through there. And this"—he takes a couple of steps toward a walled arch in the center—"is the kitchen and family room."

I follow him through the opening. A twelve-foot farmhouse table that must seat at least a dozen and a half people sits off to the side of the countertop. Six recliners face a TV on the opposite side.

"Hope you can cook, rookie, because no one else here can worth shit." He chuckles to himself.

Yeah, that's not going to be a problem for me. Cooking's a skill I had to master younger than any child should.

"Hey, I heard that."

From where I'm standing, an upper oak cabinet hangs open. A set of hands pour a cup of coffee behind it, dump in a packet of sugar, and stir the hot drink with a spoon. He's facing me when the cupboard closes.

"Good to see you again, Morgan." With a neutral expression, he raises the steaming mug to his lips and takes a lazy drink.

Why does he look so... familiar?

"It's Reed, actually," I correct him.

When he pulls the cup away from his face, I study his gray hair and the long, lean lines that slope his jaw.

"We stick to last names around here."

He rounds the barstools until he stops right in front of me, where I can get a good look at him. With weathered boots and a full mustache, I'd say he's been here... a lot longer than just a couple of summers. Then it hits me.

"Jack."

"Hart," he adds, acting completely unfazed by my unhinged jaw. "Superintendent of Iron Summit."

My new boss is *Jack Hart*. My father's friend. The man who witnessed one of the worst weekends of my life.

Of the hundreds of fire crews on the west coast, I never considered getting placed here, with him. I should have thought about this being a possibility, but I never saw Jack again after that day in the campground. I certainly never spoke about him with my dad. And in my twelve-year-old eyes, for all I knew, Jack Hart would be retired by now.

"You missed pre-season onboarding." He takes another sip. "Something that takes two weeks. You'll need to catch up in two days. Think you can handle that?"

Is he testing me?

"I think I can handle bypassing the training altogether and just get to the good stuff," I tell him.

My course training wasn't all that many months ago, and there wasn't anything I struggled with.

He lifts an eyebrow. "Guess I should hand over my job to you then?"

A new guy clomps into the kitchen, bearing the weight of a large duffel bag.

Jack stops him with a hand covering the strap. "McCafferty, this is Reed Morgan, the new recruit. I need you to train him today. I'd do it myself, but I've got... something"—he pauses like he's thinking on it—"to take care of."

"But it's—"

"I know, and I'll make it up to you," Jack promises.

In his disappointment, the guy hurtles his bag onto the counter. It snags on his shoulder-length hair.

So *this* is my new roommate. *Great.* I can see why Murphy wished me good luck. I'm five minutes in and already disappointing him. Off to a fantastic start.

McCafferty grunts and starts to stalk away. I take it as my unfriendly cue to follow him. Just before I clear the opening, I hear Superintendent Hart speak to someone else.

"I thought I said you didn't need to come."

When I glance behind me to see who he's talking to, it's Hailey's eyes that I meet.

CHAPTER TEN

HAILEY

14 years old

I reach for my phone on the nightstand and dial his number. I keep telling myself he's busy, that I'm the only lonely one on a Friday night, when he picks up on the final ring.

"Hey, Hayes. What's up?"

I sit up a little taller, hoping it elevates my mood. "Hey! Karen's picking up Grenaldough's. Want to come over for dinner?"

A voice I don't recognize lets out a whiney "Stoooop" in the background.

"If you're busy don't worry." My traitorous voice cracks on the last word, and I clear my throat to cover it up. But nothing gets by Dean.

"Hayes, I'll be there in ten minutes, okay?"

"Are you sure? You really don't have to come."

"I want to," he says, and that phrase sweeps me back to our sixth-grade bus stop. The day I met Dean McCafferty.

I was the laughingstock of the Four Eyes Committee as I boarded the bus in my first pair of glasses. Everything far away was clear, but up close, things melted together like honey. I'd already fallen behind in reading and avoided it at all costs, which meant I didn't do much of it at home either. Of course, my dad never saw me read. But it took Aunt Karen a while to catch on too.

It wasn't her fault. She was doing the best she could as the caretaker in my life. And even though I'm comfortable opening up to her, I'm always afraid that saying or doing the wrong thing will scare her away. Who wants to take care of a kid struggling in school when they're not yours? I'd be left without anybody if it came down to that. I didn't have room for error. So, I lied. For a long time.

Dean was new to my... community? It was less of a neighborhood in the sense that you weren't walking two feet from your front steps to borrow a cup of sugar. I imagine moving cities in the middle of a school year is nerve-racking enough. But if Dean was intimidated, he never showed it.

Middle schoolers can be harsh. Mine? They waited until I was trapped in a leather booth surrounded on all sides. I tried to ignore it. I fused my eyes to the bus window and kicked myself for not asking Aunt Karen to drive me to school.

"Boys don't make passes at girls that wear glasses," a girl named Molly chanted over the seat behind us.

She was even more of a "neighbor" than Dean was. The fact that we'd been in the same class since kindergarten, yet she still treated me like that... it made me hate her even more.

She was right though. No boy was ever going to like a girl with bangs and glasses.

But it didn't keep me from barking, "Shut up, Molly!"

It wasn't my finest moment, but I was humiliated. I shrank in my seat, ducking my chin inside my coat so my face was half covered.

Dean acted unbothered. He shuffled through the front

pocket of his backpack, and I peeked over the hem of my hood lining. From what I could see of the top layer—a washer and screw, a button, a couple scraps of ripped-up paper, a rainbow loom bracelet, and a handful of paperclips—it was filled with random junk he found off the street.

For the rest of the bus ride, he tinkered with the paperclips, stretching the kinky wires to their longest lengths. I wanted someone to talk to but resigned myself to the fact he didn't have time for a four-eyed girl like me.

When the bus parked in front of the school, I turned to face Dean. He was grinning at me in a pair of paperclip glasses that sat crooked on the bridge of his nose. When the other kids caught on, I found out their teasing didn't stop at me.

"You didn't have to do that," I said to him when we were the last kids left.

"I wanted to," he said back, and wore them anyway.

I never forgot that day. Since then, he's always shown up for me in moments when he didn't know how much I needed someone.

Present Day

You can do this. Just break the ice, tell him you took the job, and everything can move forward how you've always wanted it to. You can finally give him a good reason to be close to you. One that you've spent the last several years working toward.

Who knows... maybe he'll be happy for me. After all, he fell in love with a woman in this profession. It shouldn't come as a surprise to him that I might consider it too.

I take a deep breath when I spot him between the living room and the kitchen. His feet are firmly planted on the ground in front of a guy being told what to do. A new guy, I decide, considering he's wearing freshly laundered clothing.

I slow my steps so I don't have to wait awkwardly for my turn to speak to him. But it doesn't matter. He's glancing up and ending their conversation. Dismissing the other guy and pushing past him.

I put on my brightest smile like it's a layer of makeup I forgot. I don't wear much makeup in the first place, so maybe it's too much with the way he's scrutinizing me. I try to come up with something to say as he eats up the ground between us.

"Hi, Jack," is what I decide on. I gave up calling him dad a long time ago.

"I thought I said you didn't need to come," he reminds me, and I blink. Not the unintentional kind when your eyes get dry —which they are from the desert heat that's permeated the walls of this building—but the kind that's a lot like a swallow. A reset for your emotions.

I don't need to see his face to know he wouldn't be excited to see me here. He never did like me visiting him at work. His text message only confirmed it. I prepared myself for this. Already got my freak-out over with on the plane. I'm twenty-three years old and ready to handle him like the grown woman that I am. But something about him towering over me with his hands planted firmly on his hips makes me feel like I'm that small child who asked too many questions about her mom at bedtime. The one who was too eager and selfish to know he didn't want to talk about those things and pushed him away instead.

I must have rehearsed what I was going to say at least three dozen times. Convinced myself he'd be happy about this part of my plan. But the news comes out of my mouth with a wobbly delivery.

"I'm your new EMT."

His eyes bulge. Not a good sign.

"You're *what?*" he gasps. His voice bounces off the ceiling. My face flushes as the guy he dismissed seconds earlier turns his head and takes this already anxiety-riddled moment to a whole new level.

Reed Morgan is here.

In the barracks.

With my dad and ex-best friend.

I circle back to everything we talked about on the plane. Not once did he mention his career to me. But judging by the sparkle in his eyes, he's pleasantly surprised to see me. This was not part of the plan.

Jack clasps my arm. "Since when did you get an EMT license?"

My blood simmers beneath my skin. He's not happy about it. I recoil from him.

"Since I moved to Utah. I tried to tell you a dozen different times, but you never pick up your phone," I argue. A pointless dispute to bring up with a man married to his job.

"Karen never said—"

"Anything, I know," I finish for him.

I didn't realize he talked to Aunt Karen about me all that much. I mean, he used to. When he brought me home from the hospital, alone, she moved in to help take care of me. He'd leave me with her for long periods of time while pursuing his career. When it came to parent/teacher conferences and annual checkups, she became the emergency contact. My full-time not-legal guardian.

"I told her not to," I continue. "I wanted to be the one to tell you. I thought..." I push out an awkward laugh-breath and then shake it away. "Anyway, I can see now this was a very bad idea. I need to go unpack my things."

I turn away and he does nothing to stop me.

I knew it was a risk coming here. One that I was willing to take, right up until a moment ago when he treated me like I was just another member of his crew, bossing me around about all of my life decisions.

What did I expect? A "Congratulations"? An "I'm proud of you"? He didn't do that when I graduated high school.

But there's no turning back now. He'll have to get used to having me here, and I'll have to get used to his constant state of disappointment.

"How's the antiseptic stash looking?" Ben, my new coworker, says as I stare out the back window.

The EMT quarters face a wall of ponderosa pines. But that's not what caught my eye three minutes ago. I'm gawking at the newest recruit of Iron Summit. He's in a deep squat with his palms planted on his knees, and I get a full view of Reed Morgan's backside pointed in my direction. If I thought the shirt he wore on the plane was tight around his biceps, these pants fuse to him.

"Hailey?" Ben repeats.

He's the supervising paramedic I met when I arrived, and if it weren't for needing to speak to my father, I would have stuck around and let him finish the tour he was giving me. Now I've been tasked with replenishing the medical supplies for the next fire, and I'm not making a very good first impression with the pace at which I'm accomplishing things. I don't have a clue where anything is.

"Oh, uh..." I mumble, dropping my attention. I count three cans and report it to Ben.

"Huh, that's funny. Because it looks to me like there are six," he says, leaning over me and inspecting the case I'm holding.

The center folds up like a kaboodle and—*he's right*. There are three more cans I missed underneath.

I study my hands before looking up at his green eyes. "Sorry."

Ben is good-looking. With dark-brown hair and a full five-o'clock shadow, there's nothing unappealing about his face. But he's also not squat-and-stretch-for-a-mile-long-hike attractive. And with that, I'm back to staring out the window.

"Who's the guy?" Ben says, and takes a seat on the chair next to me, ready to organize a pile of gauze.

I still when I see Reed elbowing someone else. I've been spending so much time preparing to confront my father that I hadn't considered Dean McCafferty. At this rate, it won't be long before our paths cross and I'll have to face my childhood best friend.

I pry my gaze away from the window and back to my hands. "Just someone I met once," I say to Ben.

"What's his secret?"

I look up at him, confused. "I'm sorry?"

He blushes slightly. "To get you to smile like that. What did he do?"

Am I smiling? My fingers brush my lips, and sure enough, they're lifted up at the corners.

What is it about Reed Morgan? I grinned like a little girl the entire way from the airport to the Ridley's Family Market bus stop in McCall, the sound of his voice saying *Remember me, Red* running on a chronic loop in my head. I shake it to clear the fog that descends over my thoughts even now.

"He doesn't take life very seriously. Which is entertaining to be around."

I let my gaze drift to the window once more. He's picked up a shovel-like hand tool and is swinging it in the air like a lightsaber in front of Dean's chest.

I didn't realize how much I admired that about Reed when we met this morning. The fact that he's so playful. All I could focus on was my skepticism of his intentions like I do with most guys these days.

But then he sang for me.

Something I know he did to get a laugh out of me and lighten my burden.

The same thing he's trying to do for his squad leader right now. But it doesn't look like Dean McCafferty thinks *Star Wars* reenactments are very funny.

"I didn't take you as the type of girl who liked the class clown," Ben says, like he knows me intimately and we didn't just meet for the first time two hours ago.

"I never said I liked him. I said I met him once, and he was entertaining to be around. I like stability," I tell him, like I'm reminding myself.

He smiles at that, but I don't acknowledge it. I have zero intentions of leading a guy to believe I'm open to anything. Especially not one I work with. Not even if he's attractive and has a quarter-sized dimple in his smile.

"Is it often this quiet around here?" I ask, needing a subject change.

He chuckles. "Are you bored already?"

"I guess I'm just used to... busier. I worked for the University of Utah's Emergency Department before this." On average, we treated anywhere from eighty to a hundred patients in a single twelve-hour shift.

He nods and tosses the gauze into a box at his side. "Fire is unpredictable," he says. "Some days are slammed. Others are a waiting game. But this right here is what we want." He waves his arm around the empty room, pointing to the two vacant beds and lack of wounded patients in them.

"Right."

I panic on the inside. How will I ever keep busy enough to avoid my two biggest problems in this place: a father who isn't speaking to me and a deceitful friend.

But then a six-foot-something frame dodges past my window. He makes his way over to an opening in the pine trees, and my attention paves the trail he's walking.

On second thought... make that three.

CHAPTER ELEVEN

REED

"I know, baby, I'm sorry. I wish I could get out of it." McCafferty paces in a figure eight, cooing into his phone. "Aw, come on. You know I hate being apart too. It'll go by fast. I'll see you in a couple of weeks."

When Jack assigned the quarterback of the football team to train me, I thought we'd hit the ground running. Instead, I've been sitting on a cement ledge behind the barracks, waiting for him to finish his conversation. It's giving me too much time to stew about the fact that it wasn't my talent that got me this job but my father's connections.

There's a brief pause before he adds, "Love you, too, baby," and I nearly vomit onto my boots before his call finally disconnects. Maybe it's the ninety-degree heat before noon. More likely, it's that I came here to get away from the opposite gender —never mind Hailey showing up—not follow around some lovesick puppy all day.

I jump off the wall. "Ball and chain troubles?"

He glares at me, but I don't take it personally.

"None of your business," he snaps. "I'm your squad leader, not your roommate."

A smirk slithers across my face. I guess nobody told him that part.

He braces a stopwatch in front of his face and punches a couple of buttons on the side. "Standard PT test. Twenty-five push-ups. One minute. Go."

We just met and already I hate answering to him. For starters, he doesn't look any older than me. And who tied a leadership title to someone with such a shitty attitude?

I'm your squad leader not your roommate.

Real motivating.

He's reporting all of this back to Jack, and if there is one person I need to impress here, it's him. So, I drop to the cement pad and pump out fifty push-ups before the timer goes off.

If he's impressed, he doesn't make a show of it. Just jots down my number on his palm-sized pad of lined paper and moves on.

He presses the same button on his device a few more times and barks, "Forty sit-ups. One minute. Go."

Instead of the fancy gym on the west end of the building, we're using a makeshift basketball court out back, where the cement feels like it dried before it got smoothed over. Every time I lift my back off the ground, my shirt catches on the jagged texture and chafes against my skin. It's a grueling sixty seconds, but by the time the stopwatch sounds, I've got him recording fifty-eight sit-ups on my behalf. Which is a far cry past forty.

He scribbles down my number and walks away—my ever-constant signal to follow him. Add poor communication to the list of things this guy is lacking.

He points to the back of the building where a pull-up bar has been installed.

"Chin-ups 'til failure."

I grip the metal with my fists and work up and down the wall.

Twenty, twenty-one, twenty-two, I count as the timer sounds.

I jump down and wipe my palms together.

He turns to the side, revealing a two-inch scar splitting his eyebrow. I'd ask him about it if he had any interest in becoming friends. But considering he's sighing and looking bored out of his skull at my presence, I think I'd rather badger him instead.

"You can hold your applause."

"Is it praise you want, rookie? Well, not bad. But let's see if those boots were made for walking as much as that mouth of yours was made for yapping."

He approaches a wall lined with black canvas sacks. Lifts the closest one with ease and dumps it in my arms. They bow under the forty-five-pound weight, but I thread them through the padded straps until the ruck distributes evenly across my upper back. I wait for him to do the same, but he doesn't.

"Too heavy for you?"

Like a red-tailed hawk over an exposed field, his eyes narrow. "Excuse me?"

"No, it's just, you're the squad leader right? Aren't guys in your position supposed to motivate pawns like me."

"I didn't know you needed a hand hold," he mocks.

"I mean, if you're offering..." I reach out like I'm going to grab his hand, and it does exactly what I was hoping it would.

His cheeks flush and he swats it away. "We're going three miles round trip down that trail. You have forty-five minutes."

I can't hold back a chuckle.

"Oh, *we* are?"

"Yes, *we* are."

It's getting annoying that he feels the need to state my target goals like I haven't already passed all of them before this. What's supposed to make me believe it's something *he* can do? This guy isn't even carrying a weighted rucksack.

Regardless, I do what I'm told. *More* than I'm told, in fact. The first two miles I complete at a jog, making it to the halfway spot on the trail and turning back around. I came here to impress. To stand out. Not to be mediocre.

"You're gonna burn out," he warns me from behind.

His comment only fuels me, pushes me harder. I ignore the rubbing of my heels and the heavy clunk of my boots. I'm determined to make him regret underestimating me. He hasn't seen anything yet.

I flip myself around, running backward. "Going too fast for you, soldier?"

He's only a few feet behind me now, keeping an even pace. I hadn't realized how slow I must be with the rucksack on.

"Suit yourself," he says, and I flip back around and ignore his presence. I continue on until we hit the two-and-a-half-mile mark and my boots become unbearable. I've committed to pushing forward, and I won't give this guy any ammunition. Especially knowing he might take it back to Jack. I don't need either one of them proving my father right, so I keep pushing.

When we hit the three-mile marker, I wheeze.

"Take me out of my misery, Mother Nature," I whisper to my weight-bearing-support-partner-of-a-tree as McCafferty scribbles my time for the hike. He marches to the same wall we started at and retrieves a second rucksack. Forget about the bulk that tips me forward as he threads it onto my front, it's my feet that break me.

"Time for long and heavy," he says.

A layer of sweat clings to my skin, the heat curdling my bloodstream. My definition of prime shape was off. I'm not even out on the fire yet and it feels like my clothes are melting into a second layer of skin. I wipe at the sweat that rolls down my forehead with the back of my hand.

"Get used to it. It's ten times worse next to the flames," he says.

I allow my posture to sag for a second, but it does nothing to relieve the deep ache setting in.

"What's wrong? Getting tired?" he mocks.

I am. But that's not even the worst part. It's these damn boots. For the top recommended and most expensive pair on the market, they're failing me. Four hours ago, they wore marble-sized blisters on the backs of both of my heels and on the edges of my pinky toes. Every time I move, my feet shift, stretching and tugging at the loose skin. I'm one move away from breaking them open.

I refuse to look weak next to McCafferty, but I'm going to need some serious bandages if I plan on being able to walk tomorrow.

"Nope," I lie. "You just looked like you could use a break."

Compared to the grueling gymnastics he's put me through, that's all today has been for this guy, a break. He sat on his ass while I showed him how to deploy a fire shelter. The only time he's lifted a finger was to hold the opposite side of the litter as I demonstrated hauling an injured crew member off the moun-tain. It's a good thing I paid attention to those fire course training videos; I've learned nothing from him.

His hands are on his hips and I know he can sense my irrita-tion. "Do you know what today was?"

"Your *don't give a shit* day?" It's the blisters talking at this point.

"Funny," he scoffs. "It's been in the nineties most days this summer. That's pretty miserable for the mountains. The crew just got off a fourteen-day roll with a seven-day extension. Twenty-one days," he repeats, as if I couldn't total them myself. "I was supposed to be at an air-conditioned movie theater eating Junior Mints with my girlfriend. Instead, I'm here with you."

"Hey, man, nothing's keeping you here." I raise my arms in the air. "I'd be happy to take your spot if you want to waste your time on a girl who will probably cheat on you while you're away all summer."

The moment it comes out of my mouth, I wish I could take it back. I'm projecting. While Teddy never cheated, I'm jealous he has someone in his life who chose him. Who wants to spend her time with *only* him.

He stands and closes in until he's inches from me.

"If you ever talk about Madison like that again, my fist will be meeting your face. We're done for today." He stomps away.

I didn't come here to make friends.

But I certainly didn't plan on making enemies either.

CHAPTER TWELVE

REED

It's seven by the time McCafferty dismisses me from our day of hell. I have to force myself to walk without a limp to get back to my room. *Our* room. Man, I hope he doesn't come back here for a while.

Most of the crew must have taken their R&R elsewhere. It's silent in the barracks.

I hip-check the door, not caring when it rebounds off the old frame. All I can think about is getting out of these work boots.

The springform mattress creaks under my weight and folds like a pool noodle in the middle. I don't have to bend very far to tug at the thick laces of my right shoe. Raw skin grates against my sock as I rock the heel, working my foot free. A layer of flesh pulls back with the cotton, and I wince when it makes contact with the open air.

Balancing my heel on the edge of the bed, I rummage around the bottom of my bag for the only box of Band-Aids the old Safeway by my house had in stock. The wrapper husks open with little effort and the tabs fall off before I've even touched them. The strip covers up the section of raw skin about as good as my sock did. I switch to my left foot, whining like a baby.

"Got a problem there, Morgan?"

My foot slips off the edge of the mattress and crashes to the floor. From my bent-over position, I catch Hailey leaning against the wood frame of the doorway. Her arms cross her chest, amusement playing on her face as she snoops at my handiwork.

I scramble to stash the bloodied pair of socks underneath my pillow. My elbow knocks into my bag, dumping the box of character Band-Aids and half the clothes I packed onto the floor between us. I swipe at everything I can reach, but she's dangling a pair of black briefs from her pointer finger by the time I right myself.

Smooth.

My mouth cracks into a grin. I can turn this situation on its head.

I press off the mattress and grab the fabric, letting my palm brush against her finger.

"As a matter of fact, I do," I say, my voice low.

She flusters.

"I don't recall you answering when I asked where you were going next. I thought I made a good enough impression to at least get that much," I add.

Her face heats and I use the opportunity to tug the briefs free of her grasp and drop them in the opening of my bag.

Mission accomplished.

She blinks, and a smile works its way up to her eyes. *Two can play at this game,* they seem to be saying.

"See, that's where you're wrong. Your first impression was terrible," she says. "And I didn't think it mattered that you knew where I was going. You didn't plan to see me again, now did you?"

I finally break our eye contact. She's got me there.

I fit a sock over my foot and slip my boots back on, tying the laces way too tight. When I take my first step, I grit my teeth behind closed lips and pretend everything is fine. She watches my face like she's waiting for me to respond.

I'm no actor, but I must be doing a terrible job at hiding my grimace because she says, "Let me look at that."

I should not be staring at her mouth as she kneels before me, but man if I don't gawk at her red lips all parted and covered in some form of berry color.

Get a grip.

She reaches out and cradles my foot in the palms of her hands. Her fingers sweep across my ankle in a way that requires me to flex my entire anatomy of leg muscles to keep them from shuddering. The warmth of her touch seeps into my skin, and I find myself leaning closer instead of pulling away like I should be. Keeping up the facade that I don't need help.

"You're supposed to break them in, you know," she says, swiping her finger beneath my sock and peeling it away gently. "Not wear them for the first time on a training day."

I didn't get into my past with her on that flight or tell her how this job came to be for me—that I didn't exactly have time to break anything in. But I stop myself. *Remind* myself that you can't get hurt if you don't open up.

I steal the sock from her hands, slide it on, and stand. "I like to live on the edge, remember?" I arch a brow at her.

"And how's that working out for you?" she asks.

I model the box of Scooby Doo Band-Aids. "Saving the day."

I take another step and hiss through clenched teeth.

"All right." She straightens and drops her hands to her sides. "I guess those crappy Band-Aids will do the trick then." She saunters away from me, and the way her hips move makes it difficult to keep my eyes above her waist. I manage to appreciate her hair and the way it weaves in a long braid down the middle of her back instead.

"Crappy?" I scoff. "I'll have you know I paid seven bucks for quality first aid."

"Yeah, well, those overpriced stickers are half the size of the blisters on your heels. But suit yourself."

I don't want her help. The last thing I need is to look weak around here. But I'm not naive enough to believe this is a smart decision. In fact, I might not have a choice in the matter if I don't want to humiliate myself in front of McCafferty tomorrow.

"Wait!" I stop her.

She turns slowly, those deep brown eyes making me swallow before I can get any words out.

"Okay."

She cups her hand around the shell of her ear. "I'm sorry?"

"You heard me."

What more does she want? A *Scarlet Letter* speech?

"You're impossible," she says with a shake of her head as she leads the way to the EMT wing.

If I thought the barracks were quiet, you could hear a needle drop with how empty this room is. Minus a couple of medical gurneys, a locked hazardous waste box, and a long supply table, we're the only ones in it.

Hailey grabs an oversized lunchbox with a white cross stamped on the front. The first aid kit opens with the squeeze of a buckle and the pull of a zipper but might need to be shrink-wrapped shut now that it's been broken into. Supplies overflow onto the table. A saline solution wipe, a roll of gauze, and red medical tape are what she reaches for.

She gestures for me to sit in a fold-out chair across from her. I unlace my boots again and work them off my feet while she washes her hands in the sink, then she's back in front of me and cradling my ankle as she lifts my foot onto her lap.

I've had worse moments, but I'm given an I-told-you-so

smirk when the Scooby Doo Band-Aid falls to the floor with my sock. I flinch when she dabs the surrounding area with a saline solution wipe. She uses two fingers to hold a square strip of gauze over the blister and her teeth to rip a strip of medical tape.

I find myself wondering what it would feel like if those teeth sunk into my bottom lip. Would it send an electric current through my veins like her hands are now?

I clear my throat, trying to focus on something other than her mouth and her hands and her impossibly close proximity and what it's doing to my head.

"You want to tell me what you're doing here, Red?" I ask.

"Same as you, it would seem."

She's wearing a pair of blue slacks and a far-too-sexy-for-a-wildfire-crew blouse that buttons up the front.

"A wildfire EMT, huh?"

She nods. "Got hired yesterday."

My mind drifts back to our interaction for more pieces of the puzzle I think I might have missed.

Jack... I *see* the name on her phone screen. I *hear* it whispered in my father's voice inside my head. *He's been through a lot, him and his—* It hits me like a tidal wave.

Hailey Hart is Jack's daughter. *He's* the jerk who told her not to come.

The whole situation is muddy. I don't know how to make it less so besides doing what I'm good at.

My lips tilt into a smirk. "You ready to be surrounded by a whole lot of those guys you love to hate? The ones who only ask questions so they can get in your pants?"

She lifts her gaze to me. Leans in close, only a whisper from my face, and says, "I think I'm good. I handled you, didn't I?"

Heated eyes dart a path to my lips and back up again and hell if I don't wonder what it would be like to lean the rest of the way in and kiss her. Wonder if she'd yelp if I grabbed behind her neck and crashed our lips together in the hungry way I want to right now. It's impossible to think with her looking at me like that. Like she wants to lock that door and be alone in this room with me. It's messing with my head.

She doesn't need to be someone's rebound, and I don't need the distraction, but her breath is *way* too hot against my ankle not to focus on our proximity to each other.

"There," she says. "All finished. A hell of a lot better than a Scooby Doo Band-Aid."

I work my foot from side to side, inspecting all the angles. "I don't know... you think it'll hold?"

She swats me playfully on the arm. "Get out of here, rookie. You need to get some sleep."

I groan. "You can call me anything you want, but *please* don't call me that."

She offers me a smug grin as a parting gift. "Since you asked so nicely."

It's difficult, impossible really, to leave her, but I make my way to the door. I pause with my hand on the knob and turn back around. "Can I repay you with coffee in the morning?"

"It's my job, Morgan," she says.

Even though I promised myself I wouldn't let this thing between us—whatever it is—become a distraction, I still let myself want to be around her. It feels good to forget for a minute. Who knows, maybe it's what I need to move on.

"Okay. But hypothetically speaking, if a guy were ever to do such a thing... *how* do you like it? Your coffee order, I mean." I stuff my hands in my pockets.

Her eyes follow her hands as she restocks her kit. The soft glow pooling through the west windows highlights her smiling profile.

"I like it black."

CHAPTER THIRTEEN

14 years old

"Who's this girl you were hanging out with?" I nudge Dean in the shoulder as he bites into a slice of meat lovers pizza. On our stomachs, sprawled across my bedspread, we're watching *Arrow* on a twenty-four-inch flat-screen TV.

"Just some girl."

I don't buy it. Other than the guys on our high school football team, I'm the only other person he's ever hung out with.

"Sure." I consider giving him a break and letting it go, but... Why doesn't he want to tell me about her?

I tip on my right side, nudging him with my heel this time. "Come on; it's me. You can tell me anything."

He sighs like he knows he's not getting out of this. "It's the new girl," he mumbles under his breath.

"Madison Walter?!" My eyes bug out of my head.

"Why are you saying it like that?"

I press my shoulders back. "Like what?"

"With whatever weird gasp that was. As if it would be absurd for me to get a girl like her."

"No, it's not that. It's just..."

Madison Walter is beautiful. Long blond hair that skims the waist of her jeans. Crop tops that show off her perfectly milky skin. Eyelashes that fan her cheekbones when she bats them. It's not hard to see why Dean likes her. But she's kind of...

"What?" Dean presses, irritation creeping into his tone.

"I mean, she's kind of entitled. I just pictured her with one of the Johnson brothers or something, that's all."

Nate and Noah Johnson, identical twin seniors with a track record for trolling younger classmen, seem like the perfect fit.

"She's different than you think." He rolls his eyes.

"Different *how*? She wears a pound of makeup and every time she talks, it comes out all breathy and squealy." I giggle, and he glares at me. "I'm sorry. That was rude."

He sighs, scrubbing his face with his hands. "No, I get it. It's not like I've ever had a girlfriend before. What makes me think I can keep her?"

I push on his bicep so he'll stop hiding behind the pizza box. He tips backward on his forearms.

"Come on, Dean. You deserve any girl you're interested in."

And I can confidently say that because he's a twelve out of ten in the chivalry department. I can also attest to how good-looking the guy is, even if I've never been interested in him like that.

"Okay, tell me about the version of her you've gotten to know," I say. Maybe that will help me see her the way he sees her.

"Well... she likes horses and listens to country music." He's forgotten about the pizza box and is now staring off toward my closet with heart eyes. It makes me feel like a jerk for not catching how into this girl he already is. "She moved here with her grandparents, and she's really sweet with dogs." He blushes and I chuckle.

"You *have* always been a sucker for an animal lover."

"So, what is it then?" he asks.

"If you like being around girls like her, sometimes I worry you don't know me very well," I answer.

"Try me."

"Do you know why I called you tonight?" I ask.

He paws his slice of pizza around his plate as he thinks on it. "Because your dad didn't come home again?"

"Close. He came home for ten minutes, packed his camping supplies, and took off for the weekend."

He frowns at me. The genuine kind that makes me regret ever questioning if he knew me. "I'm sorry, Hayes."

I shake my head, willing the waterworks back where they belong.

"It's fine. He has to go back to his stupid job on Monday anyway."

Dean's eyebrows crinkle.

"What?" I pry.

He bites his cheek. "I mean, I wouldn't call it stupid."

I huff. "He has a teenager without a mother, Dean, and a job that takes him away from me for weeks at a time."

"Maybe he really loves it," he says with a shrug.

"Exactly! More than me. Are you really defending him?"

Dean's always the first one to comfort me when it comes to my dad. But then sometimes he'll say things like that, and it makes me feel like an overreacting brat.

He squeezes my knee. "No, I'm sorry. I think he should be around more on his time off. There's no excuse for that. But I also think his job is pretty great, ya know?"

I don't love the look in Dean's eyes as he says it. Like he's daydreaming about what it would be like to be him.

I know he's not wrong. I'm proud that his job is fighting

forest fires—he's a hero in a lot of people's eyes. I can't dispute that fact no matter how hard I try.

"Just promise me we'll always have each other," I beg him. "That nothing will come between our friendship?"

He rolls onto his side so he can look at me. Then he sticks out his pinky for me to latch on to. I twist them together and squeeze tight.

"I promise," he says.

Present Day

I toss and turn alone in my empty room. I don't know if it's the reality of being back here sinking in or the fact that it's below freezing in this ice box. I found an extra quilt in the storage cabinet I'm supposed to call a closet, but between the cement floors and the massive air vent beneath the bed, I couldn't get warm.

I pull on a pair of workout shorts and a sports bra, hoping a sunrise hike will help. A little blood flow to warm these numb extremities and clear my head.

I take the long hallway past Reed's room. The temptation to invite him worms its way from my subconscious. The place where I've fought to keep my thoughts of him until now.

The warmth of his skin as I took care of him, the heat in his eyes as he watched me. Reed Morgan ignited a fire within me that's proving hard to put out.

No distractions, I scold myself.

When I make it to the gym, I exit through the side door of the building. Gravel crunches beneath my tennis shoes and I wince, rubbing a hand up and down my arm and shooting a glance over my shoulder. I'm the loudest sound out here and the biggest target.

Focus on something else, Hailey.

The trail. The woods. The pre-dawn air.

I take in the sky—a cloudless state of midnight blue. It glows from a smattering of stars stretching in all directions. I gawk at it, missing the figure cloaked in darkness as he crashes into my side and knocks the breath from my lungs.

"Hayes? What are you doing out here?" Dean squints.

I huff out a laugh as my blood pressure skyrockets. "Oh, y'know... just thought a good bulldozing would be the ideal way to wake up."

The corner of his mouth quirks up in a half smile. "I'm sorry, I didn't see you. Are you okay?"

Okay would be an understatement. More like shaken up and thankful for the dark. Neither of which has anything to do with almost getting plowed to the dirt.

"Yep. Fine."

"Are you going for a hike?" he asks.

I roll my eyes. "No, I'm going on a bear hunt."

"Yeah, you're right. Stupid question. Mind if I join you?"

There's a very real possibility I could run into a whole host of wild animals out here. I don't have the faintest clue what to do if one approached me. Regardless of the state of our friendship, having him along might not be such a bad thing. He used to be my safety blanket. Before he went and screwed it all up.

"Sure." I hold out my arm, motioning him to go first. We don't need another collision. The next one would end in a bed of sharp sticks.

"You aren't wearing glasses," he notices.

I concentrate on his face instead of the uneven terrain beneath my feet. Under the moonlight, a two-inch mark glows white near his forehead.

"And you have a scar through your eyebrow," I retort.

His eyes drop to the ground.

Did he expect me to come back here the same person as when I left? I doubt *he's* the same.

"I got Lasik two years ago," I say. Not that I owe him an explanation.

He nods. "I stood too close to a branch my buddy was sawing. It gashed open my face when it fell, and the hair never grew back where it scarred."

Four years. Over twice the amount of time it takes scars to fade. It looks about as light as the ones on my heart. And yet, I feel guilty. For the past but also for right now. I'm sure this is his morning routine, and I'm encroaching on it. Or is it him intruding on me? I let out a sigh. Having him here adds to my already confused thoughts.

My feet pick up their pace as I sort out what to say to him. They carry me. Faster and faster. Until I'm practically running, my heart drumming inside of my chest.

What do you say to the person you used to tell everything to? Someone who was an extension of your family and now feels more like a stranger.

"Do you always walk this fast?" Dean pants.

I've managed to weasel my way around him. He's having to grind his hips back and forth to keep up with me.

"Didn't know *I'd* be giving you the workout, did you, Denominator?" I tease him.

The old linebacker nickname slips out before I have the chance to register the intimacy of it. As though we're not two people marching in a single-file line like distant soldiers readying for battle.

"No, but you've always surprised me, Hayes," he says.

"By coming back here, you mean?" I spin around and splay my arms out wide. "Surprise!"

It's light enough now to make out Dean's frown. I think it's safe to say he received my unplanned arrival as well as my dad did.

"It's a happy surprise."

"Tell that to Superintendent Hart." I turn away from him. "Seems like the two of you are thick as thieves these days."

He reaches out and snags my bare arm. "Wait."

The sudden stop jolts me around. He bears his apology in his eyes.

"Tell me how to fix things between us. How can I make it up to you?"

He went back on his promise. I don't know how he's supposed to change that now.

"After all those years watching me miss him... you made it so I had to miss you too."

He runs a palm along the back of his neck. "I didn't..."

I wait for him to finish that sentence, but he's searching the sky to pick the right words. It's taking him way too long to put them together into an "I'm sorry."

"You know what, I think this might have been a mistake," I say.

"What part?"

"Me coming back here. Us taking this hike." Because I'm a lot more winded than I should be for someone standing stalk still. "I'm gonna head back," I add.

"Hayes, just talk to me. *Please*. I *promise* I'll listen."

Had he said anything else, I'd have probably stayed. Heard what more he has to say. But that word. *Promise*. It's a bitter reminder. Why should I believe this time will be any different?

"That's the funny thing about promises. You either keep them or you break them."

CHAPTER FOURTEEN

REED

12 years old

I watch in horror as the embers lick at the bed of pine needles around us and skitter across the ground.

"Reed! What have you done!" Dad screams from behind me.

Jack races for his truck and pulls a long, hoe-like tool and shovel from the back end. He tosses the tiller to my dad.

"Start scraping away anything that can burn... sticks, weeds, pine needles. You're going to have to get kind of close," he instructs as he jams the tip of his shovel against the packed dirt. It only penetrates a couple inches below the surface, but he dumps the excess off the end and tries again.

"Come on!" He hollers at my dad, who startles from his stunned state.

He's clumsier than Jack with jittery nerves and wobbly arms. But he does what he's told, scraping away all of the random brush from the trench.

"What can I do to help?" I ask.

"You've done enough," my dad barks back, but Jack intervenes.

"There's another shovel. Bring it to me."

I run faster than I ever have before. Climb onto the tailgate and drag it back by the wooden handle.

"You saw what your dad was doing right? Trade him jobs. Work this left side now and scrape away anything that's not dirt."

The shovel feels like lead in my grip, the weight of it clunking against the ground when I transfer it to my dad's hands. Between the swept-away brush and the channel Jack dug, the right side of the two-foot fire holds steady beneath their barrier.

We get to work on the opposite side. They continue the trench while I work between them, raking everything I can find.

"Now stand back!" He motions away with his arms and hauls two coolers a few feet in front of the flames. As I watch them eat up the ground he's standing on, all I can think about is how brave he looks. How bold he has to be to command a running fire like that. The flames reach the toes of his boots by the time he dumps the ice. They sputter, sending smoke billowing overhead.

With the fire surrounded on all sides, and everything burned in the center, the active flames die down and we breathe a sigh of relief.

Well, Jack and I do. My father levels me with a look of disgust.

"What were you thinking, dammit? I told you not to wave the stick around like that! Do you know how much worse this could have been?"

"I'm sorry," I whisper. I know this was my fault. If I could take it back...

"Why can't you be more like your brothers!" he screams, and something inside of me dies along with that fire.

How will I ever be good enough for him after this? I more than disappointed my dad today. I made him realize he's better off never relying on me.

I trudge toward the truck and open the passenger door. The leather seat bounces with my jump and the hunk of metal slams shut with a pull. I don't know how long I'm sitting in there before Jack approaches my side of the vehicle. He presses his palms against the window. My reflection in the side mirror is hard to look at, my eyes swollen and red from crying.

He wraps his fists around the window frame and caps his large palm around my scrawny bicep, giving it a squeeze. "You did good out there, kid."

If it weren't for him, we would've never stopped that fire on our own. I know that. He knows that. Yet he still praises my efforts? My eyes well with fresh tears as he squeezes a second time.

"Most people freeze in fight or flight." His eyes find my dad through the driver's-side window. He's pacing with his hands threaded behind his head. "Not you. I think you would have jumped out of an airplane into that if you could. You have a future in this if you want it someday, and we were lucky to have you by our side."

Not *I* but *we*, he says. A word I'm not sure will ever describe the kind of relationship I'll have with my father. I may not have gotten what I wanted out of this weekend, but I found something better. A new dream. An answer to Jack's question.

I'm going to be a wildland firefighter when I grow up.

Present Day

A thick fabric covers my nose and mouth as I jolt up in bed.

The sleeping bag slithers from my face and down my torso until it falls in a heap on the stone floor. Strobes of golden light shine through the blind slats, and I block them with my forearm.

What time is it?

"Get up. We're meeting at the trailhead in ten. And you're not rooming in here," McCafferty barks.

"Take it up with Murphy," I tell him.

He kicks his sleeping bag back to his side and stomps out of our shared bedroom.

I groan. Between the deep ache settled in my muscles and the tender wounds on my heels, I'm not ready to be a whipping boy today.

I crawl out of my makeshift bed and bunch the sleeping bag from the top until it fits back in my pack. Shirtless and in gym shorts, I stuff my feet into unlaced boots and grab a change of work clothes to bring with me to the bathroom. Laughter sounds from the kitchen I have to pass through. I should have thought about the fact that other people would be up by now.

"That's a good look for you, Morgan." Hailey rakes my torso with her gaze as I tromp through the archway. She's leaning against the countertop, nursing a cup of coffee. Steam curls from the top of the mug.

"That was supposed to be from me." I nod at her hands.

"Got to get up a little earlier next time." A guy dressed in the same blue polo as her smirks.

Hailey swallows a sip of her coffee and sputters out a cough.

"Everything okay?" he asks, reaching for her.

My eyes glue to where he's touching her arm.

"I'm fine, Ben. It's just... the cream."

It's my turn to smirk. Serves him right for not getting to know her first.

"It's good right?" He smiles at her, completely oblivious to her look of disgust. "Nothing better than hazelnut." He squeezes her shoulder as he walks past her. "I'll see you in there."

I make a mental note to set an alarm. Today will be the last day I let anyone wake me up to watch Hailey choke down overly sweet coffee.

"Yeah, see you in there," she replies.

I close the gap between me and the kitchen.

"Your coworker seems great at asking questions."

I think about spending a day with her in that medic wing instead of whatever hurdles McCafferty has waiting for me. Even if it means sitting around for hours, it sounds more fun.

"Ben is nice," she says.

Yeah, because that's what you want in a guy, *nice*. Well, how's this for nice?

She startles when I take the mug from her hand. I slog to the kitchen sink and pour the almost mocha-colored coffee down the drain.

Damn, how much sweetener did he put in this?

The overflowing dishwasher rack needs a stiff tug to get open. There's one spot in the very back where I fit the dirty mug in. I shove it closed and open the closest cupboard above me. It's filled with ceramic plates.

"They're over there."

My eyes follow her finger to find a dozen mismatched mugs hanging from pegs next to the coffee machine.

I chuckle when I reach for the one that says *This wine is awful. Give me another glass.*

Oh, Moira Rose. At least these guys have good taste in TV.

"What are you doing today?" she asks.

I pour her a new cup of coffee and hold out the payment I promised last night. "Probably subjecting myself to a good ass kicking."

She accepts the mug and touches it to her lips to stifle a giggle. "I'd like to see that."

My eyes trace the curve where they wrap the rim. "I'm sure you would."

"Three minutes left, rookie."

Hailey and I startle at the creak of a recliner in the living room. McCafferty is eating a Costco-sized blueberry muffin and watching the weather report.

"Duty calls." I motion toward the hall that leads to the bathroom.

"What about *your* coffee?"

I take three strides forward—the entire distance that's left between us—and steal the cup from her hands. I tip it back, letting the hot liquid drain down my throat. Hailey's mouth hangs open as she watches my lips peel off her cup. I spin it to the side my mouth was just on so it'll be where she drinks from next.

"Yours tastes better," I say, taking clunky backward steps.

Her expression melts into a grin and then pinches into the one a mom would give a child who forgot to do their chores. "Two pairs of socks inside out so the seam doesn't rub on your toes."

I grin at her. "Thanks for taking care of my feet, Red." But my grin is wiped clean off as my back connects with another body.

"Where's your gear, Morgan?"

I spin on my heels, nearly tripping over my shoelaces. Jack's eyes volley between me and Hailey as if he's been standing there all this time, studying our interaction like a sociologist.

"I was told it's a good look." I say, winking at Hailey.

"It won't be when your shins are charred to the bone. McCafferty, update me."

Dean swings his recliner around so that it's facing us.

"Drilled a PT test, three hikes, fire procedures, and pulling an injured guy off a mountain yesterday."

"And how'd he do?" Jack asks right to my face.

McCafferty delivers his next update with a wicked grin. "He got blisters." His eyes dart to Hailey, and his sinister look disappears when her smile unzips.

"Ohhhhh!" A series of groans and chuckles seep into the room. Several guys round the corner, a hearty laugh leading the pack.

"Bet you're regretting everything now, aren't you, rookie?" My barracks tour guide slaps me on the shoulder.

"Ignore him. He has no tact." A Hispanic guy with frosted gray tips exchanges a glare with Logan Murphy. He slots a pair of gold-and-black-accented glasses against his nose with a single finger.

"Diego Ramirez, everybody. Mother figure of this crew." Murphy claps for him.

"Nice to meet you," I say.

Ramirez ignores Murphy's moniker and tips his head in a bow.

Murphy tosses a thumb in Ramirez's direction. "If you need an herbal remedy for those feet, this witch doctor's got you covered."

"They're called essential oils, dumbass, and I believe they helped pop out that ponytail you got wound into a knot yesterday," Ramirez retorts.

I think Murphy's cheeks flush, but it's difficult to tell behind his shaggy facial hair.

"Seems like the two of you have met," Jack interrupts.

We exchange a knowing look as Jack points to the next guy in a line of six.

"This is Hawkeem Jackson, your other captain."

A Black guy with a shaved head and piercing blue eyes steps forward and shakes my hand.

"Good to meet you, man," I say.

"So you're Walker's replacement. A rookie for a rookie. Watch out for that leg," he teases.

"Thanks for the warning."

Jack works down the line. "Returning crew member, Grant Daniels."

The guy's thumbs tug at the straps of his overalls as his bushy mustache quirks up on one side.

"What do you say, farmer... why don't you step up there and shake the guy's hand?" McCafferty drawls.

"Ya'll are gonna be sorry when I have a sixty-acre plot of land someday and you're still living out of the back seat of your trucks," Daniels says.

"You already have land. It's called a forest," Jack volleys back. Then he turns to me. "This is Wells Evans."

Blond, tall, and muscular... the walking definition of a Disney prince, I notice.

The shortest guy of the group by a foot pats Evans on the arm. "What this one lacks in brains he makes up for in height."

Evans hip-checks him back, knocking his black-framed glasses to the ground. A tuft of curly red hair gathers above his forehead when he bends to retrieve them off the floor.

"What the hell!"

"If you can dish it, you can take it," Evans says.

"And this is Owen Marshall, your beta squad leader," Jack fills in.

When Marshall pops back up, his green eyes have doubled in size from the thick frames. I shake my new crewmate's hand until I get to the end of the line where McCafferty now stands with them.

Two captains and a beta squad leader. That must make him...

"*Alpha* squad leader." He sneers at me as if he's reading my mind.

Of course you are.

"The rest of the guys are spending their time off away from the barracks," Jack says. "But, gentlemen, this is Reed Morgan. Our newest recruit."

McCafferty taps his watch.

"Good to meet you all but I'd better get to it." I shoot one last glance at Hailey. She's still smiling at me, which makes it hard to be anything but happy as I disappear to the bathroom to get dressed. They can all count on the fact that they won't be calling me rookie for long. I don't plan on quitting.

I pull on a fresh pair of green Nomex pants and strap gloves with a carabiner to my belt loop. I slip my yellow shirt on next and fit my helmet over my head.

"Grab your line pack. We're working hand tools," McCafferty says as I make my way down the hall toward the gym.

I pull the pack from my red bag, strapping it to my back. I'm thankful Murphy took me to the supply cache yesterday. It's already stocked with eye pro sunglasses, ear plugs, toilet paper, a fire shelter, two full water bottles, and fusies in the top front zipper pocket.

Dean throws a yellow bound book the size of a handheld notepad at my chest. I snatch it before gravity does.

"Your instant response pocket guide. Memorize it. Might save your life."

I shove it in my pack and follow him up the trail.

One mile in, I'm praising the bandages Hailey wound around my feet. The second pair of socks too, with the way my blisters aren't rubbing anymore. Looks like I owe her again.

But right now, all I can focus on is the fence of sagebrush

climbing up our ankles and snagging at our knees. I'm hacking it back with the curved ax tip of my brush hook, and even with the sun well shaded behind the packed canopy, I'm already sweltering. I can't imagine how it'll feel when we reach the hilltop.

"The McLeod next," McCafferty says.

If a hoe and a rake had a baby, that would be the sixth hand tool he's asked me to demonstrate today. I slam the steel prongs into the driest ground the August sun has ever made. Then I drag the straight edge in three-foot strokes to create a clean line.

"Enjoying yourself back there?" I ask.

He isn't even standing. He's slumped on a log nearby.

"Enjoying myself would be spending the day on the line, not babysitting the likes of you."

"You do make a good babysitter though," I goad him. "Anything else you're good at besides barking orders and changing diapers?"

Someone's got to make this hike entertaining.

"Watching you struggle," he says.

Branches crack under his boots as he stands.

"This is far enough." He hands me a chainsaw. "Fire is coming from the south. Keep it from spreading north."

In his hypothetical situation, he wants me to clear the row of trees in front of us so the fire can't carry through the canopy. This is the one skill we spent the least amount of time on during training. All I really remember is that it requires every piece of protective gear I have on me.

I add eyewear and ear plugs to my safety uniform and approach the first tree. It reaches a good twenty feet off the ground, with a stump around twelve inches in diameter. I know I'm supposed to determine the cutting technique next—conventional notch, Humboldt notch, open-face cut—but they all sound like a foreign language in my head.

That last one seems the most self-explanatory. *Open-face cut it is.*

Positioned a safe distance away, I line up my chainsaw in the direction I plan the pine to fall. Two cuts, one horizontal and one... *from behind? Or is it at angle?* I can't screw this up.

The blade slices halfway through the trunk's diameter and —*great*—I'm about to get creamed. It sways and tips in my direction.

McCafferty jumps to his feet and in a split-second decision, I finish the notch in the front. Wood shavings fly in my face. I only have it cleared by a foot when I hear the base snap. Gravity takes over and the whole thing topples to the ground.

It's not a clean cut by any means, but it didn't kill anyone either.

"This is why you need a babysitter. Now discard it in a controlled heap," Dean says.

I follow his orders, working under a gaping hole in the desert sky. Here, in the hot summer sun, my traitorous mind thinks of Teddy and Miles. Boating and swimming and laughing so hard my stomach aches. Or maybe it's the breakfast I skipped.

With my watch buried beneath my work gloves, I can't check the time. It's got to be noon, right? I glance over at McCafferty, who's squatting in the shade eating a turkey sandwich.

"Any chance you were going to tell me it's lunch time?"

"Waiting to see if you would notice," he says.

I set down the chainsaw, finding a small patch of shade across from him. He tosses me the brown paper sack from my line pack.

"Thanks."

I take a bite of the soft wheat bread. I know he isn't a fan of small talk but maybe if I try to get to know the guy, he might not dislike me so much.

"How long have you been on this crew?" I ask.

"Four years," he says.

"Four years and you made squad leader? Your parents must be proud."

What would my parents think if I stuck with something for four years?

As if he's reading my thoughts, he says, "All it takes is proving yourself here. Showing you can work as part of a team instead of next to one."

I chuckle softly, and he flicks his gaze from his sandwich.

"What?"

"Nothing. I just haven't seen a lot of *proving* from that tree stump."

Why am I this way? I can't just leave it alone?

"I've done my time here, and you know nothing about me." He stands and walks off with his sandwich in hand.

I can't blame him. Two days in and all I've learned is that maybe I've made a huge mistake.

CHAPTER FIFTEEN

HAILEY

Forty-eight hours. That's how long I've been here, and Jack still hasn't said a word to me since our initial greeting. As of eight o'clock this morning, R&R is over. Dispatch called the crew to their first assignment, and Ben and I stayed behind. It's only ten minutes outside of town. We can be there in five if we have to.

I overheard the incident size-up report over the radio before their buggy pulled out: a spot fire on a farm next to the highway. A hot exhaust pipe from a vehicle drug over a patch of dry cheatgrass. It lit on fire and ran for a ten-foot pine tree, a single barn structure, and a flock of sheep.

I've spent years knowing my father was in dangerous situations like this one, but being up close and personal, I wasn't prepared to feel worried about him. I try to distract myself with another too-quiet day alone with Ben, restocking supplies.

"How many emesis bags does one need in an ambulance?" I mumble. There's enough for the entire crew to get food poisoning at the exact same time.

"Oh, you'd be surprised when those come in handy," Ben

says. "I've used them as ice pack covers, breathing aids, dry bags, urine sample holders—"

"Do you actually like this part of the job?" I cut him off. "I've known you all of ten seconds, but you seem happy with... slow. No offense."

He pats me on the head. "I'm what they call an eternal optimist."

My teeth worry at my bottom lip. Does that make me a pessimist? Feeling concerned about my father while he's on the line and finding little distraction in anything else? I consider it for a moment. How much joy it brings me to take care of the people I love.

I stuff the last of the barf sacks in the jump bag. "I think I'm an altruist," I declare in some boisterous form of self-discovery.

"And you're not with them right now. That's why you're feeling anxious. Makes sense," Ben adds. He continues stocking sedatives, anticonvulsants, aspirin, and over-the-counter medications in an overhead compartment like he didn't just fill in as my therapist, validating my feelings.

My leg bounces a million miles a minute from where I'm perched on the gurney. "Well, doesn't it bug you not knowing how they're doing?"

He shakes his head. "Not really. But I don't have someone I care about on our crew."

"I don't have..." I start to lie but decide to flip the conversation back to him. "But you must have experienced this feeling at some point? To become a paramedic, I mean. Unless you genuinely love life-threatening emergencies, high-stress environments, trauma, and performing under intense pressure simply for the fun of it." My eyes widen. "I *do* sound like a pessimist."

Ben chuckles. "You sound like someone who chose this job for the right reasons, knowing you could face all of that."

I nod.

"Everyone has a story for why they do what they do." Dropping his eyes from my face, he leaves the back of the ambulance without another word.

We don't talk much the rest of the day, managing to busy ourselves until early evening and never getting our own radio alert.

"I make a mean spaghetti," Ben says as he turns off the lights to the medic wing. "You want to eat together?"

Cooking is something I've never enjoyed, but eating alone I don't mind so much. After being stuck at the barracks all day, I could use a night out.

"Thanks, but maybe another time? I think I'll take a drive and pick up some food along the way. I have a phone call to make."

"Sure," he says, ducking out the door.

My stomach churns. None of what I said to him was a lie. I haven't checked in with Aunt Karen since I got here, and she's been blowing up my phone with love life updates. Except for the part about rescheduling for another time. I don't think that's a good idea at all. Platonic coworkers don't have a spaghetti dinner for two without it ending up *Lady and the Tramp*–style. I'm already distracted enough with...

Slumped shoulders and a bobbing head take up the front door window of the building. I rush to the door, holding it open as Dean and Murphy carry a limp Reed through the opening. They're supporting him by each arm.

"What the hell happened?" I gasp when I see Reed's face. He's part pale, part green, with his head flopping all over the place.

"He's too good for water," Dean grumbles as they lay him down on the closest gurney.

"Red?" Reed croaks out.

He looks up at me like I'm a kaleidoscope of colors swirling in the most transfixing pattern. Then his grin blooms and that small depression hollows his cheek. Damn if I don't blush right there on the spot.

"*Red?*" Dean questions.

"Don't ask." Here is not the time nor place to be divulging my connection to the newest recruit. That knowledge won't win me any favors with Jack. And Dean's still not off my forgiveness list.

"I'm starting to like your office," Reed slurs, like he's either drunk or hallucinating, but I know it's because he's dehydrated. It draws our attention back to him.

"We've got to stop meeting like this," I tell him as I cradle his head in my lap. "Do you listen to any of the advice you're given?"

"I do when it comes from you," he says. "But not this drill sergeant." He waves an accusatory finger at Dean, who rolls his eyes.

I hide my amusement with the bow of my head. "I see that strategy is panning out quite well for you."

"I saved a flock of sheep today!" Reed exclaims.

"Congratulations, rookie. You graduated from kinder-garten," Dean mocks.

Reed groans and his eyes swirl around the room. I ease his head to the side.

"Okay, boys. I think I've got it from here," I say, escorting them both to the door.

The husky guy next to Dean turns around before reaching the exit. "I'm Logan Murphy, by the way." I swear his voice rattles the walls with how deep it is. I shake his outstretched hand.

"We may not have met until now, but I heard a lot about you today." His amused eyes flash to Reed. "I'll tell your dad where he is."

"Thanks," I say.

And as much as I try to dodge Dean, I nod goodbye in his direction. *Please, forgive me*, his expression reads. The same one he had yesterday morning on our hike. But I turn away and ignore it.

By the time I make it back to Reed's side, he's looking more than pale. I'm afraid he's about to puke. I find an emesis bag, place it over his mouth, and push on his back to tip him to the side—a movement that takes all of my body weight to accomplish.

Sure enough, he vomits. When he's done, he rolls onto his back on his own. With the contents of his stomach purged, he no longer looks green but flush. I graze the backs of my fingertips over his forehead.

Fever. I need to cool his body temp.

I dispose of the soiled bag in the nearest wastebasket and grab the first block of ice I can find. Recalling my conversation with Ben earlier, I slide it in a clean barf bag and hold it to his forehead. If we were at my childhood home, I'd be using a cold washcloth or a bag of frozen peas. But it's probably for the best. This medical grade slab feels far less intimate.

When I press it softly against his forehead, he wraps his fingers around my wrist, pulling me closer to his face.

Okay, not more intimate than *this*.

"I'm not any good at letting people in."

There's a deep sadness to his voice he's hiding behind, and as much as I promised myself I would keep my distance, I want to strip it all away. Find out what it is that makes him feel unworthy of being cared for. But he's not in the right mental or physical place for that kind of conversation.

I try to make light of it instead. "Mr. Cocky is not talking himself up anymore?"

"I think I like being around you," he confesses. But it's not accompanied by his usual perma-grin. Instead, he looks terrified to say it out loud. I doubt he means it in the way most people say it. We've known each other for barely three days. He's delirious and woozy and fighting a serious case of dehydration. That's a one-way ticket to a local hospital and out of this job if I don't get him in a better place.

"And I think I need to give you an IV to get some fluids in your system." I dodge his comment. "I'm going to need you to keep your arm straight and relaxed for me, okay?"

"Yep," is all he says back as his eyes wander around the room. The fact that he's still conscious is the most important thing, but I hope I didn't hurt his feelings.

Warm water douses my hands as I scrub them with soap. I towel them dry and squeeze on a pair of Latex gloves. An antiseptic wipe, a tourniquet, an IV catheter, and tape are all the supplies I gather on a metal tray beside Reed's bed.

If there was ever a time to be thankful for the extra courses and service hours I completed to get my advanced EMT license, it's right now. I'd need Ben's help to break the skin if not, and I don't want him in here.

"This might feel cold," I warn him as I swirl the sterile wipe over the crook of his arm.

He drags his eyes to the spot but doesn't flinch.

"A little pressure," I say next, and wrap the stretchy band tightly around his bicep. With the push of my pointer and middle fingers I work the inside of his elbow, searching for the right vein. None of them have the bouncy feel they should.

I slide his arm off the bed. *Come on, gravity, do your thing.*

Ten seconds, twenty, thirty-five, sixty. I keep time with the digital clock on the wall.

I lay his arm out once more and feel again. A vein in the center bulges slightly. It's not ideal but it should work.

"Okay, little pinch," I warn him, and then prick the skin. I feed the catheter in until I see blood.

There.

With a pull, the tourniquet releases, and I tape the catheter in place.

"What did you put in that thing, pennies?" he asks a couple minutes later.

I chuckle. "It's saline solution. Some patients complain it tastes like metal. It should go away quickly."

"Yep. It's gone." He smiles again.

Even delirious, Reed is happy and handsome and all of the things I should not be focusing on right now.

"See, there you go!" I say, before realizing I'm *stroking* his shoulder too and jerk my hand back.

OKAY. I officially need to leave his bedside.

"Get some rest. I'll be"—I look around for somewhere else in the room to sit other than perched over his body and decide to simply stand a few feet away—"here if you need me."

I forget about dinner and my phone call to Aunt Karen. I stay with him. Monitor how he's handling the fluids and electrolytes as he slowly slips to sleep. It's not until he's twitching that I admit, "I think I might like being around you too."

There are so many reasons why I shouldn't say that. The biggest of them all steps in the doorway.

"How's he doing?" Jack asks. As his usual distant self, his hands are wedged in his pockets. He looks more weathered every time I see him. Dark circles under his eyes, hard lines around his mouth.

"He'll sleep it off," I say.

My dad nods. "You're good at this."

We've never been great at talking or connecting. Finding common ground on much of anything. I think this is him trying to offer me a compliment?

"Thanks," I reply.

And I wait for him to say something else. Anything else. He could fill our silence with the most mundane thing, and I'd still listen. I want him to get to know me. Find out what the two of us have in common... more than just the same address. It's been years since we spent the kind of one-on-one time together that allows two people the chance to open up. Of course, I'm always wishing he'd tell me more about my mother. A dream I doubt will ever come true at this point.

I've talked to Aunt Karen about her before. It was one of the first times after my dad left for a whole summer. I was eight and she had taken me to a Payless Shoes for new light-up sneakers. Just her undivided attention had me tearing down all of my walls.

She told me how little she knew of my mother. When my parents met, the two were so wrapped up in each other they rarely made time for anyone else. They eloped at a courthouse and had me a couple years later. I remember feeling disappointed I didn't have anyone to ask about her. I wanted someone to tell me about the way she smelled or if I resembled her in any way... Some connection to make her feel real to me.

Instead, I got the ghost of her my dad always carries around. I lived in fear that the mere subject would smother him.

"Are you getting any sleep?" I study the pigmented crescents that frame his eyes.

"Don't worry about me. Sleeping on the ground is part of the job. I've been doing it for..."

Years, I know, my brain fills in for him.

I set the ice block to the side of Reed's face. Blotches of pink have returned to his cheeks. His body temperature has cooled down, so I don't think he'll need it much longer anyway. Stowed beneath the table beside me is my personal bag. I approach the side pocket filled with Ziploc bags and pull out the one labeled *Melatonin.*

"Try these," I say. "They're all natural."

I might need a nightly dose of them myself while I'm here, come to think of it.

"Thanks." He takes them from my outstretched hand. "For all of this. I'll see you in the morning."

Between his earlier compliment and this gesture now, I feel my heart swell in my chest.

Maybe he really does believe in me. Maybe the initial shock has worn off, and he's proud of this accomplishment. Even if I only chose to do it at first because I knew it would remind him of my mom.

CHAPTER SIXTEEN

HAILEY

14 years old

"You're back early."

I cup my left hand in a visor over my eyes. The sprawling pine tree in our front yard does little to block the August sun, even at nine in the morning. *The Longest Ride* by Nicholas Sparks folds closed in my lap as I leave my spot on the porch steps and approach his truck. It sputters as vehicles with two hundred thousand miles do when he slows on the gravel and shifts into park.

"I came to unload my gear," Jack says through the rolled-down window. He pops open the door and rounds the side of the vehicle, stopping at the tailgate.

Jittery nerves ping-pong inside my abdomen as I shuffle from ankle to ankle. "So, how was it?"

With a big scoop, he transfers a heap of equipment to the dirt runway we call a driveway. I'm expecting answers like "Great" or "Fun." "Relaxing," maybe. Not a confession.

"We had a fire."

I drop my book to the dirt. It sends a puff of dust billowing around my flip flops.

"At your campsite?" I gasp.

"I'm fine, Hayes. See?" He splays his arms out wide as if I haven't already done a thorough sweep from the tips of his hair to the steel toes of his boots. Same analysis I do every time he comes home. No cuts, scrapes, or broken bones that I can see. But... *is that soot under his fingernails?* How did I miss it until now?

"What happened?"

"It was a common mistake. The pyro kid I went with just wanted to have a little fun."

A kid? I thought he said he was going with friends.

A stinging feeling spreads across my chest at the quirk of his lips. It's been a long time since I've seen him look that happy. Years, even... and the fact that it was a result of him spending time with someone else's kid rather than his own has envy curling itself throughout my body until I'm having to clench and release my fists in tight balls.

"I brought you something." He breaks the silence between us. Even his voice has a melodic dance to it.

A smooth slab of wood rests in his open arms when I build up the nerve to look at him.

When he transfers the flat lumber to my hands, my fingertips brush the underside. The outer layer feels sandpapered to soft perfection.

"A piece of driftwood?"

I don't mean for it to come out sounding ungrateful, but what am I'm supposed to do with it?

He clears his throat. "I thought maybe... we could make a swing out of it?"

I tug on my ear, still unsure of what to say.

"I'm sorry." He shakes his head and turns away. "It was a stupid idea."

"Wait." I stop him. Grip the gift tighter as he tries to take it from my hands. "It's not stupid, it's just... I'm fourteen, not five anymore."

It's his turn to catalog my appearance. The peaks of his eyebrows squish together. He threads a hand through his hair and ash flakes onto his cheekbones. I don't think he's even noticed how much I've grown until this very moment.

"Right. No, yeah, I know," he stutters. "Forget I said anything." His tailgate lurches shut with a sudden shove, but I grab his arm, stopping him from jumping into the driver's seat.

"Dad, wait."

The name slips from my lips in a desperate ploy to get him to stay.

"I want to," I say. "Let's build a swing."

This time he smiles for *me*. And I don't really care if a swing is a little juvenile or maybe five years too late. I'm no longer thinking about what I was hoping would happen from this conversation. All I can focus on is that he thought of me.

Present Day

My mouth stretches wide in a yawn. How many times has it done that now? I've lost track.

There's a steady ticking like the beat of my pulse inside my head but it's coming from the wall. 4:03, the standard clock reads. I should just give up sleep at this point. It hasn't mattered how deep I slump into this fold-out metal chair; it's the opposite of comfortable. Now I'll live with a pounding headache, a ramshackle back, and an attention span in desperate need of a polar plunge. *We are no longer eighteen,* my body reminds me.

I push up with my heels to straighten in the chair. It squeaks with the transfer of my weight and I jolt my head to the side. Reed only stirs. His lips are a warm pink now, his cheeks too. I run a hand across his forehead. Cool and dry. A far cry from the clammy, pale sheet of yesterday's dehydrated skin. I check his IV next. The electrolytes have emptied into his veins in a steady drip.

I sigh in relief. He's made it through the worst part. Which is a good thing because I'm in desperate need of a shower.

As if on cue, a clump of matted hair drops in front of my eyes. I wedge the cluster into my braid to get it to stay back. The full moon casts a blue hue against everything it touches. The gurney, the floor, my walking path all lit in a soft glow that guides me out of the medic wing.

The windowless hallway is another story. A black hole of silence.

Clip clop, clip clop. The percussion instruments I call shower shoes slap against the wood floor. I slow to a scoot and paw at the wall to guide me, trying to remember which door leads to the women's showers.

My fingertips brush over the letters R-E-S and my brain fills in the rest of the word.

Made it. With a towel slung over my shoulder and a fresh uniform draped over my arm, I push open the door.

A motion light flicks on. It's dim but brighter than the hallway. I set my belongings next to a porcelain sink and twist the cap off a tube of Crest. Seconds later, spicy mint explodes on my tongue and I close my eyes, pretending it's an Andes chocolate to curb the rumbling in my stomach. Skipping dinner is catching up with me.

The hunger fuels my pace as I strip off yesterday's clothes. I leave them in a dirty heap outside the closest tile stall, then dive into the first of four empty showers and yank the curtain shut. Warm steam envelops me in the cramped space within seconds.

I spend very little time lathering and rinsing my hair and body before shutting off the water.

I whip open the microfiber drape and goose bumps pebble on the surface of my skin. I claw through yesterday's work clothes looking for... *I dropped my towel by the sink.*

"It's cold, it's cold, it's cold," I chant to myself in a naked prance to retrieve it. *Must make it back to the warm box.* Scooping up my uniform from where I left it too, I swivel for the shower.

Slap.

A warm body smacks into my bare skin, the hit so hard that I lose my grip on everything I'm carrying. A button-down shirt, tactical pants, underwear, and a lacy white bra all fall in a pile at my feet.

Reed's eyes bug out of his head as I scramble to cover the surface area of Texas with two limbs. I might as well be using dime-sized Band-Aids.

"What are you doing in here?" I swivel from side to side in a desperate ploy to get my stuff off the floor without dropping one of my arms.

"This is the men's bathroom. What are *you* doing in here?" he asks. His eyes troll the ceiling.

Men's bathroom? What is he... *the dark hallway, the fumbling hands, the braille reading...* it's all coming back to me.

"It was closer," I argue. I'm sure as hell not going to tell him that, for all I knew, I *was* in the women's restroom. I would sooner tell him I was worried about being away from him for too long than admit the truth. "I didn't think anyone would be up yet! Turn around!" I demand.

He's quick to pivot toward the opposite wall. With his back to me, I gather my stuff, making a break for the bathroom stall. I fumble around for an imaginary lock on a shower curtain as if he'll barge in here after me.

The shudder of an exhale is the only sound I hear behind the thin fabric separating us.

"Dammit, Red. What am I going to do now? Picture my grandmother all day?"

I dry my body with the damn towel that got me in this situation and cram my foot into one pant leg, hopping to pull them on. If Reed's awake, it means everyone else probably is too. Now the whole crew is going to know I showered in here.

"I'll tell you what you're going to do." I grunt as I work the pants up and button them at the waist. It takes even less time fastening the four buttons on the front of my top at the pace I'm moving. "You're going to monitor that door so I can sneak back out of here, and then you're going to forget this ever happened."

I'm so focused on shoving all of my things in my arms that I forget Reed is my patient. How on earth did he remove that IV on his own? Just savagely rip it out of his arm?

I yank the curtain back and sweep the floor for my belongings. Somehow it feels like I'm hauling out more than I brought in here when all I did was exchange one set of clothing for another. I tiptoe toward the door as if Reed didn't hear the woosh of the shower curtain or the buzz of my toothbrush when I accidentally hit the ON button while swiping it from the sink. He's still doing what I asked, stalling by the door. But I have to face him now.

When we make eye contact for the first time, I can't help but blush a little. He saw *every* part of me. Which suddenly feels very unfair. Usually when you get naked with a guy for the first time, it's because you both chose to. Not because you're flocking around a men's bathroom in a naked parade.

Reed's wide shoulders are taking up most of the exit space. I'll have to push past him to get outside. But as my pants brush his leg, he snatches me by the hips and presses me against the wall. I yelp and lift my eyes to his face as he lets the door fall shut, closing us in the bathroom alone together.

"I can't do that."

Heat soaks through my skin and seeps from the place where he's touching me to my entire body.

"Is it hot in here? Maybe we should open a window," I say, searching around the room before I remember: it's an interior wall.

"Don't deflect," he says with that look. The same serious one he used last night when he was out of it. Saying things he doesn't remember. Things he probably didn't mean.

I think I like being around you.

"You can't do what?" I question back.

He maps my eyes in a zigzag pattern. "Forget it ever happened."

I let out a frustrated puff of air. "Why not? And why do you call me Red all the time?"

He presses in closer, my body flush to his now.

"Because. You're the only woman who doesn't hide your blush under my stare."

He crowds me against the cool cement wall.

YOU.WILL.NOT.BLUSH. I repeat the command inside my head. But I already feel it. The warmth creeping up my neck and radiating across my cheeks. He's *so* close, his lips inches from mine, and I actually let my eyes fall prey to them once. He exhales, and I can taste the scent of peppermint from his parted lips.

Did he brush his teeth in the medic wing too? How long has he been up?

"I already have a hard enough time focusing on this job just knowing you're in the other room," he whispers. "I didn't need to know what you look like naked too."

My heart is galloping in my chest. Crossing a finish line I didn't sign up to race.

I swallow and rapidly blink. "It's nothing you haven't seen before, right?" Even as I ask that question, I contemplate how many women he's seen naked. I have nothing from his past to base my answer from, but I get the vibe that he's a player.

His eyes flit back and forth between mine. The heat of his hands sear into my sides, and suddenly, I feel like my shirt has caught fire. He leans in an inch closer for a second as we share each other's air. I can see it in his eyes. He's warring with himself over something. The way he's pushing his forearms into the wall behind me like he depends on them for support. But then he pulls away just enough to free his hand and pinch the base of his neck.

"Right."

Why is he agreeing with me if he looks like he doesn't want to be? At least a hundred different questions surface as I study that look.

Whatever cataclysmic spell we were both under breaks the moment he takes yet another step back, and I seize the opportunity to slip past him.

"Let's just push it out of our minds. Not make this a bigger deal than it has to be, okay? I don't want to forever remember your look of horror when you walked in here."

He grabs me by the wrist one more time, his thumb dragging across my pulse. "It wasn't a look of horror. I had to fight to stare at that ceiling," he says.

I can't fan my face as it flushes beneath his gaze, so I touch my cheeks instead. But even my palms are hot and do nothing to help. I need to get out of here!

I dodge past the threshold expecting to find an entire crew of onlookers waiting in the hallway. But no one is out here. No one is up yet. I'm back to sneaking around in order not to wake anyone else.

I chance one last glance through the crack as the door falls shut, but he's already gone.

The spray of the shower sounds seconds later with his words trailing across my mind like they're attached to a banner on the back of a small plane.

I had to fight to stare at that ceiling.

I told him not to make it a big deal, but *that?*

Now we're so far past a big deal we're a whole brush fire.

CHAPTER SEVENTEEN

REED

1 2 years old

"I think it's best if we go home in the morning," was what my dad said after we stayed up until midnight making sure the flames were officially put out. We'd emptied every last cube of ice from the coolers and soaked the bed of charred pine needles with all the water bottles Mom and a few people from surrounding campsites had packed.

I unzipped the tent at sunrise to a black line in the dirt. It stretched on and on around us. I wasn't convinced if I stepped anywhere near the eternal circle, it wouldn't swallow me whole. Everything was the color of midnight and covered in ash. A situation that still required an incident report to local authorities by Jack. My mistake was even harder to look at in the daylight.

If I could go back and make different choices, I would. I'd tell my dad I was sorry right away, and he'd not only hear it but believe it too. But it's too late for that. The damage has been done. I'm afraid I've lost his trust.

It's quiet when we pull up the driveway in Park City, the

end of an eight-hour drive spent in silence coming to an end. I'm not sure I've ever run out of things to say in my whole life, but at a loss for words was exactly how I'd describe the weight sitting on top of my chest.

"I'll unload. You can head inside." His voice is even. He doesn't even sound mad anymore. But the fact that he's still acting so withdrawn, pushing me away, stings more than anger ever could.

This weekend built a barrier between us. We're that black line that never ends. I don't know if I'll ever become more like my brothers or if there will be a day when something I do makes him proud. But right now, it feels like I could do just about anything, and it still wouldn't be enough.

Present Day

Forget it ever happened? Is she kidding?

How am I supposed to ignore the soft curve of her waist that fit perfectly beneath the palms of my hands. Or the way her hair fanned across her breasts as it cascaded down her chest. I can't stop picturing Hailey pressed up against that bathroom wall, and it's doing exactly what I promised myself I wouldn't let happen after my training mistakes... It's making me lose focus.

My first day on the line was yesterday, and I'm determined to be the best at this job. But now there's a small problem. A crimp in my plan. The superintendent's daughter is consuming my every thought.

"Failing to break in your boots, dehydration, disrespect." Jack presses his palms into the door casing, commanding my attention. My hands freeze, wrapped in shoelaces. I unwind them and roll my shoulders back. He doesn't look mad; it's worse. He looks disappointed.

"It's one thing to show up unprepared," he continues, "but had you started training with us in April, I would have let you go the moment you mouthed off to anyone on this crew. I want to be right about you, Morgan." His eyes bore into mine as if he's transferring a memory... *that night... the campsite... the fire.* A mistake I never want to relive. It was nine years ago, but the pieces all fall into place like it was yesterday.

You did good out there, kid. Maybe you have a future in this.

I still remember his vote of confidence in me. I think it played a big role in why I chose this career path for my life. But I pushed that weekend so far out of my mind that I never tied the two together until now. And even though I hardly know this guy, his opinion matters to me because of it. I want to impress him like I did back then.

A crackle sparks through the radio speaker clipped to Jack's collar and draws my attention to the staccato voice delivering a choppy message.

"*Dispatch to Iron Summit. We've got a brush fire north of Warren, Idaho, at the White Horse Campground. Sending you the resource order now.*"

He tucks his chin to his collarbone so that is mouth presses against the communication device. "Superintendent of Iron Summit. Copy that."

He draws his phone from his pants pocket and swipes across the screen. I study the movements of his mustache as he mumbles, "45.264 degrees north, 115.6765 degrees west. Command One, Garret Paxton. Air Tactical 6. Tac 3."

GPS coordinates, incident commander contact info, and radio frequencies, I determine from the limited information he whispers.

"*Department 8, this is dispatch. We need two engine crews on site,*" the static continues.

Jack drowns out the alert with his own phone call. "Murphy, we roll out in one hour. Notify Jackson."

With swift movements, he tucks his phone away and grips me by the shoulders.

"I'm taking a chance on you because I owe..." He shakes his hand as if he can physically mop away the end of that sentence. "But I will sure as hell find a replacement if you keep pulling stunts," he warns.

I'd nod if it wasn't for my stunned realization. The reality of my situation all making sense now. I didn't get hired mid-season because of my talent, skill, or résumé. I got this job as a favor to my father.

"Oh, and Morgan... stay away from my daughter."

"Saddle up, gentlemen. It's time to take Pony for a ride!"

Half the crew gathers around a two-wheel-drive commuting vehicle. It's mint green with a mountain logo and *Region 4* stamped on the back door. Long white stripes paint the sides of the buggy nicknamed after a small horse.

"Look who's on their own two feet today." McCafferty slaps his palm over the top of my helmet and jostles it around a bit. "Thought that life-saving sheep maneuver of yours might have done you in, rookie."

I vaguely remember boasting about that in my disoriented state.

"Do your worst," I say to the alpha squad leader as he assigns us all our tasks.

He saved me for last.

"Fuel duty," he calls over his shoulder, then breaks apart

with the rest of the guys to get to work. I expected toilet paper duty at this point, so I'll take it.

Of the four side compartments on the vehicle, the two that hug the back end carry Siggs—twenty-ounce red metal bottles of fuel made for saws. I slide a couple dozen small MSR-made tanks into the pipes that hold them and the corresponding bar oil beneath. With the fuel properly loaded, I double-check my own line pack. The government-issued bottles in the side pockets are still empty.

I jog to the kitchen and fill five liters of water and add two Gatorades from the fridge. I won't make the same mistake twice.

"Let's go, let's go, let's go," I hear Jack yell from the parking lot. "We've got fifty miles to cover on a thirty-mile-an-hour road. That's an hour forty minutes for you loiterers to dink around." He slides behind the wheel with Murphy in the passenger seat.

I've managed to leave it turned off for days now, but I fish out my phone to check my messages on the drive. Several sets of work boots clank against a metal strip running down the aisle as the guys pile on by rank. We all shove our line packs in the mesh-covered compartments overhead and plop down into one of four rows of dual black leather seats. As the newest recruit, I'm at the very back with Ramirez. But I'm not complaining. The view of a certain ambulance out the back window is all I was hoping to see.

Mere minutes down the road, the buggy is a party bus of noise. The clang of heavy metal tools on board, the grate of shoe soles on the rough floor, the shout of conversations as they compete to be heard, and Ramirez, my seatmate, who is belting Beyoncé lyrics four feet from my ear drums.

A pounding pulses behind my eyes, and I don't know if it's the lingering aftereffects of dehydration or the dread of turning on the phone cradled in my lap. I still don't want to think about seeing Miles and Teddy on Instagram. When it powers on, one unread text message shows up. I tap on the green icon and a phone number I don't recognize flags at the top.

Hi. How's that head feeling? the message says, and I sweep the buggy for the guy who's messing with me. No one has their phone out but Ramirez, and even he has his eyes closed, head tipped back as he warbles another verse.

I glance through the back window and find Hailey watching her lap. *Was it her?* There's only one way to find out.

How'd you get this number? I type. Seconds later, three dots pop up in the bottom corner, float there, and disappear with a new message.

It's my duty as EMT to make sure my patient is feeling up for this, it reads.

A grin splits across my face. I try to peek out the back window again, but the glass has fogged over from Ramirez's passionate lungs. *Man, he's into it.*

I swipe an arc of condensation with my forearm.

> REED: You know, you could have just asked me for my number instead of stealing it from your dad's office.

She smiles at her lap.

> HAILEY: Now where's the fun in that. You didn't answer my question.

> REED: Well, you're coming, so I'm going to be perfectly fine. How's it going back there?

> HAILEY: Ben keeps asking if I'd like a drink from his thermos. What are the chances it's filled with 99 percent creamer?

REED: Proceed at your own risk. 😉

HAILEY: What about you? Dean killed you yet?

REED: McCafferty couldn't kill a fish if he caught one by accident. But I could use a game of 20 Questions to pass the time. Ramirez is singing "All the Single Ladies," and it smells like feet in here. Interested?

His voice jumps up and down as the rattle trap buggy traverses a long stretch of gravel—Warren Wagon Road.

HAILEY: You poor thing. Sure, I'm in.

REED: Planner or spontaneous?

A part of me hopes she'll say spontaneous, but the way she clung to that safety manual on the plane... I'm going to say planner.

HAILEY: 100% planner. Stay up or sleep in?

Thought so.

REED: This is a no-brainer. Stay up.

But I imagine it. What it would be like if sleeping in meant having her in my arms. I'm not sure I'd ever want to leave that bed.

REED: Date night in or out?

HAILEY: In... by the fire. Eyes or Hair?

REED: Butt. 😅 You?

I snicker when I find her shaking her head at her phone.

HAILEY: You're such a rebel. Good thing you have really nice eyes.

Suddenly we're inching toward dangerous territory. But I can't stop now.

REED: You do too... and lips.

HAILEY: Watch it! Your driver is my father, remember?

It's a tease of a warning. A reminder that this thing—whatever it is between us—can't cross a line, even if we both want it to.

REED: Oh, I haven't forgotten. Neither has he.

She sits up straighter, holding the phone closer to her face.

HAILEY: Did he say something to you?

I don't want to worry her.

REED: Nothing I can't handle.

I catch her gnawing on her bottom lip.

HAILEY: Casual or serious?

For some reason this question makes me think of Teddy. I never used to be a casual guy. But after her... I'm afraid to be anything but. Even if the idea of Hailey and I together as more than casual makes my heart beat faster, I lie to her.

REED: Casual. You?

The three dots show up and disappear several times. I'd watch her reaction through the window, but we take a left turn, and I can't see her face when the text finally comes through.

HAILEY: Call me the queen of casual.

My eyebrows lift. The buggy takes another sharp turn, and a burst of color fills the back window. I don't have a chance to reply when my vision glasses over at the sight before me.

CHAPTER EIGHTEEN

REED

Aplume of smoke billows into the sky, thick and gray. A stretch of yellow caution tape surrounds a metal grate. A fire ten times the size of my first burns the ground. My father's voice, distant and choppy, is all I hear.

Reed, what have you done! Why can't you be more like your brothers?

The memory serpents around my windpipe, but the feeling only lasts a second. Several miles off the main road in a remote area it's clear. We've made it to the White Horse Campground.

Two engine crews with long hose lines draped over their shoulders control the scene. They've established an anchor point near the road and are drenching pine trees with arcs of water. The engine crew captain and incident commander trail up and down the south side as Jack pulls our vehicle up next to them.

"Good to see you again, Hart. This is Captain Sparrow."

The incident commander introduces Hart to his counterpart—a guy with a beard halfway down his chest. A pirate joke lingers on the tip of my tongue, but we all remain quiet in the back seat as we listen to the report.

"We've got fire at the timber. Moving uphill. Rapid rate of spread. Ten-miles-per-hour winds from the southeast. We need your crew to plug into the right flank and work north toward Salmon River." He turns his head to the side, his voice catching on the wind. I hear nothing but "Good luck out there."

Jack nods to them as he pulls the buggy off the road and onto a hiking trail. We don't make it very far before the surrounding brush is too dense. If we take our standard issued tires through this terrain, we'll get stuck.

It's not until we're diving out of the back of our vehicle that I notice the ambulance is gone. Ben and Hailey must have stayed behind with the engine crews. Jack circles his arms to gather us and shouts his debrief over the crackle and pop of bright orange flames.

"Listen up. We're dealing with extreme fire behavior. We're talking flame lengths up to fifty feet in the sage and lodgepole pines. We're keeping the crew together. Four saws up front cutting a fifty-foot swath. Everybody else with hand tools scraping behind them. We need to make it as far as we can today. Marshall, you'll be posting lookout on that hill spinning weather. I need an update every hour on the hour." Jack tosses him a radio. "Use Tac 3."

"You got it, Supt." Marshall catches the device with one hand, clips it to his collar, and slings his line pack over his back. He takes off on his own for the summit.

"What are your questions?" Jack asks the rest of us.

I raise my hand. "I've got a question."

He plants his hands on his hips, his mustache set in a firm line. "Something tells me I'm going to regret hearing it."

"How often do you think we can expect an update from Captain Jack Sparrow back there?" I ask.

He rolls his eyes. "You've been waiting the last five minutes to say that haven't you?"

I grin. "Yes. Yes, I have."

"*This is Copter 110, issuing water drop.*" The declaration comes through Jack's radio, and like a dam breaking, water gushes from the sky and drenches the flames a hundred feet from us. The helicopter arcs to the left, the blustering wind spraying a net of heavy mist over our entire bodies. The initial condensation dampens our clothing and drips down the lenses of our protective eyewear. Most of the crew drops to the ground in a plank for the rest of the deluge. I take it standing up, arms spread wide.

"What a time to be alive, boys!" I yell, shaking my body like a wet dog. I may look as though I just walked through a car wash fully clothed, but I *feel* like I just free-fell from a fifty-foot cliff.

Now *this* is what I came here for.

When night falls, the wind carries smoke away from the campground where we've settled with the engine crews. The deep-blue sky glitters with stars—a respite from the heat of a fourteen-hour workday. Clearing one mile of brush is what we have to show for it.

McCafferty was right. A day of hiking in 90 degrees is nothing like laboring beside open flames.

We dug and scraped for hours. My forearms and hands seize so badly from the fine motor strain they're struggling to support my dinner fork. But that's not stopping me from cramming in two thousand calories of beef and bean burritos as my stomach gnaws on my spine.

Jack squeezes Marshall and Murphy's shoulders as he says to the crew, "Good work out there today. Let's get some rest. We're in this for the long haul."

When he steps to the side, I see Hailey waiting in the shadows beneath a tree. She's chewing on a nail as she tracks her father's footsteps. There's a sadness in her eyes as she watches him. It makes me want to ask her questions. Personal questions that I'm afraid I'll have to reciprocate. But I give in to the pull anyway and approach her.

"Long day, huh?" She stuffs her hands in her pockets as I stop in front of her.

"They're about to get even longer I'm afraid." I sweep my eyes past the charred vegetation where the woods glow a brilliant orange.

"I heard," she says. "They're setting up a fire camp here tomorrow. This place is about to become a city."

We both scan the beginnings of that new city forming, with water tender crews and hand crews setting up tents. The idea that this fire could morph into a new animal every day excites me, no two days on the job looking alike. It's exactly what I was hoping for.

"That means you're staying too?" I ask.

She nods, and I smirk.

"What?"

"Oh, there's only one part of this new camp I'm disappointed about," I say.

"What's that?"

I take a step closer to her. "What happened this morning not happening again."

Even in the dark, I watch the color in her face deepen, like a layer of red crayon shading in the apples of her cheeks. Her eyes flare as she bites her lip.

"I thought we weren't going to talk about that," she whispers.

I lean in slightly, her back connecting with the tree trunk behind her. I inch as close to her lips as possible. Just a breath apart. Her chest rises and falls in rapid succession as I whisper against her jaw, "We're not. Casual, remember?"

Her exhale ghosts across my face. "Right." She swallows once. Blinks twice. Then she sweeps out to the side and jogs away.

I release a held breath. "You can do it," I whisper out loud to the tree. "Casual as a cucumber."

CHAPTER NINETEEN

HAILEY

"Can you believe this place? I've never seen so many tents in my entire life," Ben says as he hammers the fifth and final pole into the packed dirt and feeds the end through the corner pocket of the canvas. He pulls tight and the pentagon domes over our heads.

I eye his handy work. "Not bad."

"Not bad? This thing looks like it came from—" His sentence stops short when he realizes I'm complimenting him, not teasing. "The circus," he finishes. "And thank you."

He pulls at the collar of his uniform.

"It does look like it came from the circus. Imagine the sort of magic tricks we could perform in here." I wave an ear thermometer in a series of embellished loops.

"If you call taking care of poison oak or wrapping a sprained ankle a magic trick." He chuckles.

"Hey, not everyone knows how to do those things."

"But everyone does have Google," he says.

"Not out here they don't."

We've already had this conversation. It's not that I'm excited for someone to get hurt, but I don't do well sitting around all day.

I can't be on the fire line either. Reed's out there working with the crew, and he'll be all distracting with his tight pants and his panty-dropping dimple. I need to keep my underwear right where they are, thank you very much.

Arms full of supplies from the ambulance, Ben asks, "How long do you think this will go on for?"

"My dad was on the same fire for months one summer." I feel around with the toe of my boot for the nearest worktable. When it connects with a metal leg, I empty my arms on the surface. I yelp as a first aid kit clatters open and look up to find Ben's grinning face three feet from my own.

"I'd be okay with it," he says. It's followed by one of those long pauses and a look that implies something words don't even need to say. I squirm.

I'm going to be spending a ton of time with this guy. Potentially days on end alone in this tent. If I don't come out and tell him that nothing will ever happen between the two of us, he might get the wrong idea from sheer proximity alone. As I'm about to squash the grin plastered on his face with honesty, he changes the subject.

"What got you into the EMT field anyway?"

A loaded question that involves telling him about the dad I'm trying to be closer to and the mom I never knew.

I give him the second-best truth. "I like helping people."

"You're a fixer," he says.

"An altruist," I remind him. "What about you? I know you didn't get into this field for the occasional poison oak on a slow day."

Judging by the set line of his mouth, he doesn't want to answer that question any more than I did.

"A car accident."

I melt my back against the table, and he does the same.

"It was my senior year of high school. My girlfriend and I were on our way to the homecoming football game."

A whoosh expels from my lungs and coils around the room, making it feel smaller somehow.

"A drunk driver crossed the median on the interstate and hit us head-on."

I suck in a breath. "I'm so sorry, Ben."

I don't know what compels me to reach for his hand, but I do. Maybe it's the altruist thing. Or that I know what it's like to live without someone you love.

I may never have met my mom, but I loved the idea of her. She lived on in every crevice of our home, from the cookbooks my dad never used, to the photograph of her pretty face holding me in a hospital bed. It used to sit on my nightstand, but it disappeared just like the smell that once clung to her clothes in the closet. I haven't thought of that photograph in a long time.

He accepts my gesture as I cradle his palm.

"It's okay. It was a long time ago," he says. "I just remember it took forever for any kind of medical team to arrive. I've replayed the scenario over and over in my head, thinking if they could have just gotten there faster... but after all the medical training I've done, I know that she didn't stand a chance. She wasn't wearing a seat belt, and the windshield glass severed her carotid artery."

She bled out in minutes, I fill in for him. He stares off toward the tent wall, and I squeeze his hand once, letting him know I'm still here, still listening.

"I like to believe that had I been prepared, maybe I could have slowed it down. Given her enough time to call her parents. Given them the goodbye they deserved. Instead, I've honored her memory by making it my life's mission to be as prepared as possible. I took all of the emergency training Unitek EMT had to offer."

"Arizona? How did you end up here then?"

"It was this little brochure we found on the table of a diner once. *McCall, Idaho*, it said across the front. Picturesque mountains painted the cover. We decided right then and there we were going to move here together when we graduated. She liked the mountains, and I liked to ski. It seemed like a good fit. I know some of our friends and family would say I'm crazy to come all the way here without her. But it makes me feel closer to her, ya know?"

"Boy, do I know," I say.

"Your turn. How did you get this job?"

"I'm... from McCall."

I don't tell him the part about moving back here just to be closer to my dad. Even though he must know we're related by now, I hate admitting it out loud.

"I think Meredith would have liked you." He smiles, brushing his thumb over my knuckles.

A groan echoes from the tent's entrance. When we both look up, the blond crew member I haven't met yet is slumped against Reed. Soot covers their bodies from head to toe. I pull my hand back to my lap, but it's too late. Reed tracks the motion.

"What happened?" I ask, pointing toward the empty gurney.

Reed takes slow calculated steps, accommodating his hopping friend.

"You're the one who diagnoses injuries, Red," he says, dumping the guy on the vacant gurney and folding his arms.

What's his problem?

"Jumped from a tree branch and came down on it wrong. I

think it might be sprained," Ken Doll moans. "I'm Wells Evans by the way."

I swear his teeth glint, even with the lack of sunlight.

"Was that so hard?" I ask in a clipped tone to Reed.

"I didn't see it. Just volunteered to bring him in here." I catch Reed glaring at Ben.

"Volunteered, huh?"

He stares at the exit as if he'd rather die than be in here right now.

"Not the time for flirting people," Evans groans. "I'm not sure I'm going to be able to get this boot off if we leave it for much longer. Is it cutting off the blood supply to my feet?"

I lift his pant leg and expose an ankle the size of an apple. Ben squats down next to the injury as I gently roll it from side to side to check his mobility.

"Looks like a nasty sprain," Ben says.

"What do you think?" Reed asks me.

Is he... *jealous*? I'm not sure how else to explain him dismissing Ben like that, but there's no time to analyze Reed's motive.

"Ben's right. It's sprained. Good news is, with elevation and ice, we should be able to get the swelling down in a few hours."

"You good, Evans?" Reed asks as I work the laces open and ease his boot off from the heel.

"Yeah. Thanks, man," he says.

"Is that all you need from me?" Reed asks me.

I study him. This is not the same guy who stayed and helped the old woman on the airplane. His friend is injured and he's diving for the tent exit.

"Didn't know you wanted to be taking orders from someone else. But yes. You're dismissed, Morgan."

He scrubs at the back of his neck and turns on his heel, leaving the tent ten times faster than when he came in.

"Wow. I've never seen that guy not smiling," Evans says. "It's kind of a tragic sight."

"Me neither," I add, wondering who it was that destroyed Reed's confidence in relationships.

CHAPTER TWENTY

REED

My line pack digs into my deltoids and slumps my posture. It's all I can do not to collapse in the dirt.

One mile to go.

A cramping sensation seizes my left calf, and I roll my toes to stretch it out. The transfer of weight adds tension to my thighs and my knees threaten to buckle with each step I take. But that's not what's causing the tightness in my chest.

McCafferty treads the path in front of me, guiding us back to camp. He could balance a bowling ball on each shoulder, but it's his drive that I admire the most.

Over the last five days he's cut more trees, moved more fuel, and been the last one to set down his hand tool at nightfall. An exemplary leader who knew it was smart not to overexert himself during my training days. He saved his energy for this.

I study his even steps. Mimicking the cadence like counting sheep. It's repetitive enough to distract from the throbbing in my feet, and before I know it, we make it back to camp an hour past dusk.

It's dark and quiet everywhere but the catering trailer. In a single file line, a food crew serves us burgers and fries on cheap disposable plates. The fried aroma rips at my stomach, and I inhale a bite before I've even sat down on the wooden picnic bench. The greasy food eases the pain that's lingered there most of the day. I cram in every last bite, crumple the trash, and slide out from the bench.

"Morgan, you aren't sticking around?"

It's the first time he's called me by my last name.

In any other circumstance, it would be the *first* thing I notice. But all I can think about at this point is crawling into my sleeping bag and passing out. There's no more putting on a brave front tonight.

"I don't know how you guys do it," I confess.

"You'll get there," McCafferty says, nodding at me. Another gesture reminding me how wrong I've been about him.

"Thanks. I'll catch you guys tomorrow, okay?"

A series of good nights follow me as I stumble my way across the dark side of camp.

Signs barely visible in the moonlight stake the ground: *Shh, crew is sleeping.*

I unzip my red bag and drag the cocoon from it, spreading it out on the ground. A groan escapes my lips as I kneel to untie my boots.

"You want to tell me what happened yesterday?" A soft voice cuts the silence.

I peek over my shoulder. Hailey's standing there with her arms folded across her chest. She must have found a way to shower today because her hair isn't in a braid anymore. It reminds me of the plane and the men's bathroom. Both of which I don't want to be thinking about right now. In fact, I don't want to be thinking about anything at all.

"I'm really tired, Red. Do you think we can talk about this tomorrow?"

"You're leaving tomorrow," she says.

"I meant after work."

The loose strands of her hair wave back and forth with the shake of her head. "I overheard my dad talking to the incident commander. It's too long of a hike now, so you guys are spiking out."

"Oh." My legs finally buckle when I try to sit. I grunt as my butt connects with the packed ground.

Her brow wrinkles as she kneels before me.

"You're sore. Let me help you." She doesn't ask, just demands it. Wrapping her hands around my right thigh and putting pressure on the pads of her thumbs, she rubs up and down my leg in firm strokes.

I try to pry her fingers away, but she bats at my hands.

"Let me." Her tone is softer this time, and she loosens her grip. "Better?"

I nod. The warmth of her fingertips feels like a heating pad next to my aching muscles. She starts at my knee, each stroke shifting higher until she's rubbed circles so close to my groin I can hardly see straight.

I don't want to ask her to stop, but this feels too intimate after what I witnessed between her and Ben. If she's attached to anyone else, I need to make it clear that what we're doing, no matter how casual we claim it to be, needs to stop.

"I'm not worth your time," I say.

With all the mistakes I've made here so far, I hope she sees that. We don't need to make this any harder than it has to be. She agreed to casual. But after seeing her holding Ben's hand, even that seems like too much for me.

She pauses the motion of her palms long enough to look up at me. I try to hide it from her—the fear I felt as he touched her. Knowing the last time that happened to the girl I liked, she chose the other guy.

"I'm a grown woman, Morgan. I make my own decisions,"

she argues, and continues her pursuit down to my calves. "I don't know what you think you saw, but it wasn't it."

"You weren't just holding his hand, Red. When I walked in, you were looking in his eyes like they held something to protect."

Her hands drop from my thighs.

"Ben was confiding in me about something from his past. I was being there for him."

I shake my head. "It doesn't matter anyway. I'm saying whatever this thing is between us"—I wave my hand back and forth between our chests, which are only a couple feet apart at this point—"I can't do it."

In a lot of ways, Hailey is nothing like Teddy. Not the same free spirit or daredevil mentality. She's stable and sure. She feels safe. She makes every one of her decisions with the utmost thought, and she considers other people's feelings above her own. How does she know whether or not it was like that with Ben?

But she leans closer, the space between us disappearing. There's rapid speed to the rise and fall of her chest now, like the other day when her back pressed against that tree.

"Why not?" she asks as she wraps both hands around my thighs again. This time it's intentional. It's not for me, it's for her. "Why can't you?" she pushes.

She inches forward. So close now that I can feel her breath dancing in the air between us. And she's achingly beautiful. My insides liquefy but I fight to keep a firm grip on reality, otherwise I'm going to do something I can't come back from.

"Because. I've been the other guy before. The one who's not good enough. I can't do that again," I tell her.

Her eyes fall to my mouth. Land there and never stray.

"You're the *only* guy," she whispers, and something inside of me snaps.

I reach for her neck, jerking her to me. She lets out a soft sigh when our lips touch. I thread my fingers into her hair, letting the silky strands hold me to her. She crawls into my lap, straddling my waist. The weight of her body against me feels like a special form of torture. Her butt sinks against my thighs, and I don't know whether to rock her against me or hold painfully still through the ache.

It feels like she's feeding me the very air I need to breathe. My heart bats like a pair of wings against my ribcage, thrashing around in my chest. I could stay like this forever, believing she's mine. I want her to be mine, and the thought terrifies me.

She pulls away first, with the distant sound of laughter drawing closer. She crawls from my lap and my body protests the moment I lose her touch. It's begging for her to stay. I know we just crossed a line we can't come back from, and now I'm leaving tomorrow morning. Leaving her here alone for who knows how long with her coworker. The very thing that wasn't on my side the last time I was in this situation.

My skin still feels like it's on fire even though she's let go of me entirely. A soft giggle escapes her lips, like she just did something far out of her comfort zone. It's cute the way she's looking at me, as if I know her secret.

Her teeth draw across her bottom lip, and I almost groan out loud from the sight of it.

"Remember me," she says playfully as she stands, using my own words against me. Then she turns around and slips into the shades of gray as confusing as my heart.

CHAPTER TWENTY-ONE

REED

"That's your favorite food?" Murphy booms around a bite of bread. "Your last meal on earth and you're asking for pickles?"

I don't know why he's so surprised when he's also downing his second chicken salad sandwich. It has enough dill spears on top of it to fill a sixteen-ounce jar.

I shrug and reach for his unopened third one. "Well, if that's how you feel…"

He punches his fist against my forearm, and my radius bends to his blow.

"Murphy doesn't share food!" he barks.

"Jeez!" I rub my palm against the swelling red blotch. "I can see that."

"And you wondered where I got my scar from." McCafferty chuckles, shaking his head.

I gape from Murphy to Dean's eyebrow and back again. "*You* did *that?*"

"He's only an animal when he hasn't been fed." Marshall pats his smaller-than-average palm on the top of Murphy's head. "You're a good boy, aren't you, Murph?"

Murphy burps in Marshall's face and fogs up his glasses.

"Careful. He doesn't like to be touched unless that hand is attached to a six-foot-two Australian model." Ramirez tsks, peeling back the heel of his bread and grimacing at the soggy side underneath.

"Says the dude with the sexuality of a river," Murphy fires back.

I wince. I don't know what the issue is between these two, but a comment like that seems too far. It can't be easy being bisexual on a crew of eighteen guys.

"Relax, Morgan. I'm proud of my fluidity." Ramirez winks and ditches his uneaten dinner in the dirt next to him. He jumps to his feet and starts thrusting his hips, singing "Crazy in Love." Daniels and Evans join in and pretty soon we are an entire flock of male peacocks parading about.

"All right, children, let's save the mating rituals for R&R." Jack freezes with his Ridley's grocery sack dangling from his fingertips, connecting the dots that he just used the words *children* and *mating ritual* in the same sentence. We all erupt with laughter.

"That did not come out how I meant it to," he says, collecting everyone's trash. "All right. It's not safe anywhere but the black tonight. Pitch your tents."

I watch as the guys unearth their sleeping arrangements from their line packs and assemble them on top of charred soil.

Tents, I scoff. Who would want to be stuffed in a claustrophobic coffin when you could be looking at all of this?

A stretch of stars blink to the south where the smoke is less dense. A skittish deer prances across the open field in the same direction, seeking shelter from the fire. Untouched trees sway in the breeze, and even when the scent of smoke filters through my nose with my head inches from the black dirt, this still might be my favorite part about this job. *Nope. I don't need a tent.*

"You sure you want to do that?" McCafferty asks, poking his head out of the small zippered opening.

"Wouldn't have it any other way," I say, easing onto my back and tucking my hands behind my head.

"Suit yourself." He zips his tent closed, and I continue my stargazing until my eyelids grow too heavy to hold open any longer.

I don't know how many hours of sleep slip by before an itching sensation breaks out across my face. Half out of it, I bat against my right cheek. The prickling moves to my forehead, and I swipe it with my sleeve. An uneasy feeling draws me from my groggy state as tiny pinpricks light up a path down my neck and into the collar of my shirt. I jolt up and out of my sleeping bag, rapping at my skin like it's covered in... *ants*.

A prissy shriek gusts out of my lungs as I discover hundreds of ants crawling over my skin, burrowing under the hem of my shirt and down my...

I rip open the button on my pants, jerking them down my legs and off my feet. I'm busy stripping off all my clothes and discarding them on top of my infested sleeping bag when I finally notice every guy on the crew has unzipped the flap to their tent. They're all staring at me.

"What's the matter?" McCafferty asks with a smirk.

"There was... and they..." I'm completely naked. Waving my arms about. Trying to explain why they just witnessed a scream that could've only come from a three-year-old girl gust from my lungs. But the sentence dies on my tongue.

"Did I forget to mention fire doesn't kill ants?" McCafferty winks at me as he ducks his head back in his tent.

The rest of the guys go back to sleep after some more ribbing, but as for me?

I stay up.

"Rough night there, Morgan?"

Jack materializes out of nowhere at dawn. The sensation to scratch my face overpowers my reflex to jump.

"Are you going to be ready for today?" His eyes crawl all over me as I scratch incessantly.

"Like a cat in heat," I tell him.

His eyes follow the pattern of my hands. "Well, all right then. Let's move out."

The first mile of our hike is mostly flat. The next four are at a steep slope and require us to clear brush. Burn it too. It takes hours, the same motions over and over. McCafferty and I are paired on a saw team. He's the swamper, and I'm the retriever. Any clippings he cuts I toss in a giant burn pile behind us.

We work in hand signals, the only form of communication possible with the grind of steel against wood. But when the fuel runs out after forty-five minutes, he's the one to strike up a conversation.

"I never asked you... are you from around here? You've got the tan for it."

"You haven't asked me much of anything." I keep my tone light so he knows I'm joking.

While we aren't exactly friends yet, he no longer treats me like someone he despises. I'd like to keep it that way.

"There's a first for everything." He grabs a red Dolmar fuel can and unscrews the top.

"Bear Lake," I answer.

Why I tell him that, I have no idea. I should have said Park City. Bear Lake is the last place I want to be thinking about right now.

"I've heard of it. Doesn't it have that restaurant with the famous raspberry milkshakes?" He removes the saw's fuel cap and wipes debris from the rim with a cloth. Then he tips the spout in a slow pour. The gas leaks into the power tool.

I swallow, forcing down the knot that tries to lodge in my esophagus anytime I think about that town. I nod. "LaBeau's."

Why do I picture Teddy dunking her pickle into that milkshake and laughing in the free-spirited way I loved so much? Or her bright green eyes that stood out beneath her strawberry blond bob? Or the way she would lose herself when she sketched?

I was always in awe of her talent and how much I felt when I was with her, never knowing how to express it. It's hard to let go of.

I always knew she'd never be mine. I saw the way Miles looked at her. She painted the stars in his sky. I'm not afraid of much, but I was afraid of losing my best friends. And that's exactly what I did.

"I'm gonna get back to work," I say to him, and he studies me with a million-questions look.

He knows I can't do the job without him. But he lets me go anyway. Stays behind to screw on the cap and return the empty bottle with the rest of them. A gesture that feels more like friendship than either of us cares to admit.

"Hot buckets!" Murphy yells.

A helicopter idles overhead, dropping a box of brown paper sacks on the side of the hill we're working on. After my brief conversation with Dean this morning, I'm not in the mood for small talk. So, I study the fire while I eat my burritos.

From our steep slope, everything looks bigger: the column of smoke, flame lengths, destruction. The haze blankets the tree-tops and licks the open air above them. Flames crackle and dance for miles. Drenched in pink retardant powder, unburned fuel fights against an aerial attack. It's hard to imagine this beast ever getting under control.

Jack interrupts my wandering eyes with his situation report. "For those of you who've lost track, we've got two days left before R&R. Trends are staying hot, dry, and wind driven. Division wants us to keep working the right flank toward the head. If you were on a saw team, you're now cold trailing. I don't want anything left unchecked. Let's get back to work."

Our teams work side by side, churning up the mineral soil and digging into roots in a single file line about ten feet apart. The wind beats at the side of my helmet, my fire shield rapping against my neck. But the direction keeps the smoke out of our eyes.

I drop the wooden handle of my tool in the dirt to run my bare palm over the ground I just tilled, my knee connecting with the blunt end of a log as I kneel. A flash of yellow flicks past my periphery. Before I can check for residual heat, I turn to see what it is.

A small piece of paper flutters from the pocket of Jack's pants. It twirls a few times before catching in a patch of sagebrush a foot from me. If I don't snatch it up, the wind will carry it away. My fingers close around the worn edge as it flickers once and folds in on itself with the tight crease down the middle.

"Hart, your..." My voice wobbles with the breeze and buries itself under the rumble of the saw and the sound of branches cracking.

He can't hear me.

I unfold the glossy cardstock in front of my eyewear. Two

faces stare back at me through the scratched lenses. Not a piece of paper, I realize, but a picture, with a date on the back scribbled in black ink.

I tuck it in my own pocket before anyone else notices. When I'll find the opportunity to give it back to him, I don't know. I can't think of a single moment when admitting to carrying something so personal of his around with me doesn't stand to be awkward.

Back to work.

The toe of my boot kicks the giant log in front of me when I stand, and it tumbles in a barrel roll down the hill. Amber circles light in its path as the stump rolls a hundred feet down unburned fuel before catching on a tree root and stopping.

My eyes bulge at the sight of a dozen spot fires.

A set of boots shuffle, sending a mini landslide of rocks and dirt toward me.

"What happened?" McCafferty gasps.

"I..." I try to formulate my thoughts. How could I have been so reckless? "The log..." I try to explain. But how do I tell him I was distracted without showing him Jack's picture?

"It's okay. We'll put them out," McCafferty says.

The individual hotspots are spreading. At least ten feet by ten feet now.

"What the hell happened?" Jack yells, his boots raking the hillside.

"I..." I fail to speak again. *I have to fix this!*

I pick up my Pulaski and skid toward the fires. The mattock blade grubs the soil with each raking motion, clearing away as much brush from the flames as possible.

"Supt, it was my fault," I hear McCafferty say from behind me. "It was an oversight. I should have flipped the log."

He shouldn't be taking the fall from me. He doesn't deserve

to pay for my mistakes. But I can't worry about that right now when inches from my face, the flames sputter and sizzle. The stubble that's slowly grown into a shadow of a beard singes at the tips, my fire shield doing very little to protect my cheeks.

"Yes. You should have," I hear Jack say back. "Air Tactical 6, this is Tac 3. We need a water drop forty-five degrees..." His voice fizzles out as he walks upwind toward the crew.

"Marshall, you're with Jackson. Evans and Ramirez, you take those two on the south side. Daniels, you and I will get those three on the west. You know what to do," Murphy says to McCafferty.

Dean marches over to me and pulls me out of the way so Marshall and Jackson can take over. "Come on. You heard what he said. You're with me."

"You didn't have to do that." I trudge along to keep up with him.

"You've had enough mishaps for your first season, don't you think?"

Dehydration, fire ants, smoldering logs all come to mind. I grip the back of my neck. "I owe you one."

We both hack at the sagebrush around our new hotspot. It's farther from the black than the others with a lot more fuel around it.

"Yeah, you do. You can put in a good word for me with Hailey," he says, and I stop moving.

"Wait, what?" *There's a problem between the two of them?* I fish through memories of their interactions since I got here. They've hardly spoken.

"Just... tell her I'm sorry, okay?" he asks.

He's working smarter. Cutting back big swaths at a time with full upper body strokes. But I'm moving faster. I've almost made it to the soil when I say, "What makes you think—"

"Come on, man," he cuts me off. "I saw you kissing her before we left."

If I wasn't gripping my hand tool so tight, I would have dropped it.

"We're just casual," I tell him. *Convince* myself. What even makes him think she'll listen to me?

"Uh-huh. Do you cradle every woman's face that you're not serious with? Because from where I stood, it looked pretty passionate."

Wait... my eyes zero in on him. "Why do you need to apologize to her?"

"We weren't talking about me. Why are you avoiding my question?"

I don't know if it's the smoke inhalation or this confusing circle of questions, but I'm lost.

"That's none of your business," I toss out.

What did he ask me again?

"Just like whatever you have going on with her is none of mine," he argues. "Not unless you do something to hurt her."

That's when I drop my tool. "I would never..."

He smirks. "That's what I thought. I want to believe that you're not an arrogant asshole who always needs to be on top, but rather someone who fights for what he wants. I know you're probably not going to listen, but can I give you a piece of advice? It might help you."

I pick up my tool and cut the last swath of brush closing off the spread. "I'm listening."

"From now on, choose the hard, right choice over the easy, wrong one."

With our hotspot under control, he drops his tool and points to my mistake.

"Dig a four-foot-deep cup trench beneath that log to keep it from rolling again."

And I do. For several hours on bended knee.

That first hard, right choice lands me with a burning sensation that begins at my ankle and spreads up my calf.

CHAPTER TWENTY-TWO

HAILEY

His lips feather against my skin, trailing in an arc down my neck. He draws my top to the side and brushes his mouth over my exposed collarbone. Chills race up the arm he caresses with the back of his hand.

"Is this what I've been missing?" he whispers against the shell of my ear, and my body erupts with euphoric need. I tip into this feeling. Chasing the high that is Reed Morgan's touch. The warmth of his breath, the sound of his groan, it's all I can do not to...

"Earth to Hales."

The fog lifts from my daydream to reveal an oversized palm waving in front of my face. I blink in rapid succession until the figure comes into focus. I should have known. Ben's the only one who has ever called me that nickname. It's burrowing beneath my skin like a tick I can't get rid of.

"What? Sorry..."

"I lost you there for a second." He presses the back of his hand to my forehead. "That seems to be happening a lot lately. Are you feeling okay? Is the heat getting to you?"

I don't know, is it? We *have* hit record temps over the last few days. Our medic tent is more of a sauna than a protective shade cover at this point. Cooked from the inside out would be the definition of my body right now. I lick my chapped lips.

Water. That's what I need. Three long pulls and I've drained half the bottle. It sloshes as I dump it over my palm and slap the remainder against my cheeks.

"Better?" He smirks.

I nod.

"Well, that's good, because someone's here to see you."

I pitch the empty bottle in the dirt and jolt upright.

He's back!

But the air deflates from my lungs.

Eleven days. That's how long I've waited for this twitter-pated feeling to be spoiled on the wrong person.

A filthy version of Dean waits in the tent opening. He edges closer with his hands in the air. "I come in peace."

I'd ask him how it was out there, but the sooty outline of eyewear, the sunburnt skin, and the singed facial hair all answer that question for me. It's been a couple weeks since our failed morning hike. What do I say to him?

"You're back," I decide on. More like deadpan, and he cringes.

How am I supposed to pretend I'm happy to see him when nothing has changed between us?

"We are," he responds. "For R&R. Does this mean you're talking to me again?"

I search for Backup Ben. He's not exactly best friend material, but he'd make a good wingman if he hadn't up and disappeared on me.

"Yeah, I guess it does," I say. Because what else am I supposed to do when I'm trapped in such tight quarters?

Tiptoeing would be a generous way to describe the last few

steps Dean takes in my direction. "Hayes, I'm sorry for hurting you. I hate the way things ended between us."

I plant my hands on my hips. "You mean the day you told me on my porch steps with my father waiting in the car for you that you'd gotten your red card? That he recruited you to work for him?"

Even now I see it—the guilt on his face. Equally as vibrant is the passion I saw in his eyes the day he left. The same joy my dad always had for this job.

His ash-covered hair drops in front of his eyes, and he combs it away from his forehead.

"Yes. That's what I'm apologizing for."

I shake my head. "You promised me we'd always have each other. That nothing would come between our friendship."

He takes another step closer. "You left before—"

I hold up a hand to stop him. He's as close as I need him to be to deliver this message. "Before what? Before you came back from your first roll? Was I supposed to wait around for you to finally explain to me why you joined Iron Summit behind my back instead of just telling me? I already did enough waiting for one person in my life. I didn't have it in me to do it for two. *You* left *me*."

He scratches his jaw, dropping another layer of ash on the back of his hand. "And you ran?"

Challenging me looks painful for him, so he must be desperate enough to even ask that question.

I fold my arms. "No. I moved to a place where I could start over. There's a difference."

He crams his hands in his pockets. "I didn't know how to tell you when all you ever talked about was how much you hated this job. It became my passion, Hayes. I *love* what I do."

He's right. Once upon a time, my dad's absence was all I could talk about. I felt it everywhere here. It's another reason why I moved away. And now... do I have any merit in staying mad at Dean when I'm working on the same crew as him, my dad, *Reed*? Who, for that matter, I'm not holding it against?

I purse my lips. It's not about this job; it's about not trusting that Dean won't hurt me a second time. Whenever I let someone in I subject myself to that hopeless feeling. I'm choosing to do it with my dad, but I don't need to with Dean too. Not anymore.

"I'm happy for you, truly. But it doesn't mean we can pick back up where we left off. We don't know each other like we used to. You were more than my friend, you were my family, and it felt like that didn't mean as much to you as it did to me."

Defeat transforms his features. "So, that's it then? We just work on this crew together, and I don't get to talk to you?"

It must show that this reality pains me too because he presses on.

"I can't find out about your day or"—he cradles his chin and raises an eyebrow—"ask about your crush on the rookie?"

My eyes flare. "I don't have—"

"I saw you kiss him." His lips tilt in a side smile, and for one moment I consider what it would be like to confide in him again. Maybe it would be easy to slip back into that place where we talked about everything. There's a very real possibility he knows Reed better than I do at this point—what his favorite color is, where he's from, if this casual thing between us involves anything more than a physical connection. But asking Dean any of those questions would be the very definition of opening up. We're working together, and that's it. I need to keep it strictly professional if I want to protect myself.

"You can tell me the real reason you're waiting in my medic tent," I finally answer.

He sighs and hikes up his pant leg, exposing a rash of blistered skin that spreads upward from his ankle.

"Poison oak."

"I'm not the only one," he says as five other guys waltz into the tent.

"Ben?" I holler, and he materializes. "We need hydrocortisone and Benadryl."

We treat them with antihistamine by mouth, swelling and itch relief by topical cream, and an empathetic pat to the shoulder before sending them on their less-than-merry way. I feel relieved when Dean finally leaves the tent. It felt like stripping the bandage from a fresh wound having that conversation with him, and it's a welcome distraction to focus on cleaning up the scattered supplies that litter the table instead.

"Poison oak, huh?" a gravelly voice asks from the doorway.

Jack.

I drop everything but the half-empty bottle of calamine lotion clutched in my fist, giving him my full attention.

Is he favoring one leg or is it my imagination?

"You too?" I ask. "I can help!"

He shakes his head. "I'm fine."

I rock back and forth, unscrewing and re-screwing the lid.

"Your crew will need cold compresses off and on for the next two weeks. It'll help with the itching while they wait for the rash to clear."

He backs up. Tucks his helmet beneath his arm and bobs his head. "I'll send them here when they need it." Then he turns on his heels.

"Wait—"

Is that all he came here for? A status update? I thought we shared a moment the last time I saw him. But he's still acting just as distant.

I straighten, forcing back the building tension. "I can walk you out," I offer. It's to the back of his shirt, but I don't wait to see if he heard me. I follow him. Maybe he doesn't want to have our conversation in an enclosed space where anyone can walk in. I don't either.

When he holds open the tent flap, I smile.

As it swings closed with a thwap, he blurts out, "You don't belong here," and I drop the open bottle of calamine lotion. It splatters all over the ground, along with my faith in us.

CHAPTER TWENTY-THREE

"What?" A mousy voice I hardly recognize squeaks out of me.

Am I really asking for him to repeat what he said? I don't think I need to hear it again for as long as I live.

"You don't belong here," he says again. I focus on his voice this time rather than the words coming out of his mouth. It sounds so withdrawn. As if I'm a statue he's having a one-sided conversation with, not his own living *breathing* daughter.

I pinch the bridge of my nose, clutch the sleeve of my shirt, fight the moisture in my eyes. None of it is making me feel any better. Neither is the empty pink bottle helicoptering at my feet. I bend over, pick it up, and pitch it in the tin trash can a foot from me.

Pain splinters in the center of my chest and spiders throughout my bloodstream until everything feels unbearable. My skin, the air, his presence, it's all too much. I can't stay here trapped in this silent prison.

For once, I disappear first.

I sprint in the opposite direction of camp, my lungs fighting for clean air. A wooden bench stakes the end of a gravel road, and I collapse onto the seat. Something sharp digs into my back. *What on earth...*

A bent metal plaque drilled to the slats reads *There my heart lies, scattered among the pines.*

I huff. "Fitting."

Three scoots and I no longer have to feel it pressing into my shoulder blade. I fixate on its meaning instead.

What do I do now? How do I stay here?

I turn these questions over and over, wondering if they'll always be hypothetical or if an answer will ever come to me, when a shadow shades my face.

"You okay?"

I gaze up toward the sky, and the sight of him is all it takes for the tears I've been holding back to cascade in droves down my cheeks.

He sits down next to me. The wooden planks groan with the weight of him. *Is that stubble on his cheeks?* It wasn't there the last time I saw him. Then again, neither was the inch of ash blanketing his clothes.

I turn away to wipe my eyes on my sleeve.

"I'm fine," I say.

Reed places a warm, solid hand on my knee. "You don't have to pretend with me."

"I'm not," I lie. Because this is what I do now. I keep my iron clad walls up. Because if I don't, I get too hopeful for things that never come to pass. Like the idea that Reed could be my shelter from the storms of life.

"Yes. You are. You want to know how I know that?"

I finally turn and look at him. "How?"

"Because we're more alike than I care to admit."

He runs his hand along my cheek, brushing away the strand of hair that's slipped from my braid and tucking it behind my ear.

"Well." He chuckles. "In one way, anyway. You'd never forget to break in your boots or skip water when your body is screaming for it."

I hiccup.

"You'd also know that ants live through fire, and it would be worth your time to set up a tent so they don't ravage your sleeping bag in the middle of the night," he continues.

I laugh out loud. "Did that actually happen to you?"

His eyes glance sideways before he smirks at me. "No."

Liar.

"And you sure as hell would know what poison oak looks like before kneeling on top of it."

I cringe. "You got it too?"

He winces. "You'll always be way more prepared than me. But that's not the point."

"Then what is?" I ask him.

"You're afraid to let people in."

He says it like he knows the feeling intimately. I don't deny it either. I can't. I've been disappointed, let down, looked over, and forgotten enough times in my life not to hide behind the structure I've built around my heart.

"But he doesn't *deserve* to be let in," I argue.

"Maybe not yet."

He holds out a folded picture to me no more than four inches all the way around. The edges are tattered but the faces are clear. I suck in a breath.

"Where did you get this?"

"It fell out of your dad's pocket on the line," he says.

It's the one that used to rest on the nightstand in my bedroom.

"You want to tell me about it?" he asks.

I shake my head. I wouldn't know what to tell him. I've had a million questions go unanswered about it myself.

What hospital was I born at?

How long did she hold me like that?

Did she love me?

Questions I've been too afraid to ask after he shut me down the first time.

The rustle of a nearby tree sweeps me back to that night: the last time I saw this picture.

"Daddy, will you tell me a story?"

"Okay. One story, then it's time for you to get to bed."

He tucked me under the weight of a heavy quilt, and I looked out the window to see the branches of a pine tree swaying.

Wind. It reminded me that he was leaving soon.

"Once upon a time..." he started.

"No, Daddy. A real story." My small hands reached over to the nightstand and hugged the gold frame. "The one about me and Mommy."

He peeled my fingers off the frame and set it gently back where it came from. "It's getting late, Hailey. We should get you to sleep."

"But you promised," *I whined.*

He shook his head. "There is no story. She's gone."

A flash of grief passed over his face that night, and I hated seeing him like that.

Whenever he started to look that way, he'd always leave for work early. So, I told him it was okay. I dropped it, even though it wasn't. At least not to me. But I didn't want him to leave me yet, so I learned to ask for a different story.

I kept things surface level after that. It was my fault he didn't want to stick around. I pushed him away.

But Reed's never once made me feel afraid to ask hard questions or tell him what I'm thinking. He feels safe to open up to.

"It's a picture of me and my mother," I say. "The only one that was ever taken."

Even now, I study her in her hospital gown, looking exhausted but enamored with the newborn version of me wrapped in a tight bundle in her arms.

A tear slips from the corner of my eye and I shake my head. "He wouldn't carry this around with him. He doesn't care."

Reed touches my hand. It's a simple gesture, but one I feel to my core.

"I don't think caring is the problem here, Red. I think the man cares a whole lot more than he lets on. There's a reason he's hiding this in the pocket of his clothes. He's protecting himself."

"From what?"

"Maybe himself? But what do I know." He nudges me with his knee. "I'm just the rookie who doesn't ask questions, remember? You're the inquisitive one."

"I can't ask him that," I say, holding out the picture.

I want him to take it. Give it back himself. Throw it away for all I care, because I can't look at it anymore.

"You should keep it. Wait for the right time." He closes my fingers over it, tucking it in the palm of my hand. Then he changes the subject. "What are you doing with your days off?"

Spending time with you, my heart wants to say.

I slip the picture in my pocket and stand. He stands too.

"I... don't know. I guess I'll head back to town. Get away for a couple of days." A trip that involves saying goodbye to him and riding in an ambulance with Ben.

I decelerate my pace.

He slides in front of me, sweeping his palms beneath my thighs and wrapping my legs around his waist.

"Change of plans," he whispers with that dimpled smile I've come to love.

It's hard to stay sad with him looking at me like that. I palm the crown of his fire helmet and fit it over my head.

"It looks better on you," he says, dropping his gaze to my lips.

Suddenly, all the air sweeps from my lungs. "Does it?" I ask, pressing my fingertips to his jaw.

When we're nothing but a breath apart, our smiles finally touch.

"You're mine tonight, Red."

CHAPTER TWENTY-FOUR

HAILEY

"How long has this place been open?" Reed asks as he takes in the chipped paint of the evergreen walls and the one random missing tile from the drop ceiling with the duct work showing.

Grenaldough's is old, *yes*, but in the most charming, small-town way. Residents don't seem to mind the dated wallpaper in the back either, from the way the line always stretches the entire length of the self-serve salad bar. People come here for the food. It's not uncommon on a Friday night to wait an hour for good pizza.

But my attention is elsewhere. On the lazy grazing of Reed's fingertips against my hand, to be exact. A simultaneously soothing yet distracting pattern that has me forgetting all about the painfully long commute back to the barracks earlier. Listening to Ben drone on about the upcoming Brundage ski season was not my idea of a relaxing scenic drive.

I net my fingers with his hand. I can't focus enough to respond to his question with him touching me like that.

"At least since I was eight," I reply. "Aunt Karen and I used to eat here on Friday nights. Sometimes twice a week if I was lucky."

"The candy connoisseur is that good of a cook, huh?" He gives my hand a playful squeeze.

"She has her talents."

"Like raising you," he says.

"Like raising me," I confirm.

His hand slips into the back pocket of my jean shorts as he leans in close and rasps against the shell of my ear, "Is this okay?"

The punctuated swallow that bobs down my throat leaves me speechless.

Hah, is that okay...

Is it okay if the room catches on fire? Because his hot palm feels like a branding iron burning through the denim fabric. I tilt my head onto his shoulder in acknowledgement. A good thing, too, as he breathes in through his nose and moans around an exhale. My face flushes at the sound.

We really should have had them deliver.

"It smells so good in here. Beats that last MRE meal any day," he says.

I raise my head off his shoulder. "I thought the helicopter crew was doing food drops?"

"We got into some pretty steep terrain on our last day," he admits.

An unsavory churning seizes the pit of my stomach. Not only did I miss him while he was gone, but I worried about him too.

Only... people doing casual don't worry. Which means I need to focus on a different feeling.

Empathy? Compassion? *No,* neither of those screams casual.

Curiosity? *Yeah.* I can act interested without seeming attached.

"What does an MRE meal taste like? I've always wondered."

"I don't know about all of them, but this was some sort of chicken and mashed potato situation that's right up there with the texture of sludge. I think chalk mixed with a tablespoon of water might be better."

I imitate a gag reflex. No wonder he's moaning over pizza.

"Did your family have a Friday night dinner ritual growing up?"

"No. We were more of a fend-for-yourself kind of household. In high school, my brothers and I got good at ordering from an app and having it delivered."

A strong urge to wrap my arms around his waist takes over. Again, with the pesky not-casual feelings.

"Did your parents work late or something?" I ask instead.

Coming from a single parent household, I always had this vision of the perfect all-American family—a mother, a father, at least two children, all under the same roof. Reed had all of that and his reality is still not what my naive mind imagined.

He nods. "All the time. But they tried when they could."

I question whether or not I imagined a frown tugging at the corners of his mouth with how swiftly he shrugs it away.

It doesn't sound like they tried hard enough, I think to myself. But I'm pretty jaded in that department. What my dad did... the word *try* wouldn't even be considered in the same zip code.

Reed was right earlier. We are more alike than I thought. Which means he knows how it feels to be forgotten. And I'll remind him he's worth all the time and attention as much as he needs to hear it.

"Thirty-six," a teenager in a white polo and visor hollers from behind the pick-up counter.

"You sure you don't want to eat here?" I ask, pointing toward an intimate corner booth in the back.

Reed slides the flat box from the counter and rests it on his forearm.

"I seem to recall a certain someone preferring a date night in. Not sure where I'll find a fire, but..."

My smile blooms. *He remembered.*

"Can I take you somewhere then?" I ask, knowing just the place.

He holds out his free arm to me and I loop mine through it. "I go where you go, Red."

He ushers me past the row of wooden booths. There's only ten of them. But with the high-back seating, you can't see the occupants' faces until you're passing their table. That's precisely how I've missed these two until we're passing the last one.

My gaze lands on a shift dress accentuating *very*-there cleavage and blond curls. Not sitting across from the girl but with her on top of his lap and his hand on her thigh is Ben. Eyes closed, she inches in close to him, turns her head toward us, and presses her lips to his ear, whispering something that makes him flash a dangerous grin.

"What the hell," I whisper, eyeing them both down.

"What's wrong?" Reed's attention tracks to the booth. "Is that Ben?"

"Shh, keep your voice down," I scold.

"Why are you whispering? Ben's not allowed to take a girl on a date?"

I toss my bangs as if they'll shield my eyes from the cheating taking place before me.

"Not *a* girl... *that* girl. Madison Walter."

His pupils dilate. "*Dean's* girlfriend?"

She licks the shell of Ben's ear and then giggles, and I jerk Reed's arm toward the exit.

"Hurry, before they see us."

Reed's chest puffs up even broader than it already is. What is he going to do, start a brawl? He looked like he wanted to deck Ben the other day, and I can't say I'm Madison's biggest fan, but this is not the time or place for a fight.

Before we can clear the door, bright blue eyes swivel in our direction and widen in delight.

"Oh my gosh, Hailey? Is that you?" She jumps from Ben's lap and rushes over to us. "I didn't know you were back!" Her boobs smash against my chest with her hug.

"Oh... hey, Madison. I didn't see you there. Yeah, I moved back about a month ago."

"No way!" she squeals. "I thought for sure you were getting out of here for good when you left."

She's never been very tactful about other people's feelings judging by the way she's cheating on her long-term boyfriend.

"Guess I couldn't stay away."

With her smile brighter than ever, she turns to Reed and pins her arms behind her back, swinging from side to side. "Hailey, we're being rude. And you are?"

I expect him to hold out his hand when he greets her, but he wraps his free arm around my shoulders instead. "Reed Morgan."

"Reed." She samples the way it sounds coming out of her mouth, and I hate it.

"Iron Summit firefighter," he adds.

She releases a puff of air and avoids eye contact with him. Then, like a wig, she puts on that smile once more.

"Well, it was nice to see you, Hailey. We should get together sometime!" Her eyes dart to Reed and back to me again. "Ya know, like a *girls'* night kind of thing," she adds, making the g pop.

In all the years I've known her, we've never had a girls' night.

"Yeah, sure. See ya, Madison."

She scampers away, and I level Ben with a glare.

Just as we break through the exit, I hear my coworker calling after me.

"Hales, wait!"

The door to Grenaldough's swings closed in his face. He pushes it back open.

"Hales!" he says again.

I spin around. "Don't call me that!"

"Hailey, I'm sorry! I didn't know until today, okay?"

"You knew *today*?" I close in on his personal bubble.

"Yes. She comes around the clinic sometimes when the crew is on duty."

"And she what, told you she was there to sell Girl Scout cookies all the other times?"

"No. She said she had a friend on the crew."

"Hah. A friend? And you believed her?"

"Why the hell wouldn't I?"

"No, you're right. Most people don't go around lying to their first loves and cheating on them with the first thing that moves. What are you still doing with her if you know full well she's already taken?"

"I think you of all people should know what it's like to feel lonely," he says to me.

I don't have time to react to his judgment. Reed's hands get angry for the both of us, tightening into fists at his sides as he steps in front of me. For a moment, I'm terrified he's going to do something stupid and ruin his firefighting career. But then he says, "You're lucky I love my job. Now apologize."

Ben cowers in a sheepish slump. "I'm sorry, Hailey. I should have never said that. It's me who's lonely, and it shouldn't come at the expense of anyone else."

I should accept his apology. But I can't do that when he's put me in the worst position.

"You better get back to your date," I say, and he takes that as his cue to leave.

When he spins on his heels, Reed's hands relax.

"And I thought McCafferty was the asshole," Reed jokes.

With my mind on Dean, I leave Reed for his truck.

We aren't even talking, Dean and I, but he deserves to know this. *What am I going to tell him?*

"Wait. I'm sorry. You could have handled that situation all by yourself. I shouldn't have stepped in. And I'm supposed to be defending Dean to you, not making stupid jokes."

"Dean was my best friend. Did he tell you that?"

Reed and I are the farthest apart we've been all night, and as if he senses it too, he reaches for me. His fingers skate down my palm until they thread between my knuckles. "Implied it. I don't know what he did to ruin that, but he regrets it."

"I know he does. But it doesn't change anything for me."

Just when I thought we'd gotten all of the hidden information out in the open, Madison had to go and do this.

Reed crowds me against his truck door, shielding me from witnessing Madison and Ben stepping out onto the sidewalk.

"Dean's going to be so upset. He's loved her since we were fourteen," I whisper.

She's not looking, but Reed glares at Madison anyway. "Doesn't anyone stay true to the person they're with anymore?"

I don't think he notices, but his grip tightens on my hand as he says it.

Who hurt you, Reed Morgan? I still don't know.

I cradle his face in the palms of my hands so he doesn't have to look their way. And even though it's weirdly poetic, I say the first thing that comes to my heart.

"Not everyone is looking on the other side of the fence. Some people notice the beauty in their own backyard."

CHAPTER TWENTY-FIVE

REED

"You grew up here?"

We walk the long stretch of gravel driveway that leads toward a single-story log cabin. The property is nestled in a grove of pine trees overlooking Payette Lake. Minus the plateau mountains, it looks so much like Bear Lake my heart squeezes tightly in my chest.

I haven't stopped replaying what Hailey said back at the restaurant, treating her words like a fortune cookie for my life.

Not everyone is looking on the other side of the fence. Some people notice the beauty in their own backyard.

I've spent a long time wondering why I wasn't enough for Teddy. But Hailey freed me from that thought tonight. I know now... I *was* the other side of the fence. Nothing I could have done would have changed that fact.

Miles was safe, her first friend, the right choice. What she needed from him I couldn't give her. And I don't blame her anymore.

With my eyes locked on Hailey, my first thought is *What if you're my right choice?*

It's a dangerous thought. One that I nod away like the string of a balloon that's been freed to the sky when she says, "You want to see inside?"

A dusty old mat with a birdhouse print touches the front door. She slips a small gold key from beneath the rubber bottom and fits it into the lock, turning it then pushing the door open.

The place is as rustic on the inside as it is on the outside. Every piece of furniture except for the couch looks handcrafted from knotty pine. Large woven rugs in rich browns and greens blanket the floors.

I set the pizza box on the kitchen counter before approaching the fireplace hearth. There's a picture on top—Hailey in a green cap and gown, embracing an eccentric-looking woman's waist. Aunt Karen, I'm guessing. *Where are you, Jack?*

If I didn't think commenting on it would hurt her feelings, I would tell her right now what a prick move I think skipping her graduation was. At least my parents did that much.

"Any chance your dad is coming back here?" I ask, spinning around to face her.

"He's married to his work, remember? He rarely leaves his office at the barracks. He even put a cot in there. Chooses to sleep on it over his king-sized bed here." She points to the first room in the hallway, where there's not a wrinkle in the bedspread.

"I mean, *I* wouldn't pass up the king. But I can't say I understand everything there is to know about Jack Hart."

"Me neither."

Our mutual chuckle fades into a semi awkward silence. Here we are, alone for the first time, no one to interrupt us, and I'm not sure what to do next. I know what I *want* to do. I haven't *stopped* thinking about kissing her since it happened the first time. But now that it's been eleven days, I don't know what she's thinking.

She drags her bottom lip between her teeth as she takes a

breath. Her eyes flit to my mouth and linger there, studying the shape of my lips.

If I start kissing her now, I don't think I'll ever stop.

I break our trance and flick my eyes out toward the big bay window in the kitchen. "You should show me that rope swing."

Her cheeks turn to my favorite color, and her braid flicks down her back. "Okay," she says.

On an outstretched limb of a pine tree overlooking the lake, two woven ropes knot at the top and thread down through the sides of a wooden plank. She runs her hand down one of the frayed strands and sweeps the layer of pine needles covering the seat.

"I'm not sure this is all that safe anymore." She tips her chin to the sky, inspecting the threadbare jute.

"I'll catch you if you fall," I say, holding the swing steady for her.

She wraps her slender fingers around the rope and scoots back onto the seat. It wobbles slightly and she turns her chin to peek at me.

"I promise," I add, and press my hand to her lower back as her feet lift off the ground.

The higher she goes, the more she clings on for dear life, until her feet touch the clouds. Her braid oscillates with the wind as she grins over her shoulder. It's the freest I've seen her since meeting her three weeks ago. And that look on her face? Well, it steals a piece of my heart I'm not sure I'll ever get back. I'm not sure I even *want* it back.

"Do you ever wish you could fly without having to be afraid of the failing part?" she asks with her eyes closed.

The answer hangs on the tip of my tongue. A confession.

You make me feel like I can fly.

I let the wind drift her back and forth, slowing her down. She's so at peace that she doesn't seem to notice. Doesn't flutter open her eyes until I'm gripping the sides of the ropes and pulling the swing to a stop in front of me.

"All the time," I whisper.

For the briefest second, we hover there, inches apart. Her studying me. Me wanting her.

Kiss me, Hailey, I silently dare.

Watch me, her eyes seem to say as she fists the front of my shirt and hauls my lips to hers.

I've seen passionate kisses in romantic movies before. Moments when the characters forget where they are and how to keep their hands to themselves.

But I've never experienced anything quite like it until right now.

A kiss where the line between want and need is so blurry I forget we're outside for anyone to see. I simply give in to my desire to be closer to her. To find out if she tastes the same as the first time we did this. I groan when I'm met with the velvet flick of her tongue and briefly pause at the woosh of oars on the water as a canoe drifts by. Scooping her thighs from the seat, I have the wherewithal to carry her up the front porch steps to a place more private than this one.

The cabin walls echo with a thud when I kick the door open and press her back to it. Her pelvis grinds against my waist, and I see stars. So many stars. They're flickering behind my eyes. Exploding into brilliant beams of light. It's so bright now that all I can do is *feel*. It's too much and not enough all at once.

When I pull back, a war wages between our eyes.

You're the superintendent's daughter. An intoxicating distraction.

And I'm the guy who wasn't supposed to fall again.

But she's brushing her thumb across my swollen bottom lip and telling me where to take her with a whisper in my ear. And so my feet carry us there, to the second door on the left, as if there was no other choice.

The instant we're through the door frame, I discover what a different person I am on the other side. Not confident but *nervous* now. Her childhood bedroom blankets her in amber light, and I'm unraveling like her hair from the braid I just freed. I drop her back against the bed and watch the silky strands fan across her bedspread. She looks like a fallen angel waiting for me to make the next move.

I dip over the mattress, hands framing her shoulders. "Do you have any idea what you do to me?" I say in a strangled whisper.

Simply being in her presence, it's hard for me to concentrate on anything else. I study the way she swallows and shakes her head at my confession.

What a silly question. How would she know what she does to me? It's not as if I've given her any indication. I'd have a hard time believing those words too if I was her. And even if she's not saying them back, the want in her eyes conveys everything I need to know.

I fist the neckline of my shirt and pull it over my head. Her eyes roam my torso, wandering the trail of hair that disappears beneath my waistband. She grazes her fingertips there, and I shudder at her touch, fantasizing about the way it would feel to have her hands all over my skin. With a start, her gaze flicks to the window, and I have to lean away from her as she pushes onto her elbows.

"Is it too bright in here? Should I close the curtains?" she asks.

"Leave them," I say, brushing her bangs from her eyes.

She sinks against the comforter. "Okay. Should I..." Her

fingers fiddle with the hem of her top, and I smirk.

"Do I have to stare at the ceiling this time?" I ask.

"Do you *want* to stare at this ceiling this time?"

She drags her shirt over her head and tosses it on the floor. The sight of her beneath me in a nude bra matching the milky color of her skin is enough to make my mouth run dry. I already know what's waiting underneath that small scrap of fabric, but it's different this time. She's funneling her arm beneath her back instead of fleeing a men's bathroom, and I'm anticipating the straps giving way instead of feeling like an intruder.

"Is that a trick question?" I ask as she slides the silky cups away from her body in a slow, sensual movement.

She shakes her head.

"I want to see all of you," I say. I can't stop looking at her.

A nervous smile tugs at her lips. "It's nothing you haven't seen before, right?"

It's that same question she asked me at the barracks. She thinks I've done this a lot. I swallow and lie on the bed next to her. The corners of her hazel eyes pinch as she draws figure-eight patterns over my face.

"Reed?"

It's the first time she's called me by my name, and all I want is to hear her say it again.

"Is everything okay?" she asks.

Distracted, I nod. I've never wanted her to see me as a one-night-stand kind of guy, but if we're going to take this any further, she deserves to know.

"I've only ever been with one person," I admit.

Her eyes widen. I can't blame her for being surprised when everyone in my life thinks the same way about me, and everyone in her life has given her reason to believe that's just how guys are. I wasn't able to convince her on that plane that some guys are different. That *I'm* different. I just hope being honest with her now will show how seriously I take this. That this moment with her matters a great deal to me.

"It was dark. I was drunk. It was fast. I was hurting. It was a rebound thing, and I barely remember it."

She reaches for my hand and winds our fingers together. Something I wasn't expecting... Sympathy.

"I want this to be different," I tell her. "I want to take my time with you and remember what it feels like to hold you close to me."

She shifts in my arms so that she's cradled against my chest and draws my palm down to her lips, kissing the center.

"I want that too," she says, and for this moment, I pretend we're more than casual. I lean in and kiss her like she's *mine*. Slow and steady like a canoe rocking in time with the ripples in the water. She gives, I take. I pull, she pushes. We kiss until I've memorized every dip of her mouth, every stroke of her tongue. Until we're both left panting and wanting more.

She reaches for me first, gripping the button on my pants and tugging down the zipper. I help her work the denim down my thighs, chuckling when they meet the laces of my boots.

A faint blush pinkens her cheeks. "You could always leave them on."

I raise one eyebrow. "Boots? *Only* boots? That does it for you?"

She lifts onto her elbows again and nibbles on her bottom lip like she's imagining it. "I mean... it doesn't *not* do it for me. You look good in those boots. But I think I might like them even better when they're on the floor with the rest of your clothes." Her eyes heat.

"Off it is."

She giggles as I bounce around on one foot, tearing the laces free and jerking them off by the heel. I ditch my pants beside them before kneeling over her and dropping my mouth to her chest. In a slow dusting, my lips feather from her sternum to her breast. Her back arches as I work the button of her jeans open and shimmy them down her long, lean legs. Lying there in nothing but her underwear, I kneel at her feet.

"I am the luckiest guy alive." I grin against her skin and hold her gaze while trailing my mouth from her ankle to her knee, her knee to her thigh. My fingers track over the same sensitive skin my lips touch, and she sinks her hands into my hair, groaning my name.

Bam.

"What was that?"

We jerk apart.

I shuffle, bent in half, to her bedroom window to get a good look outside. Jack Hart steps away from his pickup truck, headed straight for the porch steps.

CHAPTER TWENTY-SIX

Hailey covers her exposed chest with her arms, meeting me where our clothes lie in a heap on the floor.

"I thought you said he wouldn't come back here!" I hop in the most awkward angle to get my pants over my hips without fully straightening.

With wide eyes, she hisses, "He *doesn't* come here!" She drags her shirt over her head, stashing her bra beneath the bed.

"I can sneak out the window," I suggest, sizing up the small frame. I'd have to turn to the side to make it through the narrow opening, but I think it could work. I'd do just about anything right now to avoid the repercussions of my boss finding me alone in this bedroom with his daughter. But I remember the small problem with that plan.

My truck is in the driveway.

"I can have anyone I want here," she argues. "Just... give me a minute with him before you come out, okay?"

I search her face as she brushes the strands of hair out of her eyes and straightens her shirt. Then, she disappears through the doorway.

The front door creaks open and I perch on the edge of her

bed, unsure of what to do. Afraid I royally screwed up on all accounts.

"What are you doing here?" I hear her ask him in the entryway.

I stand from the bed so I can pace back and forth while I wait for his answer. Whatever he comes up with, it will say a lot.

His heavy boots clunk against the floor, the sound getting louder, which means he hasn't suddenly decided to retreat into the night and leave us to it. Perfect.

I know she's strong enough to handle him herself, but I can't help peeking around the corner to take in the situation and make sure she's okay.

I can barely make out the slope of Jack's nose past the wall between us. He'd have to crane his neck to the side to see me from where he stands.

"I came because I thought we could talk," he says.

She's fidgeting. I hate seeing her this way, like she's a cat stuck in a storm, cowering before his thunderous gaze.

"Oh. Okay," she says.

When his eyes stray toward the hallway I duck for cover.

"Why don't we sit down." She guides him to the living room.

"You're home." He says it like it's taken seeing her in her childhood space for him to believe it.

"The place looks the same," she says, making awkward small talk.

"Yeah, I guess it does, doesn't it? I haven't been around here much since you left."

A low laugh bubbles from her chest. Not a happy sound but irritated. "You weren't around here much even before I left."

He sighs. I can see more of his face now from the recliner he's sitting in. His eyebrows pinch together. Just talking to her looks painful for him.

"If there was one good thing I could ever do for you it was protect you. What I said this morning... that you don't belong here... I meant in a place you aren't safe." He drags a hand over his mouth. "Incident command posts are functioning homeless communes, Hayes. The camps are dirty and hot. They're an epicenter for viruses and illness. Things I don't love the idea of you being exposed to. I didn't mean to imply I don't want you around, that you aren't great at what you do, or that I'm not incredibly proud of what you've accomplished."

Wow. That was... unexpected. But did she even hear him?

Hailey's staring out the kitchen window, as if a home video is playing across the glass.

"Did you know I went on that swing out there today for the first time since we built it nine years ago?"

I expect her to look at him for his reaction. But her question was obviously rhetorical.

"You told me you had some jute rope lying around that you weren't sure what to do with," she continues. "You even let me drill the holes in the seat."

A soft smile graces her lips.

"I was so happy that day. Hopeful that this material object would be the very thing that would bring us together."

She blows out a breath.

"But then your phone rang. You stepped away to take the call, and I sat on that swing staring out at the lake for *hours*. I knew with one pump of my legs I could start it on my own. But I wanted you to do it with me. I waited for you and..." Her voice cracks before she ever finishes the sentence, and my heart pitches in my chest.

Come on, Jack. Say something.

But he's sitting there, stalk still, not touching her.

"I waited to feel that same joy I felt when you brought home that wooden plank from your camping trip."

Camping trip? Wait... how many years ago did she say it had been since she had ridden on it? *Eight? Nine?* That would make me...

No.

My heart sinks like it's made of lead.

That would make me twelve. And that wooden plank I can clearly remember him tucking under his arm... that was for Hailey.

Dread coils in the pit of my stomach with the secret I've been unknowingly keeping from her. The one where I went on a camping trip with her father that she wasn't invited on.

"It was the first gesture you ever made that showed you thought of me," she whispers. "I was ready to feel like I was floating on that swing. But you never came back." She shakes her head. "You never *come* back."

Jack stands and clears his throat. But he pinches the bridge of his nose and says, "I thought I could do this. You came home, and I thought—"

"That things would be different this time," she finishes for him, like she can relate.

Anguish grips his features. "I don't know how to do this, Hayes. How to be a good father. I know I've failed you. I'm so sorry."

I hear his boots clunk against the floor as he backs out of the living room and through the front door.

Like hell he's sorry! If he thinks he's going to just leave her here crying without making sure she's okay first, he's got another thing coming.

I burst out of the bedroom and rush to her, wrapping her in my arms. She quakes against my chest.

"Shh, it's going to be okay," I whisper into her hair, then press a kiss to the top of her head.

She tries to grab on to my arm as I chase after him, but her fingers only trail at the hem of my shirt.

"Reed, no," she calls from behind me, and I pause my steps. "He wants to go."

"He's your father, Red. If he can't see for himself, he needs to know what he's missing out on."

It takes everything to leave her there, but it's something I have to do.

He's almost at his truck when I step onto the gravel driveway and call out, "Why do you shit all over her, huh?"

He doesn't turn around to look at me when he speaks next. Not that I'm surprised. "Stay out of what you don't know, Reed."

Be damned my goal of getting him to trust me. She doesn't deserve this.

"No, you know what, I won't stay out of it." I reach for his arm and jerk him around. We may be the same height, but the man hasn't taken a day off in years, and he carries the fatigue around with him like a weighted blanket. I could rip his arm right out of its socket if I'm not careful.

"I know more about her in a few weeks than you ever have."

He pulls himself free and continues his march toward his truck. But I stay no more than two feet behind him.

"Did you know she likes her coffee black? Just straight black, no sugar. Or that she eats M&Ms in the order of a rainbow."

He reaches for the door handle and stops. I take it as my sign that this is working. That I'm getting through to him.

"She likes it when you sing the lyrics wrong to a song when she gets anxious. And her eyes..."

He yanks open the car door as he whirls around.

"Don't tell me about my own daughter's eyes!"

"Why?" I press in closer, getting right in his face. "Because—"

"Because I know what they look like! There isn't a single moment I don't spend seeing them everywhere I go. So, stay out of it! This is the last time you'll be defending her to me."

Jack jumps in the front seat and slams the door shut, peeling his truck away in reverse.

This moment might have risked everything I've worked for over the last month, but I don't care. I'd do it all over again for her.

REED

You can learn a lot about a person from their childhood bedroom.

Judging by the trophies that line the top of her oak dresser, Hailey likes soccer. And the cork board tucked behind them with a dozen different push pins through the photographs? Dean really is her best friend. Was, I guess.

A crack of thunder rattles the window. I never did close the blinds, and dark clouds form an angry vortex in the sky. A summer storm is coming.

Her chest shudders in the cradle of my arms. This was not the date night I had planned for us.

Grenaldough's pizza still sits uneaten on the counter. She cried herself to sleep shortly after he left, and I don't know if she wants me sleeping in here too, but I couldn't leave her that way.

I notice goose bumps along her shoulder and drag the edge of a patchwork quilt made of old high school T-shirts up to her neck.

She's sentimental.

There's a patch on one of the corners that says *Bald Eagle*

Powder Puffs with a screen-printed camo football below the lettering. I didn't have to see this one to know she's tough.

The way she allowed herself to open up to her dad tonight. To get *that* vulnerable, knowing there was a good chance his words would hurt her, was another level of bravery altogether. I've never done that with my parents.

For a long time, I assumed we all had our scars from our youth. And that we heal them by moving on. Doing better for ourselves as adults.

But if there's anything I've learned since leaving home, it's that the past follows you wherever you go. You don't get to hide it away when it's in a glass box of insecurities. There's no key to lock it shut and throw it thirty feet deep in a lake. You actually have to face it.

For me, I don't think I'll ever feel worthy until I tell my father I still think about that day.

I'm a hypocrite though. Offering advice to Hailey and Jack when I haven't even called my parents since I got here.

In a slow, continuous movement, I drag my arm from beneath her head, transferring her to the nearest pillow. Then I slip from the room and make my way to the front porch, careful to keep my footsteps light.

The phone rings four times before he picks up. "Reed?"

"Hey, Dad."

"It's good to hear your voice, son. How's the job been?"

Exhausting. Exhilarating. Hardest thing I've ever done. "It's been great. How's everybody else?"

"Oh, you know your mom. Always filling up the schedule."

So do you, I want to add.

"How are Rex and Ronny?"

I ask to be polite. I know if I don't, he'll tell me anyway.

"They helped me get the restaurant shut down for the season last week."

Of course, he brings up Bear Shore from a question like that. At least with the place winterized, it guarantees six months before I have to hear about it again.

Nice, is all I say back until our conversation hits a lull and he clears his throat. "So, uh, has your crew heard about that fire in Warren? A news reporter claims it's up to 64,000 acres."

"Yep. Been working on it since it started," I say.

"Really? Are you okay?"

His concern surprises me. But I smile, looking through the window to where Hailey sleeps.

"Nothing an EMT can't handle."

The line goes silent for a second, and all I can think about is that day nine years ago. This is my chance to tell him how I really feel.

"Hey, Dad..."

"Yeah?"

"You remember that weekend we came camping here..."

A bunch of garbled tones filter through the speaker, and his voice muffles as he says something to someone on his end.

"Reed, I'm sorry. I've actually got to go. We have a big case load, and your mom is on my tail to finish the paperwork before tomorrow."

"Yeah," I manage, because what else am I going to say? *It figures you'd be too busy to have this conversation with me.*

"We'll catch up soon, okay? Tell Jack I said hi," he says.

You mean the guy who's doing you a favor? "Yeah, I'll tell him."

I hang up before even saying goodbye, because what's the point? This conversation was never about me, as usual.

A feeling simmers at the surface, white hot. Anger? Resentment? Blame? Maybe a combination of all three.

And I'm not sure it's even him I'm mad at anymore. I chased myself out of town. I messed around with that stick to get his attention nine years ago. It's me who's too scared to tell anyone how I really feel.

When I get back to her room, I tuck my phone next to Hailey's on the nightstand, toggling them both to the silent setting. We could use the uninterrupted sleep.

It takes a while for my mind to settle down with the image of a burning campsite and an unworthy kid haunting it. But the low rumble of thunder in the distance becomes enough of a sound machine and eventually, I drift off to sleep.

CHAPTER TWENTY-EIGHT

HAILEY

I can't see a thing.

At the crack of an eyelid, brilliant white light blinds my retinas.

Where am I? What time is it?

I bat at the surface next to me, reaching for the familiar rectangular object.

It's too far away.

I try to roll to one side but there's an arm draped across my midsection. The person it's attached to groans and furls me in tighter.

I fight through the haze, scratching at my eyes. I try to push Reed's big body off me with no luck. If I could just... get... a little... I swing at the phone with the finesse of an octopus arm, and it sails off the nightstand and thumps to the floor.

Super.

I'm going to have to go about this another way. I wiggle my body up, down, side to side, testing which direction grants me the most leverage. When my chest slips lower with the scoot of my butt, down it is. With no footboard, I flop off the end in a blunt thud to the floor.

Wow, okay. I'm awake.

I swipe up on the dark screen and stand.

Eight missed calls?

Seven say Dean. One says Jack.

I rub at the puffy circles that ring my eyes.

I was crying. Jack was here. I've been working. Reed was... *Reed. Working.*

Reality crashes in on me.

Eight missed calls and it's light out!

"Reed!" I slap at his arm and he sits up with a start.

"What? What is it?" He scans the room, swinging his head frantically. Then he groans at the surge of light.

"My phone's on silent," I say, switching the sound on and off again to be sure I'm seeing it correctly. "How did my volume get turned off?"

Reed scratches the back of his head. "I thought you could use the extra sleep on your day off."

"Yeah, I could! Except it's past nine now and we missed a dispatch call over an hour ago!"

He throws himself out of bed and runs to the living room. He turns on the TV, flipping to Channel 7 News, and we hear the detailed report we would have gotten from my dad or Dean if we hadn't missed their calls.

"The White Horse fire burning across the Payette National Forest developed a massive shift overnight when a thunderstorm swept the area. The fire that was once contained on the northern border hopped the Salmon River. High winds and lightning in the area are making it difficult for crews to stay on top of the spread that has burned an estimated 103,000 acres at this point. Forest Service officials say if they don't get ahead of this thing, we might be in for a long summer."

I grab the remote from his frozen hand, punching the OFF button and flinging it on the sofa. "We gotta go! Now!"

Reed's the first one in the truck.

"I'm so sorry. I shouldn't have done that. I didn't even think—" He shakes his head and clenches the steering wheel in a firm grip.

"Let's just hope we aren't too late, or we're all screwed," I say.

We ride in silence, with Reed barreling twenty miles an hour over the speed limit through Warren Wagon Road and me hanging on for dear life.

A call comes through the truck's dash with Reed's phone connected to autoplay. He answers it.

"Where the hell are you!" Dean's voice screams through the speaker.

We jostle back and forth when the paved road gives way to gravel.

"Five miles out," Reed answers.

"From where?"

"What do you mean from where? White Horse!"

"You need to turn around," Dean says.

"Why?"

"Because we're not there, man."

"Where the hell are you then?"

"The crew had to turn down the job, Morgan. We can't work with a seventeen-man team."

Reed's eyes grow wide. "No. We... we can still do it. I can be wherever you need me to be."

"We *needed* you to answer your dispatch call almost two hours ago."

The line goes dead and Reed slams a palm against the dashboard. "Dammit! I should have listened to him."

"Woah, it's okay. We'll fix this."

"How, Hailey?"

I wince when I hear him use my first name.

"This is what I do. I screw shit up! Dean, my dad, *your* dad. They're all right about me. I manage to make the easy, wrong choice every time."

I don't know what he means by that, but I can't help tying those words to me—*easy, wrong*.

I pull out my own phone and dial the number I've had memorized my whole life.

He shocks me when he picks up on the first ring.

"If you're calling to defend your boyfriend, it's too late, Hayes. Dispatch is already sending out another crew. That's how this thing works."

"Dad, please!"

The name sounds foreign on my lips, but desperate times call for desperate measures.

"Please do this *one* thing for me."

He lets out a shaky exhale through the speaker. I don't ask for much from him, but I can't be the reason Reed loses this job. I've seen how hard he's worked to prove himself here. He deserves a second chance.

"Okay. Let me make a call."

"Thank you!"

We park on the side of the road and wait. One minute turns into five. One nervous knee turns into two shaking knees. Then the phone rings again—Reed's. Even with it disconnected from the truck and pressed to his ear this time, the volume's loud enough I hear my father's voice.

"Morgan, make sure my daughter is safe and then meet us at the McCall Smokejumper Base. You've got forty-five minutes. This is your last chance; don't blow it."

"Thank you," Reed says.

"I didn't do it for you," Jack answers.

Reed looks over and smiles at me when he says, "Yes, sir."

He ends the call and drops the phone in his lap, pulling back onto the gravel road.

"Wait. What are you doing?"

"He told me to make sure you're safe, and that's exactly what I'm going to do."

"At the campground? Reed, please! The crew is spiking out again. Probably for an entire roll this time. You can't spend two weeks without an EMT. Ben will be staying back to hold down the medic tent. You guys need me."

"I'm sure dispatch has already thought of that," he argues.

"Fine, *I* need you. I can't spend the next two weeks wondering if you're okay! There could be bears out there! Or a coyote!"

His eyebrow peaks and that damn dimple sinks into his cheek.

"I didn't realize they taught you bear defense in EMT school."

I slap him on the arm.

"Wow. I take it back. Maybe they did. You've got the arm of a major league pitcher."

"And you've got the reflexes of a dairy cow."

He chuckles, spinning the car around.

I don't know if I got him to agree because he feels sorry for me or if having me along makes sense. But somewhere in my heart, I'm hoping he did it because a part of him needs me just as much as I need him.

CHAPTER TWENTY-NINE

REED

So *this* is where the elite work.

The McCall Smokejumper Base sprawls in all directions. To take it in all at once would be impossible, so I start with the first thing that I see.

Protected behind barbed wire fencing and a keypad-controlled gate, a wooden structure stands three stories tall. It connects to various platforms by a harness-and-rope system. *A training course.*

A snapshot of a dream I imagined for myself years ago, jumping out of planes and parachuting into fires, flashes before me. This is what I've been waiting for.

The visual tour ends with the steely glare of my superintendent on the other side of that gate.

Reality slaps me in the face—*not a smokejumper*—and I slam the truck into park.

Grabbing my gear, we take off in a sprint toward the open access point.

"This your idea of safe, Morgan?" Jack scolds as his eyes flick toward his daughter.

What was the non-selfish reason for why I didn't drop her

off at the fire camp? I try to recall… anything other than simply *wanting* her here. But he's right. It was egocentric of me to put her in unnecessary danger.

The crew is already surrounded by gear, waiting on a holding pattern.

"Listen up, gentlemen," a pilot shouts over the roar of the engine.

Jack abandons our conversation for the crew and we have no choice but to follow him.

"The canyon pinching the Salmon River has a seven-thousand-foot elevation. We can't get our aircraft down there, so you'll be dropped at the highest point on the north side," she says. "You'll have to hike the rest of the way in. Our aircrafts can transport nine of you at a time. We'll take the first group and come back for the rest."

As captains, Murphy and Jackson split the crew into two teams. Jackson's group funnels into the smokejumper plane first, along with Jack.

"Dad, wait…" Hailey calls out.

He pauses in the doorframe. "I can't do this with you right now, Hayes. I know I owe you an explanation, but there are a lot of lives and properties at risk on the other side of that river."

Hailey juts out her chin, her eyes burning with a challenge. "You know as well as I do that anything could happen to you guys out there. You'll be miles from camp. You don't have a single person on your crew who knows more than standard first aid and CPR. I'm your on-site EMT for the next two weeks." She doesn't ask, just demands it like the stunning force of nature that she is.

Even as the silence prevails between them while he thinks it over, she holds her posture strong.

"Please don't make me stay here worrying about you. I've

done it my whole life. I've already lived without her. I can't lose you too."

He grabs her by the shoulders and hauls her into his chest. He's *hugging* her.

"Promise me you'll stay close. I don't want anything to happen to you either," he confesses.

"I promise," she says, and I don't miss the quake in her voice.

When she lets go, he makes sure I'm looking at him before he motions to the wood-shingled building behind me. "Get her some gear."

CHAPTER THIRTY

HAILEY

The hike to the river's edge is brutal, with the wind whipping the heat in a northwest current. Thick black smoke gusts around us, leaving a layer of soot and ash on our sweat-drenched clothing. We're a dismal shade of charcoal. I don't even want to think about the sorry condition my eyesight and hair would be in had I not borrowed the protective eyewear and neck shield from the smokejumper base.

We stick together, hugging a single file line down the rocky slope as the flames continue to hiss and smolder around us. I'm right behind Reed but have to take two steps to every one of his to keep up. He reaches back, closing his gloved hand around mine as we shuffle down the side of the dusty hill.

At the bottom, a patch of river rock leads to the water. The wind slices against the current, rippling in tight divots across the surface. The heavy weight of my pack and the blunt force of the wind nearly knock me sideways.

The next gust chops Reed's words of "I can carry that for you" into fragments before they ever reach my ears.

I turn down his offer and instantly regret it, my eyes bulging at the insurmountable climb ahead. What a waste to have to hike down just to trek out again. But this time, the crew is digging lines as we go.

Reed says something else, but all I can I make out is "follow Dean."

Only, Dean's legs are just as long as his, and I can't reach the same rocks and ledges his boots find. So, I slip and slide, one time landing both palms on a sharp rock. It takes me cutting my hand to consider that maybe I made a mistake in coming with them.

What will I do next? Stub a toe? Break a knee?

"Hayes, your glove is on fire!" Dean screams, knocking it from my hand and stamping on it with his boots.

Yep. I'm a safety risk.

"Let me help."

It's been four painfully long hours since I made the mistake of getting a little too close to the flames, and no one believes me when I tell them I'M FINE. Not Dean, not Reed, and certainly not my dad, who responds to my pleading in typical fatherly fashion: "You can't perform first aid if you're injured or exhausted."

"I'll keep it light," I insist.

He lifts a tool with a steel-clawed end and lets the handle fall toward my chest. I miss it, and it plows into the ground.

"Pick it up," he says.

I do.

"Now slam it into that pile of brush right there." He points to a bunch of spiny plants.

I teeter backward a bit with the heavy end over my shoulder and, likewise, fall forward with the sharp teeth. I grin when it breaks the dirt's surface and nets half a dozen branches. Maybe too many branches, I think to myself, when one snags as I pull it toward me and it rips the tool from my hands.

"Do that a hundred more times and tell me if it feels light to you."

Okay, he's got a point. I'm in no shape for this.

"I can't just sit here all day and do nothing," I say. "I promise I won't overdo it."

He chuckles as if that's not possible but helps me pick up the dropped tool anyway.

"Okay. Go for it. We need all the help we can get if we're going to sleep in the black tonight."

I start to seriously doubt my dad's sanity. I don't know why I hadn't considered our sleeping arrangement. I sure as hell will guarantee there are no flames nearby if I'm expected to be dreaming for any length of time out here. I get to work, clawing and pulling.

The crew is an unstoppable machine that only breaks for a fifteen-minute standing lunch. My admiration for their endurance is riding at an all-time high. My arms are noodles by the time dinner rolls around, and just the thought that I'll be sleeping on this rock-hard ground makes me want to cry into my poor excuse of a square pillow.

"Did anyone see the ass on that helicopter pilot?" Murphy asks as he pumps his eyebrows up and down. He situates his tent in the semi-circle we've formed.

"Dude, I sat in the seat behind her, and that ripe peach was my perpendicular horizon." Evans whistles.

I smirk. "Is this what you guys do out here? Talk about girls? You're one pillow fight away from a thirteen-year-old's slumber party."

Jackson winks at me. "Join us! It'll be fun! That reminds

me"—he turns to the guys—"remember the time I tried to set Hart up with my aunt May on R&R?" Jackson says.

With those dusky blue eyes, his aunt had to have been pretty.

When they're all loud laughter, my dad says, "Dial it back. There are female ears present now."

I blush. "I don't mind."

"See, Hart? I bet Hailey would like to play this game," Dean says.

Now that I'm out here in the woods with him every day, I won't be able to dodge talking to Dean forever like I'd hoped. But for now, I avoid returning his smile by zeroing in on my dad's reaction.

"Absolutely not," he barks.

"What game?" I ask, my curiosity getting the best of me.

"Oh, come on, Supt. It'll be fun! You can tell her all about how she—"

"Not funny, McCafferty," my dad says, and I hear this rumbly sound follow it.

Is he... *laughing?*

I look over at him, and his shoulders bounce.

He *is* laughing.

I'm sure I've heard my dad laugh at some point. But for the life of me, I don't remember it. It's the most lighthearted sound.

I don't know why it's taken me so long to understand it. In this light, with these guys... He belongs here. I may not know this version of him that they do, but I want to. And I think this game might be the way to do that.

"I want to hear it!" I burst out.

Mostly because I can't believe my dad dated someone. When did he have the time?

With an eyeroll, he begrudgingly lets Jackson continue.

"So, Aunt May was here for the winter carnival last year.

It's this big event the town hosts where businesses have elaborate sculptures carved out of ice and enter them into a competition. She's a huge fantasy fan. And when she saw a sculpture of a dragon, she asked Hart to take her picture riding it. But he couldn't figure out how to get the camera open."

"Surprise, surprise," Ramirez says, and the whole crew laughs along with him.

I glance at my dad and he's touching his mustache in nervous strokes, but he's still smiling.

"She was sitting on that thing for a good three minutes until he finally got the shot," he continues. "And when she stood up... she ripped the crotch clean out of her pants."

"No!" I gasp.

My dad's cheeks blanch. It's endearing.

"He had to fashion his coat into a diaper to get her out of there."

He looks at me then, and we share the first smile we have in a long time.

I like this game. Done Me Dirty, they call it. I've been on a lot of awful dates in my life, so it's not hard to come up with one. Maybe slightly more embarrassing with my father *and* a guy who I'm crushing on present. But if I want them to be vulnerable with me, I need to be vulnerable back. One dirty dating story for another.

"I'll go next," I offer.

CHAPTER THIRTY-ONE

REED

My teeth clench when Hailey starts in on her dating story.

"The first EMT job I ever took was with the Public Health Department. I was assigned to a homeless outreach program, and one of the guys I was helping was a transplant from Texas. We'd conduct health assessments, treat infections, administer vaccines, but this guy didn't need any of that. He needed a job.

"I hated seeing people struggling to get a start in life, so, on my own time, I helped him get a new suit and lined up an interview at a local restaurant we partnered with to support shelters. After a few paychecks, he offered to repay me by taking me out to dinner. He was nice to look at," she says, and blushes slightly.

I force my jaw to relax, but the sensation transfers to a clenching in the pit of my stomach. It's ironic to be out in the middle of the vast wilderness and feel stuck in such tight quarters.

"I thought, why not. If anything, I was new to Utah and could use a friend in the area. At first, it seemed sweet when he asked me a million questions about myself. But then he started dodging the ones I asked about him." She takes a deep breath that lifts her whole chest and continues. "We were at this really popular Italian place in downtown Salt Lake. It took forever to get our food. So, when he finally *had* to tell me something, he said that he got laid off from his job in Georgia and moved to Utah for a change of scenery."

"Georgia's not Texas," Marshall pipes up.

"Thank you, Captain Obvious." Evans chortles.

Where is this story going? Because now I don't just feel possessive but protective too.

"His excuse was that he grew up in Texas but moved to Georgia for a year after graduation. That wasn't the only part of his story that didn't add up either, and a week later, he was arrested at work. The head chef recognized his face on *America's Most Wanted*. It turns out, blond Jeremy Scott stole a famous piece of pottery and tried pawning it for money. It launched a full federal investigation against the guy who was now posing as Evan Banks with dark hair."

"Wow." Dean chuckles, but it either doesn't get her attention or she's still upset with him.

I breathe a sigh of relief. I was afraid that story was going to take a dark turn.

"Yeah, well, not everyone is as good at dating as I am." She smirks at Marshall and then says, "What about you?"

"You mean, what's it like to get turned down every time you ask someone on a date?" Murphy jokes.

Marshall pushes his glasses up the bridge of his nose. It makes his pupils twice as large when he does it.

"It's okay, Marshall. Logan Murphy wouldn't know what it's like to put himself out there. He hasn't been on a date in four years," Ramirez says.

Here we go again with these two. Murphy frowns. I didn't

think it was possible for the burly guy to experience this emotion but... is that *pain* in his eyes?

"I'll have you know, I went out with this girl one time," Marshall starts, "and she was beautiful. Like, blond hair big boobs kind of hot. I took her to the state fair, and while we were waiting in line to ride the Ferris wheel, a few of her friends spotted us and stopped to say hi. They were giggling and whispering and squealing and nudging her. She was blushing, so at the time, I thought they had to be talking about me, right? How good looking I was?"

"Let me guess, she lost a bet," Ramirez says, choking on his water.

"Yeah, to your grandma," Marshall throws back, and everyone laughs—even Ramirez, who lives with the grandmother in question.

"Anyway, she blushed even harder and then reached into her pocket and pulled out her phone. She said, 'Would you take our picture?' so I wrapped my arm around her at the same moment she shoved her phone against my chest."

This poor guy.

"But jokes on her." Marshall reaches into his line pack and unearths a picture of four blond girls with the whitest teeth I've ever seen. He's grinning from ear to ear.

"Now that we've established that Marshall is a stalker," Murphy says. "Jackson." He nods in his direction. "Your turn, man."

"First white girl I ever dated asked my father if we were from Africa," Jackson says. "He's a fourth-generation Louisianan."

"At least she didn't ask if you had a speech impediment." McCafferty covers his face with his sleeping bag.

"Madison asked you that?"

Dean tenses, his mouth slightly agape when Hailey acknowledges him.

"She made me nervous, and I stuttered in front of her," he admits.

I'm liking this Madison girl less and less the more I learn about her.

"And you're still going out with her?" I interject.

He glowers at me. Whether fitting or not, Done Me Dirty is not the time you break the news about a cheating girlfriend in front the entire crew.

"How many times have you been an idiot here," Dean fires back, "and Hailey seems to still be interested in you?"

"Dean!" she squeaks.

But a playful smile bends McCafferty's lips, and he slaps me on the upper back. "I was kidding. All right, Morgan. Let's hear what you got."

Looking back on my dating history, it's fairly platonic. What you'd expect from a typical high school and one year of college experience. I don't talk about this part of my life, so I'll keep it vague. With everyone's eyes on me, this is the only thing I can think of to say.

"I spent an entire summer trying to get a girl to fall in love with me."

"You're joking," McCafferty says first.

Everyone's eyes narrow when they realize I'm serious.

"I wish I was."

He asks the second question too. "And how did that work out for you?"

"Well, I'm here, aren't I?" I shrug at him.

"But did you take off your shirt for her because... *damn*," Ramirez says, smirking.

"Keep it in your pants." Murphy grunts at him.

"What! You can't tell me the guy doesn't look good with an eight-rung ladder for abs."

"And that will be the end of our game," Hart interrupts.

A few more jokes get thrown around before everyone crawls in their own bivies. Even after my ant debacle, I still don't understand how they can stand sleeping in a mummy bag with a net over their faces. But I got luckier than the rest this time; mine happens to have enough room for two.

In the dark, my sense of sound heightens tenfold. Everything feels closer: the crack of limbs buckling, the steady whistle of insects, and the whoosh of the wind circling us. I should be passing out. Rendered unconscious after what I put my body through today. But it's my mind I can't turn off.

There aren't pieces of Teddy and Miles everywhere here like there would have been had I stayed in Bear Lake. But sometimes, like when I make the stupid decision to bring them up, they squat in my mind rent free.

"Reed?" I hear Hailey whisper into the dark. I helped construct her own bivy close enough to mine that they're practically touching. I assumed she was asleep, but who am I to say when I can't make out her outline.

"Yeah," I respond, staring up into the night sky. Not even the brightest stars stand a chance against the smoke that drapes in the air.

"You want to tell me about her?" she asks.

I dip my head to the side she's lying on as if we're in the same bed together and I can see her face.

We still haven't talked about Teddy. We haven't defined what we are to each other, and I'm afraid she'll see herself as the rebound girl if I'm really honest with how I once felt about Teddy. So, I make the choice to pretend like she meant less to me than she did.

"About who?"

"Your summer girl."

"There's not much to tell. I spent six summers with her, and she fell in love with my best friend."

"Did she know how you felt?" she asks.

My cheek rubs against my sleeping bag with my nod. "Yeah. She knew."

"How?" She sounds flabbergasted.

I sigh, realizing I can't downplay the truth anymore. "She got in an accident last summer and lost her memory. All the moments we shared together, they were gone just like that. I guess some stupid part of me hoped I could help her get them back. So I spent the summer recreating those moments. But it only led her to remembering him."

She slips silently from her sleeping bag. I only know she's done it when I hear the zip of my own. It's barely wide enough for my body, but I draw back to the edge, and she tucks her hips in so she's flush against my skin. I help her close the net, distracted by the heat of her breath warming my lips.

"I'm sorry," she whispers.

"It's okay," I tell her. "It was always meant to be him; I just didn't want to see it at first."

"Reed." She breathes my name.

I love when she says my name.

"You deserve to be someone's first choice. Someone's everything."

I sweep her bangs out of her eyes and brush my knuckles against her cheek.

But I can't be your first choice, Hailey, my heart says. *Somebody's already taken that place in your life, and I'm not sure you have enough room for anyone else.* Especially if she knew that person chose to spend time with me over her.

"I'm not sure I'll ever be first choice material," I admit.

The fingers of her left hand clutch the back of my neck as she kisses me softly on the mouth.

Once.

Twice.

Three times.

Then she melts against my chest and whispers, "You already are."

CHAPTER THIRTY-TWO

HAILEY

I wake in the crook of Reed's arm.

When did I fall asleep?

He brushes his lips against my temple, and for one moment I forget that I'm spiking out with my father and his eighteen-man crew who are all going to witness me leaving this sleeping arrangement.

Nothing happened, but they don't know that.

"Good morning," Reed says, curling my soft body into his hard one even more than it already is.

"This is becoming a habit, me falling asleep on you," I say, unzipping our shared sleeping bag.

He grips my hip and I yelp as he pulls me toward his chest. "I can't say it's one I'd like you to break anytime soon."

I scroll his face in the morning light.

My gosh, this man is beautiful. Even with a shirt on.

I touch the hollow in his cheek, letting the tip of my pointer finger sink into...

The tent walls quake.

What was that?

They billow once like a parachute and then shudder, faster and faster.

The fire.

We wrestle and stumble out of fabric. This sleeping bag was not made for two. Reed tugs at the opening first, his broad frame shielding my body as he yanks at the zipper.

A rush of air tornados through the hole. Dirt, pine needles, leaves, all fly inside our shelter. I can't see anything. I have no clue what's making that chopping sound.

And then as quick as it blows in, the dust storm calms. It hangs in the air for a minute before I catch the whirl of the black copter blade soaring into the sky over us. Two paper sacks are thrown near our faces.

"Lucky bastard. If I had Madison here..." Dean murmurs, except I miss the rest of his sentence as I blow out a breath.

It's just breakfast delivery.

"I really need to tell him about her," I whisper, more to myself than to Reed, and another shaky breath gusts from my lungs.

"Let me do it," he offers, brushing his hand down my cheek.

I wish I could trap all of my problems outside this canvas bubble. Stay in here forever with him.

"I can't let you do that," I say. "He's finally starting to let you in. It needs to come from me."

He frowns when I pull away from his touch, running a hand down my braid where it's plastered to the back of my neck.

I miss showers.

I slink out and snatch up my breakfast sandwich, hoping the helicopter chaos is my answer to escaping unseen. I work the wrists of my bunched shirtsleeve down my forearms as I stand and squint into the daylight.

No such luck.

The *entire* crew stares back at me.

I don't know if we ever were one, but I guess Reed and I are not a secret anymore.

I might as well be picking dandelions.

If I thought my hand tool was heavy yesterday, how it feels today is laughable. Sweat trickles from my hairline toward my eyes and I wipe it with the back of my glove, smearing another layer of soot across my already caked forehead.

I need a break.

Grabbing a bottle of water from my borrowed line pack, I drain a full liter down my throat. Thank you, Air Tactical 6; it's still cold.

My stomach growls. How long has it been since I ate?

Slipping the pack to the ground, I rummage through the front pocket. My hand closes on a crinkly corner, but much to my disappointment, the item packaged in aluminum foil and plastic is an MRE meal.

Nope. Won't be needing that.

I stuff it back in. I think it's Marshall's? He could use the extra calories.

With a second sweep of the front pocket, I pluck out a bag of trail mix. I can't tear the top off fast enough when laughter steals my attention. Even though it's the fifth time I've heard it since last night, I don't recognize who it belongs to until I see my father's head tipped back at something Murphy said.

Will there ever come a day when it doesn't sound foreign to me?

He catches me staring and approaches my resting spot.

I pop a red M&M in my mouth.

"You like it here," I state. A truth that seems to set him free when he gazes with adoration at his surroundings.

"What's not to love?"

I chew two orange M&Ms, the chocolate melting on my tongue.

Had you asked me before now... the sight of charred ground, burnt trees, and smokey skies would not be something I'd have categorized with the word love. But now that I've been out here, seen it for myself, I know that's not what he's talking about. Or rather, *who*.

The guys sawyering and cutting and protecting this land are his family. And in the past, that realization would have broken me. But as I've gotten to know them personally, it's a bond I admire. Even now, I watch Ramirez with his frosted tips humming, and Murphy with his burly beard and larger-than-life smile shaking his head at him. They're two very different men working together as one. Even Dean and Reed seem to be in sync. Something I didn't want to mess up by letting Reed take the fall for Madison.

"He was right. You do eat M&Ms in the order of a rainbow," my dad comments, taking a seat beside me.

I add three yellows to my mouth.

"Who was right?" I turn my body so I can face him, even if he has a hard time looking at anything other than pine needles and his own two feet when he's around me.

"Reed."

My cheeks pinken. Here we go. I brace myself for the lecture to stay away from him.

"I'm sorry for barging in the other night," he says instead, taking me by surprise.

"I'm always glad when I see you home," I admit.

He finally looks at me. Really *looks* at me. Lets me see his pain.

"I've been running for so long I've forgotten how to stay," he says.

Something compels me to reach into my pocket and pull out that picture Reed gave me. I slip it in his palm.

"He was right about you too, you know. Looks like you were staying closer than you think."

He holds out the photograph of me and my mother and regards it with a sad smile. "How did you get this?"

He doesn't need to know Reed found it. "It fell from your pocket on the line," I say.

A puff of air expels from his nose. "It was snowing the day you were born. Did I ever tell you that?"

A look of sympathy must pass across my face.

"Yeah, I guess I wouldn't have." He drops his chin at first but then lifts his eyes to ask, "Can I tell you now?"

"Please."

"It was snowing," he repeats. "Big fluffy flakes that stuck to your eyelashes when you stood beneath them. It was a mile-long walk to the car with the way your mother was waddling. By the time I got her tucked in the front seat, she was laughing uncontrollably at the frost that had fused to my eyebrows and beard. Said I looked like Scrooge."

I picture it and giggle.

"Probably not my finest look." He returns my smile. "She labored for twenty-seven hours. It was like you didn't want to leave her."

My eyes mist over.

"But she was determined to bring you into the world in your own timing. We paced that hallway until you were ready."

A hot tear rolls down my face as I savor the thought that she wanted to keep *me* close just as much. It's the first piece of my mom I get to hang on to.

"At five in the morning, you came quietly into the world,

wide-eyed and curious. She held you, staring into your eyes. We stayed that way for a long time."

His bottom lip quivers, and I don't know whether to give him space or reach for his hand.

I decide on the latter.

"But then she started feeling dizzy and asked me to hold you. Somehow I hadn't noticed that the doctor and nurses had left the room. We were all alone in there, and I had no one to call on for help. At that point, I'd worked for years in crisis situations, but as I watched blood gush from the end of the bed, I froze."

I squeeze his hand as tears break free from his lash line, repelling down his cheeks in long streaks.

"Our doctor thought everything was fine. She'd stitched up her tear and went home for the night. It happened so fast, the hemorrhaging."

I can see the guilt he's been carrying around all these years, and I don't know how to fix it besides telling him, "It wasn't your fault."

He swipes at his eyes and lifts his head, pain radiating from every pinched groove and downturned line on his face.

"It's always been my fault, Hayes. When your mom died, a part of me died with her. The only thing she left behind were those eyes, and I couldn't bear to look at you. I wasn't cut out to be a single parent."

I see them now... all the ways he's been scared.

I shrug. "I think I turned out okay."

"I don't know how to make it better between us," he says.

I've been in this place for a long time. The one where he's at the wheel but I'm giving the directions. I think it just comes naturally to me now to be the one with the plan.

"We take it one day at a time," I tell him. "We start over."

I don't need a caregiver or financial support anymore. What I need is a family.

"We all make mistakes," I continue. "I just want us to be there for one another through them."

"I don't deserve you," he says, squeezing my hand back.

I wrap my arms around his neck, and he circles my middle. The small, broken girl inside of me screams for joy.

"You deserve all the best things this life has to offer, Dad."

CHAPTER THIRTY-THREE

REED

"Dude, is that what I think it is?"

McCafferty picks up his chainsaw and plows into my shoulder to get by me. We're dealing with a potential structure threat at a ranch property today, and he isn't wasting any time following dispatch's orders in protecting it.

"No," he grunts, yanking on the ignition string even though we're a good sixty yards away from the open hay field and stretch of pines we're making a fire break between.

This is too good to let go of, so I keep up with his pace.

"Really?" I yell over the motor. "Because it looks to me like a tampon string is hanging from your nostril."

He whips around and the limp fabric strand slaps him in the cheek.

I grin even wider.

"I get bloody noses in the summer. Sue me!"

"And you couldn't have stuffed a wad of toilet paper up there? Did your girlfriend pack your line bag for you?"

He smirks and revs the four-stroke engine. "Nope. *Yours* did."

Touché. I deserved that.

Now that the entire crew knows Hailey and I shared the same sleeping bag, it won't be the last girlfriend comment thrown my way. It can't vex me when I like the sound of it a little too much.

I watch her now, standing with Jack, and heave a sigh. We steal kisses whenever given the chance, but I'm not any closer to knowing what she's thinking. The most private conversation we've had was one about her dad a week and a half ago. If I can't have her to myself, I'm glad she has him to keep her company.

Or did, I think, as she sweeps her hand down his arm in a *Be right back* gesture.

Where is she going?

She jogs several feet, sizing up trees on the outskirts of the property until she ducks behind one. It's out of view from everyone except Dean and me. He's turned away from her, so I guess it's only me who can see.

What is she doing?

She pinches between her shoulder blades and reaches up the sleeve of her shirt. A bunched ball slides down her arm and away from her wrist, black lace dangling from the tip of her finger before she stuffs the undergarment in her pocket.

My mouth parches.

"Morgan, are you coming?" Dean asks.

I pry my eyes away from my unintentional voyeuring. "Yeah," I say, hoping it doesn't come out sounding strangled. I will now be thinking about *that* for the rest of the day.

I jog ten paces to catch up to him.

"Dude, Madison would *love* this place," he says, gawking at the string of Appaloosas corralled behind a gable barn.

"She would?"

That designer dress and uptalk voice screamed valley girl to me.

"She loooves animals," he drawls. "Wants a whole herd when we buy a piece of property together someday."

"You guys are planning to *live* together?"

The moment it leaves my mouth I scold myself. *Quit being so judgmental.* Of course the guy plans to live with his girlfriend. She's perfectly committed as far as he knows.

"Is that so hard to believe?" he asks.

"No, it's just..."

I should tell him. For three very important reasons: we're alone, he brought her up, and Hailey won't have to. I know she asked me not to, but that *look.* I hated seeing her so worked up. There may never be another opportunity like this again, even for her.

I stop before we reach the end of the fence line.

His eyebrows sink together. "What? Why are you looking at me like that?"

Think, Reed. You've spent every day with this guy for weeks now. You can figure out what to say to him.

"I..."

"Well?" he presses.

"...was wondering if you could show me the technique for felling one this big?" I ask, turning toward the 150-foot pine that towers over us.

I am such a chicken. I'm not at all prepared to be operating heavy machinery with a heart racketing around in my chest like this, but it was the best thing I could come up with. I hand him the chainsaw for good measure.

"Woah! Reed Morgan asking me for advice?" He grips the handle from my outstretched hand.

"Hard right, remember?" I wink at him.

"Look how far you've come, my friend."

Friend? Finally. Except now I'm a friend who's keeping a secret.

Judging by the size of these pines, this property has been here for years. A rickety fence with rotting wood stakes the perimeter. It's going to be impossible not to collapse it with these tree breaks. I crane my neck, sizing up the skyscraper before me. Maybe asking for help wasn't the worst idea; I'm not sure where to even begin.

He stalks the circumference with me. "You need to evaluate for disease, dead branches, rot, and the proximity of neighboring trees. What do you see?" he asks.

The most I determine from my clockwise rotation is the natural lean direction. Out of all the trees we could have come across, this one's by far the healthiest.

"A southern lean," I reply.

"And what are your escape routes?" he asks next.

I point in two forty-five-degree angles.

"Look at you. Learned a few things in that training of yours. Okay, stand to the side of me and I'll show you how to make the cut."

"Ya know, this would have been helpful my first day of training. That tree almost took us both out."

I move out of his way and he winks at me.

"Now what would be the fun in that? See what happens when you ask nicely?"

With his body at an angle to the stump, he performs a series of three cuts—two forming a wedge in the front and one from the back—before the whole thing buckles in a final collapse on the hay.

He flips the kill switch. "And *that* is how it's done," he says, whipping off his glasses. "Your turn."

We work for hours side by side. He lets me practice; I perfect the technique. He tells me what a good job I'm doing; I throw out a praise kink joke. It's like we've been doing this more than a day, more than a few weeks, more than half a summer together.

The afternoon melts into twilight, and I step back to take in our work.

"We're out of fuel again," I say.

"I think we should call it a night anyway." He rounds up our gear and turns for the crew's meeting spot.

"Wait!" I shout.

After the hours we've spent together, this is either the best or worst idea I've ever had.

"I met your girlfriend."

When he turns around, his eyebrows are pinched together. "When?"

"R&R."

Real specific, Reed. I tilt my head back so I can gauge his reaction with my helmet out of the way.

Not mad... *yet.*

"Hailey and I were picking up a pizza at Grenaldough's, and she was there."

Okay, looking *slightly* more bothered now.

"With another guy." I land the blow.

He looks at me like I'm crazy. Like this has to be some kind of joke.

"No..." He chuckles and shakes his head. "She was shopping with her mom that day."

"I saw her, man."

"Stop." He pinches the bridge of his nose through his visor, his helmet jostling from side to side, and then he turns on his heels.

"Wait!" I cover the same hay-smashed boot prints he makes until he finally swings around.

This is backfiring. I don't want him to go back to camp until we've talked this out. It would just upset Hailey.

"She wouldn't do that. You don't know her."

It could be the red from the setting sun casting a hue on his face, or he could be about to blow a fuse. I'm going to wager the latter.

"Okay." I throw my hands in the air. If I can't defuse this situation, this bed of grass won't be the only thing crumpled beneath his boots.

"I've known her since we were *fourteen*," he explains.

"You're right; I don't know her. I didn't want Hailey to have to be the one to tell you. Don't be mad at her, okay? She wanted to, there's just—"

"No right time to drop a bomb in someone's lap that their girlfriend is cheating on them. Thanks, rookie. I got it." He chucks his saw on the dried crop and stomps away.

CHAPTER THIRTY-FOUR

HAILEY

"You saw Madison at Grenaldough's?"

Dean storms toward me, kicking over a bale of hay. My eyes widen at his volume and then shrink beneath his intense gaze.

Reed told him.

I glance around.

"Looking for your boyfriend?"

"We wanted to tell you, but—"

"But what, Hayes? I'm not privy to that kind of information from you anymore? I know I screwed up with us, but you've known for years how I feel about Madison."

"I know," I say, tugging on his arm as he pushes past me. Digging the heels of my boots into the ground does nothing but drag me along with him.

He could scream in my face. He *should* scream in my face. But even that wouldn't devastate me quite so much as his watering eyes and sagging head.

"Then why didn't you say anything?" he whispers.

What's worse than blindsiding him? Answering *that* question.

"Because..."

Think, think, think.

"You used to tell it like it is."

Not about this I didn't. But he wants honesty?

"It's not like we've been talking. And I've always hated her, okay? She's never deserved you."

He glares at me. Ditches his gear in a pile and busies himself with his sleeping arrangement. "That wasn't so hard, now was it?"

"Dean, please," I plead, reaching for him a second time and drawing my hand back after I discover he's already flattened out his sleeping bag and is zipping himself inside.

"I need some space." He rolls to his side and I have no choice but to honor his wishes.

I'm several yards in the opposite direction before I'm berating myself. I should have told him. What was I waiting for, a moment that wouldn't hurt as much? Well, that moment doesn't exist.

"Red?"

I must look ready to claw my own eyes out. He's approaching me slowly.

"I told you I would tell him," I say to Reed.

He cradles me against him. "I'm sorry. I was trying to protect you."

I want to be mad at him, but all I feel is sad for Dean. I melt into Reed's arms the moment he touches me. "No, I know."

"It's going to be okay," he whispers into the strands of hair that tangle around my face. "Speaking from experience, he just needs some time."

I nod—or nuzzle my nose, I'm not sure which—into the comfort of his shirt. Even after endless hours of sweaty work, it still smells like him.

"It's been almost two weeks without a day off," he says. "I think we could use a little fun."

Leave it to Reed Morgan to be thinking about fun at a time like this.

I tip back so I can meet his eyes. "What exactly do you have in mind?"

His face morphs into the brightest most infectious smile as he grips my hand and takes off across the open ranch field, towing me along.

"Where are we going?" I shout. With all of the trees cut down, it looks so desolate now. For a moment, I feel sorry for the owners. But the alternative would have been losing the entire property, and even the thought of that is a shame. Especially this part of it.

"Look at how majestic they are," I gasp as our steps slow beside a herd of grazing Appaloosas. I run my hand along a spotted coat, and the horse whinnies when I lean my cheek against its muzzle.

"Wow. Bear defense, horse whisperer... I've got my very own Steve Irwin." Reed watches me with an amused grin.

I smirk over my shoulder as I round the perimeter of the two-story barn. "What can I say... my talents are endless."

"I have no doubt." He chuckles and skips to catch up to me. "What else should I be preparing myself for?"

"I guess you'll have to wait and see," I say, pressing my ear against the barn door. I jiggle the handle but the latch clangs near the top.

"Hailey Hart," he gasps, gripping his hips. "Are you *breaking* into a barn?"

I fiddle with the flappy clasp, giving it a good tug. "I don't see any breaking, do you?"

The door hinges groan as I slip inside the small opening. He follows after me and toes the door shut behind us. Light spills through the gable windows that line the second story.

A John Deere factory threw up in here. Everything from excavators to dump trucks and riding lawn mowers to a lone combine with hay bales on the side fill the barn. Not a single animal stall in sight.

"I can't believe you broke into a storage shed," he teases from behind me. "I was supposed to be showing *you* the fun time."

I spin around to face him. "So... show me then."

He surveys the space until his eyes catch on something in the back corner.

"Bull's-eye," he says, weaving us through the heavy machinery. His broad shoulders block the object he's beelining for, but knowing Reed, it's a good time whatever it is. When he finally stops in front of a pile of hay, I step to the side to take it in—white with black spots and two giant horns protruding from the head.

"A mechanical bull?" I gasp.

"Don't knock it. People have their things." He winks at me.

"And by things you mean a one-way ticket to a concussion?"

He tromps through the straw, searching the ground until he finds a black cord snaking through the golden clump. In a squat, he plugs it into the nearest outlet. "Have you ridden one before?"

With a skeptical glance, I eye the rusty hinges. "Well, no, but..."

"You might like it. Here." He holds out his fire helmet to me.

I back away. "There's no way I'm getting on that thing." It's dangerous and reckless. We're miles from the nearest doctor, and not to mention, we snuck away from camp. This bucking bronco isn't going to be quiet.

He closes in on me. "I'll catch you if you fall. That promise worked once before, right?"

"That was a *swing*, Reed. Not a tornado on a stick!"

He chuckles and runs a hand through his disheveled hair. All of this seems to be amusing the heck out of him and also not changing his mind with the way his helmet is *still* outstretched.

"Let me see that thing." I bump him out of the way to get to a metal box standing a couple feet tall near the outlet. A series of dials spreads across the top panel—buck, spin, speed. I release an exasperated sigh, pointing a finger at his chest. "Keep it at level one and whatever you do... don't laugh." I snatch the protective headwear.

"Wouldn't dream of it." He winks at me again.

I fit Reed's helmet over my braid and hike my leg over the bull's back. "This is a terrible idea," I mutter to myself. "What am I supposed to do with my hands?" There's barely a slippery hump to clutch onto.

"You're supposed to swing your arm in the air like this." Reed grips the waist of his pants with one hand and lassos the other arm above his head, prancing about.

"All right, Buffalo Bill."

"Ready, cowgirl?" He closes his hand on the speed dial.

I shake my head.

The mischief in his eyes when he says, "You might like it," has me forgetting to grip on tight, and the bull starts to sway with the twist of the dial. I lurch forward, clinging to the faux animal's back for dear life. A loud clanking rings from the machine my legs are choking as it bucks me forward and back, side to side. Faster and faster, it jerks.

"This is not level one!" I holler right before it pitches me off the side into the bed of hay.

Three seconds. That's all I lasted.

He yanks the dial to the off position and the whole barn

quiets as he dives next to me, sending a vortex of straw swirling around us. I can't stop giggling.

"So, what'd you think?" He brushes away the random pieces that landed on my face and removes my helmet. He's practically draped over top of me and the weight of his body sends a swoop low in my belly. My laughter stills.

"I liked it," I whisper, losing myself to the midnight sky of his eyes. His tongue wets his lips and my gaze traces the glistening path.

"What else do you like?" he whispers back.

Somehow the air feels more charged with the bull turned off. In every intimate exchange I've ever shared with someone, it's always felt one-sided. It's been about what makes *him* feel good. I've never considered what I might like before. No one asked.

"I don't know what I like," I admit.

He threads a hand in my hair and works his fingers in slow circles, massaging my scalp and the base of my neck with the perfect amount of pressure. A sigh escapes my lips.

"What about this?" he asks. "Do you like this?"

I swallow and nod. Then he leans in closer and my eyes flutter shut. I think he's going to kiss me. I can feel his breath ghosting across my lips, and I *want* him to kiss me. But just when I think our lips are about touch, I feel a tingle skitter down the shell of my ear. The proximity of his body, his warm breath, his sultry voice when he says, "How about this?" My back arches toward him.

"Yes." A broken gasp leaves my lips.

I want to tell him I need his mouth everywhere, but he's already brushing it down the column of my neck like he read my mind.

I groan his name.

He drags down, down, pressing a kiss to my collarbone. "Do you like my mouth here?"

I finally get the courage to say it out loud. "I like your mouth everywhere."

He touches his lips to mine, and I forget where we are. It's brief. Not nearly long enough for me before he's pulling back and making space between us. Pushing off the palms of his hands and standing. I instantly miss the weight of him pressed against me.

"I have something else I want to show you," he says, holding out his hand.

"Okay." It comes out in a breathy stutter.

I'm stumbling when he gets me standing. Tows me behind him until he's hopping up on the first rung of a wooden ladder. *Creak, creak, creak,* it squeaks with his bounce. When the shabby step doesn't give under his weight, he helps me onto the first one. Ten planks later and I'm pulling myself over a wooden platform at the top.

"Wow. It's like a little home away from home up here," I say to the twin-sized mattress on the left and the free-standing desk on the right. "And look at that view," I add, peeking out the small window to the land below. Mini figures of our crew stake out camp on the grass surrounding the couple's wraparound porch. None of them seem to be bothered by the ruckus our bucking bull just caused.

Reed's hand grips my braid, pulling it to the side. His palm closes in on my hip. "I like the view in here better," he whispers against the exposed skin of my neck, and my body instantly reacts to his presence. With one hand curling around the edge of the desk, the other fists his hair.

"What else do you like?" I spin in his arms, volleying his earlier question back at him.

"I like you," he answers, taking the weight of the world out from under my legs as he grips my thighs and fastens them around his waist. He plants me on top of the desk, nudging my knees apart and making room to slide between them. Then he kisses me, even softer than before. I can feel a tremor in the hand he has at my neck as if it's taking a Herculean effort for him not to drop it lower on my body.

"It's impossible for me to keep my distance from you," he gets out as his mouth charts a rough path to my collarbone.

There is a very real possibility that after this fire season Reed will leave and never look back. I could be opening myself up to getting hurt and left behind again like the other men have done in my life. But if I allow myself to live in that fear, I'll never know what this could be. And this feeling... I need more of it. Keeping my distance from him is driving me insane.

"I don't want you to keep your hands to yourself." I'm panting now. Forcing air into weathered lungs. I reach for the hem of his shirt and he shudders when I touch the sliver of exposed skin at his waistline. "You asked me what I like... I like being with you. I like"—I graze my hand down his chest—"touching you. And I have an IUD... We can take this as far as we want to, and you don't have to worry about that part."

"The only thing I'm worried about is not having enough time with you." He draws a blanket off the desk chair and spreads it out on top of the mattress. Then he jerks me from the edge of the desk like he was waiting for that last string of willpower to snap. Waiting for permission to carry me over to the small mattress and tug my shirt over my head before laying me on top of it. My naked skin pebbles everywhere the cool night air touches.

"It drove me insane knowing there was nothing underneath here," he groans.

I pause, blushing. "You saw that?" *How embarrassing.* I need an excuse for why I took it off, but all I come up with is the truth. The reason why most women hate wearing one in the first place. "I was hot, and it was uncomfortable, and—"

"And I like it better when it's off," he finishes for me, flattening his tongue over my nipple. I arch into his touch. *Is this what it feels like to be desired by someone?* The way he takes his time working from one side to the other, leaving nothing untouched. He barely pulls away from my skin enough to tuck his forearm in the hem of his shirt and lift it over his shoulders.

He asked me what I liked. *This.* He hovers over me shirtless. *This is what I like.*

There's very little room to spare from what we're taking up on this mattress, and all I can think about is how there couldn't be a more perfect place than this. It feels too good. Like one of those daydreams I'd have while working in the medic tent. I'm second-guessing if this moment is even real when he pulls off my pants and underwear. His hand rides up my thigh and—*nope*—this is definitely real, the way he leans over me and works small circles between my legs that sends me into another galaxy. One far, far away from this little barn we've found ourselves in. My eyes drop shut.

"Do you like it slow?" he asks, matching the speed of his hand to the pace he's exploring my lips with. It's intoxicating. I haven't even touched him yet, and I don't know how to when the sensation he's urging is tensing every muscle in the lower half of my body. It's winding tighter and tighter the more time he spends, and all I want to do is tip over the edge. It's so close.

"Faster," I say, and his lips stay slow but his hand... I cling to the sheets. My eyes fly open and stars burst across his face as I crest over that edge and fall apart in his arms. He doesn't stop until every part of me sinks into the downey fabric.

In a hoarse whisper he says, "I knew you'd look like that."

Suddenly I'm wishing I had a mirror. I'm sure my hair is a

mess and my braid in shambles. I've never wanted to look more perfect for him.

Perfect. That's the exact word he uses when he says, "You look perfect when you come."

"Spontaneous Reed is my favorite," I blurt, my cheeks hot.

I want to hide my face in my palms. That was the least sexy thing I could say. But judging by the crushing kiss he gives and the urgent hands that remove the rest of his clothing, I don't think it was the *wrong* thing to say. In fact, with the way he's looking at me right now, I don't think anyone has ever said that to him before.

"*Everything* about you is my favorite," he says, nudging my nose with the bridge of his.

For the second time tonight, words leave me. Well, except one. "Everything?" I ask. He hisses when I close my hand around him for the first time and line him up with me.

"Everything," he groans as he presses inside of me.

My daydreams will forever be filled with the sounds and expressions Reed makes as he gives himself over to me. I liquefy with every thrust of his hips and clench of his thighs wrapping my waist until the sight of him losing control burns itself into my memory.

He shudders and collapses around me. "I take it back," he says, sweeping a lock of hair out of my eyes. "If I thought the men's bathroom shower was a problem, I don't know how I'll ever concentrate again after that."

I bite my cheek. *Me neither.*

"We should probably get back," he says, but doesn't move.

I'm not ready for this to be over, his arms around me and my legs snaked around him. I know being vulnerable is not easy for him, so I do it for the both of us.

"I don't want to go back," I admit.

He rolls to the side and gathers my underwear and pants

from the floor, helping me slide them up my legs. He lets out a deep groan like he's disappointed to see them going back on, but he's not stopping when he tugs my shirt over my head too. Then he kisses me just once and says something I never expected him to say.

"We'll have time."

And we will, *tomorrow*, when we have forty-eight hours off.

I'm just not sure it'll be enough.

CHAPTER THIRTY-FIVE

REED

Seven-day extension.

Three of the worst words to wake to after spending twenty of the shortest, most earth-shattering minutes of your life alone in a barn with the girl you're falling for.

I didn't even have time to kiss her good morning. The first stop on the get-McCafferty-to-forgive-us tour involved getting up before everyone except Jack. Which wouldn't be a problem if my body didn't feel like it had taken on The Rock in a back alley.

Slamming a double-edged ax into tree stumps ought to be interesting today. But what's another hundred and sixty-eight hours of this place? Piece of cake.

My limbs drag through the tent opening.

"Regretting begging to come back here after that dispatch call the two of you missed?"

I still haven't apologized on my and Hailey's behalf for that. Not officially. But I'm about to when I catch the fade of Jack's smirk.

Oh. He's joking.

"Add twenty-seven years of this job and you've got my physical condition," he says.

The groan that accompanied my exit must have been audible.

"Just the guy I was hoping to talk to."

"If you came to talk about my daughter—"

"I'd like to work on McCafferty's team today," I interrupt him. "I don't think he'll assign me himself, so I need you to do it."

His head tilts.

"I... can do that."

"Great! Than—"

He stops me with a hand to the chest. "If you do something for me in return."

Here we go.

I pull back, giving him space. He takes up a lot more of it when he's trying to act authoritarian.

I haven't forgotten that he's told me to stay away from his daughter. Not only have I actively disobeyed that request multiple times, but I've now—as he would see it—defiled her in a barn too. What if he knows about that? It's baffling he hasn't kicked me off this crew yet. It must have been one hell of a favor he owed my father.

"That camping trip," Jack starts, "think it can stay between us?"

My eyebrows pinch. *Meaning...* Then they rise high enough to meet my hairline. *This has nothing to do with my father.*

"You want me to keep it from *Hailey?*"

I should be elated by his request. At this point, I've waited too long to tell her I've met her dad before. But why does he care so much?

"No. I want you to pretend it didn't happen," he clarifies. "I just got my daughter back, and I can't ruin that by making her believe I didn't *want* her around."

But he didn't invite her on his weekend off. I'm no psychologist, but isn't that the definition of not wanting someone around?

"What did you want then?" I ask. Because I know for a fact she would have jumped at the chance to be close to him had he let her.

The muscles in his jaw harden with his swallow. "I wanted her mother back. Can you just do it, please?"

The reality of his answer hollows out my chest cavity. It had nothing to do with Hailey.

"Okay," I agree. "I won't say anything. But respectfully, it's because I don't want her to hurt over the past any more than she already does."

He winces.

It's a truth he already knew, but nonetheless one that needed to be said.

So why does this feel like a bad idea?

A gloomy shade of gray hovers over our crew. It seeps into the long drag and pull of ax swings and smothers the banter of eighteen men. We're simply a metronome, keeping time with the sky. A hot, barren wasteland of doubt with Jack as our guide.

"I'm sorry," I say to the back of Dean's dingy shirt for the sixteenth time.

The silent treatment was not a part of my plan.

"We're supposed to be—"

"A team," Jack finishes for me. "It seems the two of you have forgotten how to work together in the last twenty-four hours. Good news!" He claps a hand on Dean's shoulder, his ax over his own. "We've got a rogue section of the fire burning a mile up that slope. Figure out your escape route and work your shit out while you're there," he says, slapping the extra radio against Dean's chest.

Tandem hiking. This ought to be good.

Thank you, I mouth to him, but his acknowledgement is a flash to Hailey. A reminder to hold up my end of the deal. A promise I'm not sure I'll be able to keep.

Twenty feet in front of me is the distance Dean retains on this climb. *Thp, thp, thp.* I sputter against the onslaught of debris showering my face. An avalanche of dirt and foliage fragments follows the careless clunk of boots and hack of his hand tool.

"Do you think you could—"

That sentence is silenced with a snarled ball of sagebrush tumbling toward my face. I catch it one-handed in midair and dump it with the others in staggered heaps along our path.

No talking. Got it.

"Let's start here," he says when we come upon a section of the fire that juts out like a finger. He tags a tree bough with a brightly colored strip of ribbon. Hot pink, to be exact. That'll be hard to miss.

"Does this mean you're talking to me now?"

Everybody knows silence is my version of torture, so I'm certain I imagined it when he says, "You were right. That first day we met..." he starts, and I slam my eyes shut, knowing exactly where he's going with this. I didn't want to be right. Not about this. "You said I shouldn't waste my time with a girlfriend who would probably cheat on me while I was here."

I lean my weight against my hand tool and blow out a breath. "I was an asshole when I said that to you. I didn't know the first thing about your relationship with Madison. It was coming from a place of insecurity."

"Well, I'm not sure anyone can be more insecure about it

than me. The first time she cheated was only three weeks into my first summer on the job."

"*First* time?" A breath gusts from my lungs.

And he stayed with her? Then again, I remind myself, *you didn't up and leave when your girl picked the other guy either.*

"I have no idea who you saw her with, but he's at least number five by now."

In the interest of being fully transparent from here on out...

"It was Ben."

An amused look transforms his face. "As in that twat from the medic tent?!"

"I don't like him either." I smirk.

We both chuckle.

"Why do you stay with her?" I ask. It's a fair question now that I know this isn't her first offense.

His posture wilts with his upside-down smile. "Why does anyone stay when their person wants to be with somebody else?"

The answer to that one is simple. *Because you love them.* But I don't think that's what he needs to hear. "Because it's hard to let go."

He nods.

"And you don't just get over your first love because they want somebody else," I add.

The hem of my shirt catches on a sharp stick, snagging a hole in the fabric. With the constant stream of sweat gathering along my hairline and pouring toward my eyes, I work my finger through the circle and tear a strip.

"You let yours go, didn't you?"

I nod, fashioning the homemade bandana around my forehead. Much better.

"Add that to the laundry list of reasons why I'm jealous of you."

"Jealous?" My jaw hinges open. "Of *me*? The screw-up who will never live up to his parents' expectations?"

"Dude, have you seen yourself?" he argues.

"You mean with all the mirrors out here? Not lately. Why? Something wrong with my beard?" I stroke the short stubble of my five-o'clock shadow.

"What beard?"

We laugh together.

"Not *what you look like*, your *life*. You've got this gorgeous girl who can't take her eyes off you and a superintendent who you've managed to win over in less time than I ever did. For the record, man... I've seen the way you doubt what you deserve, and it's not true, that lie you tell yourself. That if you show up as you, somehow it won't be enough. You already are more than enough. You're one of the best guys on this crew." He throws a small branch near my feet. "Don't tell the others I said that."

I smile. I didn't know validation could feel like this.

"Thanks, man."

He taps our saws together. "Don't mention it."

With a clean slate between us, we spend the day talking. He tells me about his cowboy ranch plans, and I tell him all about Bear Lake. I remember what it's like to have a friend again, and for the first time in a long time, I let go of the fear of being myself with someone else.

"We need to call it," he eventually says as the fire pumps thick charcoal clouds toward the moon. We made a 95 percent dent on our line today, but it's way past dinner and becoming increasingly difficult to see.

"Tac 3, descending the hill," Dean blows into the radio speaker.

"*Roger that*," Jack's voice transmits back.

I catch a glimpse of the sky as I hoist on my line pack. Are those storm clouds? It's looking ominous now with the fading light.

Crack.

I squat to the ground, shielding my head. A snap, a whoosh, and a gust of wind domino behind me. Then a thud and a scream, like they happen in the same breath, rattle the black earth beneath my feet.

I turn around, and my own scream lodges itself in my throat.

It wasn't thunder but a twenty-foot fallen pine. And the screams are coming from the body trapped beneath the trunk. Dean's scratching and clawing at the bark with his gloves. He compresses the sides with his palms and shoves against the weight of the limb like he's trying to bench press it toward the sky, but it doesn't budge.

I drop everything I'm carrying and run to him. I straddle the trunk, wrapping my arms around its girth, and bury my weight into the heels of my boots.

Come on, come on, come on.

I lift. The tree doesn't flinch. It's too long, too heavy. I need my saw.

I run back to where I dropped my equipment and spot the familiar handle. Everything feels like it's moving in slow motion, including me, as I pump my legs to get back to him. Faster and faster I run, until I'm at his side and the knife-like grooves of the saw eat at rough bark. I grind it a foot below his thigh. In seconds, my makeshift bandana is soaked and dripping on his pant leg.

The sound of his tortured wail claws at my heart.

"You're okay," I tell him as his terrified eyes sear into me.

Back and forth, back and forth, his screams propel me on. The groove I've made is at least a couple inches deep now, but it's not enough. It'll take me an hour to get through this by hand. I need an electric saw.

But it means I need to leave him.

His face is twisted in agony. I can't tell if it's sweat pouring from his forehead or if he's crying now, but his cheeks are drenched too. He's still pushing and scratching and wrestling with the log, but all he's doing is wearing himself out.

I give one last glance to the crush injury and notice a red pool gathered in the dirt. Down on my hands and knees, I try to figure out where it's coming from, but there's nothing visible.

He whimpers, and I tear another section off the bottom of my shirt, wrapping it across his forehead to protect his blinking eyes. I hate the thought of leaving him here all alone. Every minute that passes, his struggle lessens, and I have no choice.

"I have to go back for a chainsaw," I tell him.

He's fighting to keep his eyes from closing. If I leave him, will they close completely? What if he never wakes up again?

"DEAN, look at me!" I scream.

He drags his head from where it lolls against the dirt.

"I *will* get you out, okay? *I promise.* I'll be right back."

I shove my palms against the ground and jump up, ready to break away, when an explosion sounds several feet in front of me. I duck and cover once more and have to shield my eyes from the light. I gape in horror as a patch of sagebrush lights on fire.

CHAPTER THIRTY-SIX

HAILEY

"They should have been back by now," I mumble to the dark. It's a good thing the crew is spiking out in this open field. I'd have tripped a dozen times anywhere else with my pacing.

"Everything okay?"

My whole body jolts, and I clutch at my chest. When I whirl around, a warm strobe of light shines in my eyes. I shield them with the back of my arm.

"You scared me."

"Sorry," my dad's glowing outline says.

"No, it's okay, I just... how are they still working in this?" I wave a hand in front of my face just to be sure my surgically enhanced eyesight hasn't degraded. The chances of that are slim, but the alternative might be worse.

"It's the storm. It can make things darker out here. I got a comm from Dean thirty minutes ago though. They're on their way back."

With a step to the side, I can see beyond his bright light, and a hint of concern sinks his eyebrows. Like a jack in the box, fear pops to the surface and gets my feet moving.

"I'm going to go find them," I tell him, racing for my medic kit.

"I'm coming with you." He unclips the radio from the collar of his shirt, tossing it in the air. Murphy catches it. "You're in charge," he shouts. "Make sure it stays on."

"Sure thing, Supt. But what about you?"

"McCafferty has the extra radio. We'll call if we need anything."

Without the light of day to guide our movements, it's a stumbly climb up the side of the hill. Even with our headlamps turned on, I find myself feeling around for branches and gripping on for leverage. Brush rakes over the palms of my open gloves.

Keeping track of distance is proving impossible too. With nothing but the sound of sharp stones grating against dirt where the terrain has been cut away, my mind swirls with the most outlandish possibilities.

What if they're trapped?

What if they're injured?

What if we can't get to them?

We smell it before we see it, the air filling with thick smoke. We both climb faster, closing in on the cloud of billowing gray, and then... my heart plummets in my chest.

Fire. So much fire. It forms a giant arc around a channel of trees.

"I can't see them from here!" I scream as I stumble closer. Trip and fall on a jagged rock. It pierces my left hand, and my palm stings as a sticky substance oozes from my skin. It's so hot, so intense as I close in, but I can't tear my eyes away from the orange barrier that's keeping me from them.

Where's the opening?

My dad's in front of me, blocking the sea of orange I'm ready to fight. I think I hear "Hailey, stop!" but my feet, my hands, my entire body scream and pound against him, saying: *Don't you dare! Don't ever stop until they're safe from this!*

He curses when he touches the spot his radio used to be. "We need a water drop."

I dodge around his body. I can't wait for him to figure out what to do next, and I refuse to believe that it's too late. There *has* to be another way in.

I dive back down the hillside, and my dad catches my hand. I drag him with me. We're both sliding now. He's hollering something else, but the crackle and hiss are covering up whatever it is until...

Over there. I make out what he's trying to communicate from the point of his finger.

A hot pink ribbon flutters from a tree branch. There's a small patch of soil the size of a pillow beneath it.

As fast as our legs carry us, tripping over sticks and sage, we run for it.

Where the black line ends.

CHAPTER THIRTY-SEVEN

Dean cranes his neck as far as his pinned body will allow. His eyes travel to where mine gape at the tip of the hot tree. Rushing in a raging arc toward our escape route, flames eat up what's left of the unburned fuel.

This is not happening.

If I leave him here, he'll die. And if I stay, I'll die with him. With bleak options I try again, refusing to give up. I won't let this tree stand between me and my friend.

I move farther up the trunk where it's narrower and heave on the stock with no success.

Dean's head lolls to the side, his eyes starting to lose focus again, and I rush back over to him.

"No, no, no. You've got to stay awake."

I watch the flames creep closer and climb the unfallen trees to our right as I scream toward the sky: "I can do this!"

An ember shower rains down over our heads, dropping hot ash onto our helmets and beards. It singes the tips of our hair to burnt black crisps.

A strangled something falls from Dean's lips. It could have been a whisper, a scream. I can't tell when all it sounds like is the sputtering and sizzling of fire so close I can feel the hair on my arms wilting under the heat.

Minutes. That's all I have left before we're nothing but ash.

I make out the syllables of my name. He's chanting, "Morgan. Morgan. Morgan."

I can save you, I mouth back.

He shakes his head. Using strength I didn't know he still had, he grips my shirt with his fists and hauls my ear close to his face so his lips are pressed against it.

"Some things are bigger than you and me. You can't do this one alone."

No. He doesn't know what he's asking. I've never been able to rely on anyone but me. I'm not leaving him here to die, and he's not sacrificing himself just so I'll live.

"You have to go," he says again. "Please." He's begging now, and my eyes well with tears. They burn at the corners.

"I can't lose you too," I say to him.

I've lost enough friends to last a lifetime.

"You won't," he says back.

In all the pain he's in, he actually smiles at me. *Smiles.* A look that breaks my heart in half.

But what he doesn't know is that our escape route has already closed off. There's no way out for either of us.

It's an out-of-body experience, learning you're going to die. There's nothing left to tether you to the ground. Everything is finite, nothing invincible. So, you give yourself over to fate. Hope it won't hurt like hell when you finally let go for good.

That's the last shred I'm hanging on to. Hope that Dean and I are supposed to walk away from this. That we have a purpose we've yet to fulfill. It's the only thing carrying me through the motions of deploying the one piece of five-pound equipment I hoped I'd never have to use.

I start with his line pack first, shaking it to the right and stripping his fire shelter from the case at the bottom. Gripping the handle on the end, I pull off the outer box, rip off the red Velcro that secures the whole thing in a tight bundle, slip it out of the plastic bag, and fling it in the air. The bright green cocoon unfurls as I shake it to its full length.

I drag it over to his body. It's less than ideal in every way. He's supposed to be facing the ground so the radiant heat doesn't blister his airway. If that happens, the passage in his nose will swell enough that it won't matter. He'll no longer be able to breathe.

I consider the other unfortunate part of this situation: I'll never be able to cover his whole body.

But nothing about this situation is ideal. We're out of options.

I tuck his arms close and tilt him to the side so his nose is near the dirt. Then I wrap the tarp around as much of him as I can in a matter of twenty-five seconds. When I know he's somewhat secure, I deploy my own.

I have no idea if this will work but I dive into my shelter anyway, wrapping the edges around his exposed calf and ankle that stick out beneath the log next to me. I lie flat as a pancake with my face pressed to the earth, wrapping my right hand around his foot and squeezing once to let him know I'm still here.

In less than ten seconds the aluminum and silica fibers rattle with the wind, the sound like a freight train inches from my ear.

I'm having a difficult time not doubting that this piece of foil can withstand the two thousand degrees of radiant heat it was designed for.

I've done a lot of dangerous shit in my life, but never anything that left me feeling as scared as I do right now. I've only ever had to worry about myself.

The gritty smell of dirt is the last sense I register before a highlight reel takes me deep into the recesses of my mind and away from our reality. All the things I've ever wanted to say to the people I love surface.

Dad, I know we're fundamentally different, you and me. You're strong and steady, and I'm the waves in the sea carrying you to places you didn't ask to go. But all the good parts of me, the way I was able to show up for this team all summer, they came from you. You are the anchor of our family, and I never told you that enough.

Miles and Teddy, you are my greatest memories. You both drifted into my life when I needed you. Because of you two, I'll always know what it's like to grow. I'll never regret our time together. It taught me how to love. But I've held on for as long as I can, and while I know I'll always carry a part of you with me, it's time to let go.

Dean, you are the epitome of my greatest teacher. Thank you for taking a stubborn, selfish kid like me and molding him into someone who's learning to slow down enough to open up and let people in.

Jack, I'll never understand what it is that you saw in me at that campsite all those years ago, but I believed in myself because of you. It got me here, and I hope I made you proud this summer.

And Hailey—pelting drops—you changed my world—melting heat—you showed me home—letting go—I fell in love with you.

CHAPTER THIRTY-EIGHT

HAILEY

I never knew fire could burn a heart to ash without ever touching it.

In my dad's arms, the devastation works its way up my chest. It expels from my lungs in a wail, but I don't care. I'm already hurting, so I let myself imagine them—a vivid daydream that plays out in front of me.

They're walking together through the burning wall of flames. Reed turns to Dean and quips a line that has Dean's head tipping back. Then he wraps his arm around Dean's shoulder and gives him my favorite smile. The one that says life's too short without adventure. He tells Dean with a single look that this summer changed him. That he never imagined finding a friend while working on fires. That after just a few short months, he'd walk through flames for him.

Then he looks at me. As if he knows I'm waiting for him on the other side of this thing. He sees me, and it feels like coming home.

It's just a daydream, but it's *my* daydream. One where Reed is mine and there isn't a world where we aren't together in it.

One where I'd find him in a thousand lifetimes just to love him like this.

But as daydreams do, it melts away. The red-and-orange outline of their bodies collapses into nothing. Nothing but... *rain.*

As if it was released with the breath I was holding, it falls from the sky. Heavy clouds, black as the ground we stand on, shed giant drops. The thick sheet smothers the heat and soaks the ground.

I swipe at the hair clinging to my face, obstructing my view. In a field of black, I make out two green tarps three hundred yards in front of us—fire shelters hugging a fallen tree.

"Reed! Dean!" I scream in their direction.

The tarps aren't moving. Fear claws at the inside of my chest.

We sprint for them, leaping over branches and charred sagebrush.

You were too late, an anxious voice threatens.

I worked as an emergency trauma technician for three years, and I'm afraid to face what lies beneath this aluminum. I know I'll never be able to unsee it for as long as I live.

My dad peels off to the left side of the tree, and I grip the edge of the fire shelter on the right. He's quicker than me, whipping back the material like it's routine. Dean's lying there in a contorted fetal position.

I tear at the material, pulling it away from Reed's body. He's shaking all over, his nose pressed to the dirt. He startles when I sweep my hand across the side of his face. The rain drenches his hair as he pushes up to his knees.

"Hailey?" he croaks, and I forget all of my medical training. Without assessing potential injuries, I climb onto his lap.

"You're okay." I gather up the hair that's grown longer at the nape of his neck and use it to pull him close.

Reed reaches up to tangle his fingers with mine. "You're hurt," he says, gripping my biceps, sliding my arms down his chest and inspecting my palms.

I'd forgotten about the cut. The blood is already clotted.

"I'm fine," I insist. Nothing a piece of gauze can't handle.

While he cups my hands to his chest, his head slants back. A happy chuckle makes its way out of his parted lips. "It's... *raining*." He holds out his hand, letting the drops collect in his palm. "It's *actually* raining!"

It lasts no more than five seconds before his eyes flare, and he whips his head to the side. "Dean."

I climb off his lap and we both stumble over to where he lies.

My dad is pawing at Dean's clothing and the sprawling area around his body.

"Where is it?" He talks to himself while digging through ash.

"It's there." Reed points at the dilapidated heap of shattered parts that barely resembles anything electronic.

But there's only one thing I care about, and it has nothing to do with a radio. Dean is unconscious.

"How long has he been like this?" I ask as I kneel beside him.

Reed's eyes dart around, as if searching for something in nature that could tell time. "He was still awake when I covered him."

I drop my ear to his nose and mouth, then tilt his head back and lift his chin with my fingertips. His jaw slackens with the movement, and I peer inside the opening.

Nothing is obstructing his airway.

"He's still breathing but I need one of you to monitor his chest while I take his pulse and look at his leg, okay?"

"I'll do it," my dad says, dropping to his knees and cradling Dean's head between them.

Reed's pacing. "What can I do?"

"My medic kit." I press my pointer and middle fingers against the side of Dean's neck and count.

23... 24... 25...

It's too slow.

30... 31... 32...

My stomach flips. A clenching seizes the hollow center as the minute mark draws to a close.

38... 39... 40.

The contents of my stomach pitch up my windpipe and onto the ground next to me.

You were too late, it says again.

But it doesn't matter. The numbers speak for themselves. Dean's kidneys are failing.

CHAPTER THIRTY-NINE

REED

In a sea of black, I search for red. The rounded handle pokes out beneath the fire shelter and I discard it to get to the medic kit.

"Do you have a knife in your pack? I need to cut off this section of his pants," Hailey says, wiping her lips with the back of her sleeve.

She just threw up, and now she's looking at me, eyes laced with desperation like she's depending on me for this *one* thing. And my hazy thoughts slip back to that day at the airport when I lost my grandfather's pocketknife. It didn't mean much to me two months ago. But now? It would mean *everything* to have it in this moment for Hailey and Dean.

It's Jack who thrusts a wooden handle into her waiting palm.

I drop into a crouch. I already know this can't be good with the way Dean's previously loose pants strain around his leg. Hailey uses the tip of Jack's blade to poke a hole two fingers wide in Dean's cargos right below his hip. Without moving the limb, she shreds an opening, exposing skin.

I have *no* idea what I'm looking for, but the area beneath his crush injury is more of a swamp now. A puddle of red-and-black gunk that has doubled in size. With his pant leg ripped away, I can see a jagged branch impaling his thigh just above his knee cap.

Hailey presses her fingertips against his pale skin. As if it's been replaced with rawhide pulled taut, the tissue doesn't dip with her pressure. I have next to no medical training, but even I understand skin shouldn't look like that.

"There's saline solution and bandages in the side pocket," Hailey says, pointing to the first aid kit I'm still clutching.

All I see is the spot where Dean's torn flesh hugs the broken branch. "We need a chainsaw and a helicopter. You can't fix this problem with a Band-Aid," I argue to the only one of us with a medical license.

Let them in, let them help. I hear Dean's voice inside of my head.

But they *are* helping. It's me who feels helpless.

"Go," she says to me. "We've got this handled."

The only thing that has me walking away from her is knowing that this was the decision I should have made all along.

I don't bother with my line pack. There's no fire shelter in it anymore, and it'll just weigh me down. Leaping over charred branches to the top of the hill and sliding the slippery slope to the other side, I find the crew halfway down.

The sight of all fifteen of them hauling our gear in a single file line nearly breaks me.

"Morgan, what happened? You guys have been gone for hours."

Between the heavy rainfall and the collective headlamps, I blindly guess it's Ramirez leading the pack.

"I need a chainsaw and a helicopter!"

Murphy lifts the radio to his lips and presses the call button. "Iron Summit to Copter 105, we've got a down firefighter in need of medical care. Our location is five miles northeast of Appaloosa Ranch."

"*This is Copter 105. We need to get rid of the water on board. Estimated thirty minutes.*"

"We don't have that kind of time!" I shout at Murphy.

"They'll get here as fast as they can," Murphy reminds me.

Between the fallen tree, the sudden fire, the gush of rain, and the lack of a helicopter, it all feels so out of my control. Doesn't anyone get how long he's already been waiting? But I *can* control one thing. I'm getting this tree off my friend.

Ramirez slips a sawyer pack off his back without question and gives it to me. My knees nearly buckle when the weight transfers from his arms to my upper body. "We'll be right behind you," Ramirez says, and I nod, not even sure he can see it.

It takes longer to terrain the slope uphill than it did going down it. But I keep my focus on the path ahead and the cadence of the footfalls matching my own behind me. I'm not alone in this, I remind myself.

There is a collective gasp when we reach the black. Even I had a hard time telling until now how far the burnt ground stretched.

"I could use some more light," I call out, and a couple of guys circle around the trunk that's trapping Dean's leg. I slide on protective eyewear and start up the saw. The second the metal grinds an inch into the wood, somebody screams.

CHAPTER FORTY

HAILEY

Dean's eyes fly open, and his shrill wail pierces the air.

"It's okay, it's okay." I hover over him, pinning his upper body down with the weight of my hands.

Is his skin clammy? I can't tell with this rain. But the coloring of that leg... One look and I knew this wasn't going to be good. We're running out of time.

"Get it off!" His face contorts in agony as Reed rakes the blade back and forth, bark chips flying in all directions.

"Dean, look at me." I stroke my fingers down his cheeks. I'd give anything to have superhuman strength, to hurl this log off of him and take away his pain. But even that wouldn't give him the instant relief he's looking for.

"We're going to get you out of here, okay?" I tell him. "You just need to hang on a little longer."

He thrashes his head, moaning, "I can't. It hurts!"

Reed stops the saw.

Dean claws at my skin like he'll never know a moment that isn't bound by pain, and it's tearing me up inside seeing him like this. I grip his cheek to get him to face me again.

"I know it hurts." My voice quivers. I've been calm up until this point, puking incident aside. Acted the way a professional EMT would, not the scared girl who couldn't forgive her best friend and wasted what could be her last summer with him just to watch him die right before her eyes. But I'm desperate to help him. How do I make him forget?

I look to the one person who has been that for me, the comfort and calm in my turbulent summer. Reed's patiently waiting for the command to continue. He offers me a subtle gesture that says *You already know what to do.* I know because he's shown me how. And then, as ridiculous as I sound, I start to sing.

"Electric boobs, below her shoes." Dean doesn't freeze like I did on that plane. But his shaking relaxes as he focuses on my face.

"You know I read it in a wagon seat, oh, oh," I continue.

It's my dad's voice who belts out the next line of "Bennie and the Jets." It would seem I got more from him than I originally thought—pitchy lungs to be specific.

"Isn't it *boots*?" Daniels asks.

Reed laughs, and Dean is... *smiling at him.* It's a soft, weak smile, but it's there.

One by one, new voices join in until the whole crew is singing Elton John in the backcountry of the Payette National Forest like it's an anthem to the trees.

When Dean's distracted enough, I nod for Reed to continue, and we keep singing through his cries. The chainsaw makes a clean break, and then Reed does the same thing on the section above Dean's hip.

"All done, buddy," Reed says to him.

Dean rakes his heavy eyelids open so that he's looking up at Reed. "Whoever... taught you... how to use that... did a damn... good... job," he gets out.

Reed chuckles, a sad laugh that sounds trapped inside his throat.

"And whoever... taught you... to sing like that... did too," Dean says, grazing my arm.

I shake my head furiously as I cling to his hand. "I'm sorry I didn't tell you about her. I'm so sorry I wouldn't let you in."

His arm quivers as it hovers no more than a couple inches off the ground, and he whimpers. He's trying to reach for me, and I'd let him if I thought he could. I'd hug him if I could. Instead, I press his arm back down and tell him not to exert himself.

He's getting blurrier by the minute as my tears mix with rain, my sleeve a useless towel with how sopping it is. I brush back the wet strands of hair matted to his forehead as he gets out a weak "You let... him in... and... that was all... that mattered... to me."

At first I think he's talking about Reed, but then his gaze finds my dad before eventually making its way to the sky, staring at a fixed point, the fight slipping from his eyes. Defeat takes over the weight of his limbs and he stops struggling, lying limply against the ground.

"Dean, stay with me!" I clamp my fingers to his carotid artery. His pulse is more of a hum now. This can't be the end for us; there has to be more. I *need* more time.

"Hayes, step back. We'll get him transferred," my dad says, looping his hand beneath Dean's armpit. He and Murphy work at a quick pace to support both sides while Reed stabilizes the log. They gently guide Dean's body on top of heavy orange plastic, snapping together buckles. Pulling tight on the straps, the sked stretcher forms a U-shape with a flat end beneath his boots.

"Let's go," my dad says, dragging it over the ground behind him just as the chop of copter blades splits through the sky.

CHAPTER FORTY-ONE

REED

"We don't have to start a fire if you don't want to," she says as she lays out a blanket in front of the hearth.

It's amazing how much Hailey has learned to read me. She's right. I don't want it.

I slide two logs onto the metal grate and strike a match, touching it to the center of the pile of wood. It ignites in a ripple as it spreads across the timber.

I can barely look at it.

"I want you to be warm," I tell her as I toss the match into the kitchen sink and carry over the picnic-style dinner I made.

"I'm not really hungry," she says, staring into the hearth.

I don't blame her. Eating is the last thing I can think about with Dean still in the hospital.

I shift the wooden charcuterie board to the edge of the checkered quilt.

"Have you heard from your dad?"

She taps her phone screen and shakes her head. "Not since Dean's parents got there an hour ago. The surgery will take a while."

When I sit, I pull a pillow with me and she lies down,

resting her head in my lap. Her body is no longer blocking the fire, and I hate that it's the brightest thing in the room.

"What are you thinking about?" she asks.

Do I tell her the truth? That all I've thought about since the moment they hauled us out of those woods is how much I want to leave this place? That everywhere I look I'm reminded of my shortcomings?

I study a frayed edge of wool on the rug beneath the coffee table. With Dean out for who knows how long, they ended our crew's fire season a couple weeks early. I have no idea what I'm going to do with my life now, but I can't just sit here waiting.

"Have you ever been to Silverwood?" I ask her, running my fingers through her wet hair. A waft of vanilla fills my lungs, and I take a deep breath of it.

Her eyebrows bend as she looks up. "No, why?"

I lean back on my palms. "We should go."

"What?" Hailey pushes off my lap to an upright position.

I can't tell if she's *good* shocked or *bad* shocked by my suggestion, so I continue.

"Yeah, we could leave in the morning. Be there by noon tomorrow and come back tomorrow night."

"Reed, you can't be serious!"

Bad shocked I see, but I still smirk at her. "I thought you liked my spontaneity." The last time she said that we were tangled up in a barn. A moment that seems infinitely lighter than this one.

"I do," she says, gripping my hands. "I really do, but I also like what an incredible friend you are. What about Dean? We can't just leave. And my dad... he won't say it, but he's a mess. He needs me."

People never tell me the truth. Instead, they skirt around all of the reasons why they don't want to go along with my plan instead of just coming out and saying what they're really thinking. That if I don't take life more seriously I'll wind up alone.

But I tried that. I made up this vision in my head over the summer. It started out as more of a mirage of what Hailey and I could be, but then it morphed into this real idea that went beyond a few months. I saw us traveling the world together, seeing a sunrise in every city. I saw a future. But what I failed to consider was the fact that she'd left McCall once already. And for her, this summer was about making amends. It was about never leaving again.

"Yeah, no, you're right. He does need you," I say, trying my best to hang on to her fingertips when the idea of us feels like quicksand.

A look of fear drifts across her face, and she pulls the strings of my hoodie.

"And I need *you*," she says.

Isn't that what I wanted? Someone to finally choose me? But the terrifying, selfish truth is that I wanted her to choose *only* me. I'll forever have to share Hailey Hart with her father, her best friend, and anyone else who comes into her life. She keeps the people she loves close; she doesn't run from them like I do.

"We never talked about it," she says, her eyes shifting back to the fire.

"Talked about what?" I ask.

"What you'd do at the end of the season."

Not what *we* would do, but *you*. That "you" stands out like a broken bone.

"Yeah, I guess we didn't," I say.

She holds my gaze and sweeps her thumb across my bottom lip. "Let's just wait. See what tomorrow brings."

"Okay," I say. Because I'm afraid if we say anything else to each other, it will end in goodbye, and out of everything that might come next, what I want is *her*.

I reach over and draw her onto my lap. She smells like a candle, and I'm lost the moment I'm caught in her intoxicating flame.

My eyes snag on the single freckle that dots her cheekbone beneath her right eye. I brush my thumb across it, in awe of how beautiful this woman is, and wonder why she chose me. I study every crease, every hint of pink that spreads across her cheeks and lips. I want to memorize how it feels to have her in my arms, terrified this'll be the very last time.

My palms drift to her backside and inch beneath her shirt. Her skin shudders under my fingertips as they lift higher and higher. I'm met with nothing but bare skin.

"Still driving me crazy, I see."

A fractured giggle escapes her lips. "You said you liked it when it was off."

I let my fingers explore. "*Oh, I do.*"

She draws closer by the underside of my biceps, and we stay there for a long time, lost in each other's eyes.

I don't know how to face what comes next, mine silently tell her.

I don't either, hers war back.

When our staring contest threatens to tip into tears, I want to run. I can't cry right now. The only ability I have left in me is to lay her down on this quilt. I can't think about the idea of Dean in the hospital or the thought of us losing him. But I can *feel.* I'd start with a kiss if I wasn't so lost in my head right now. I sigh and touch our foreheads together.

"You're the only place in the world I want to be," she says, and it stops me in my tracks. I marvel at how she always says exactly what I need to hear. If she can do that for me, I can be vulnerable too.

I kiss the corner of her lips where she smirks when she thinks I'm funny and the spot above her nose where her brow furrows when she's concentrating. I kiss the apples of her cheeks where, even now, she lets me see just how much I make her skin flush. I kiss her like it's the last thing I'll do on this Earth because kissing Hailey Hart is my favorite thing.

I've never asked her about her experience with other men. I don't need to. The confused stare she gave me when she said she didn't know what she liked was enough of an indication that no matter how many guys have had the privilege of being in her life like this, they took it for granted. They'll never know the girl who melts at the brush of lips against her neck. And I'm glad they won't. She saved that for me.

We take things slow, savoring the moment. The very definition of making love, and it terrifies me—the words hanging on the tip of my tongue. I don't know how to keep looking in her eyes without them spilling out of me, so I flip her onto her hands and knees. She eases back against me, pressing her palms into the floor. I grip her hips and together we let the rush of tension take over. The spark between us urges our pace until we're nothing but melting heat. A fire that burns brighter than all the rest. The only one I don't ever want to put out.

When we collapse, spent on the blanket, I tuck her up against my chest so we're spooning. We lie there for a long time, not saying anything at all. It's not until she's finally dreaming in my arms that I let go. I let her in. Nothing left to stop me.

"I'm in love with you, Red."

CHAPTER FORTY-TWO

REED

Sleep. That's what I should be doing instead of barreling down Highway 95 at three in morning. But after I called Jack, I couldn't stay.

Rhabdomyolysis, he called it: a form of kidney failure caused by the breakdown of muscle tissue.

I wanted it to be me. I wanted to give Hailey her best friend and Jack his squad leader back. Change every decision I made over the last twenty-four hours.

Instead, I did what I do best: put my phone on silent and left town.

I roll down the window and let the wind drive everything away. Well, *almost* everything.

A heavy metal concert is ravaging my stomach, forcing me to pull off at a random diner to quiet it with a hamburger, fries, and a raspberry milkshake.

A waitress with a shock of red hair slides a glass across the gingham tablecloth. I take a long pull of the watered-down fruit through a plastic straw.

"How is it?" she asks with a southern drawl.

"It's not LaBeau's."

It's rude but honest, my answer. I hoped that it might taste like home. Give me some indication of where to go next.

"Do you think I could have a pickle to go with it?" I ask.

"Honey, if you think a pickle is gon' save that sorry excuse for a drink, you're sorely mistaken." She chuckles.

"You could have warned me, ya know." I dunk the straw a few more times before taking another sip. *Nope*. Still tastes like a diluted Crystal Light packet.

"Now why would I have done that when I needed somethin' to keep this job interestin'."

"What's wrong with your job? It seems"—I scan all the empty chairs—"delightful."

"I was gon' be a sky divin' instructor at your age. Biggest mistake I ever made was walkin' away from that."

Sounds like we have a lot in common.

"Why did you do it then?" I ask.

"The only reason you ever change your plans... For someone you love."

Someone you love. The words are like pinpricks wrapped in guilt.

"It's worth it though," she adds. "Every bit of the stayin'." Then she rests a picture next to my plate. She's at a farmers' market with a wicker basket full of fresh fruit and flowers, holding the hand of a small child.

"Lucy's my reason for everythin'."

A smile tugs at the corner of my mouth. "She looks like you."

"I knew I liked you," she says, bumping into me. "Nobody says that." She swipes her picture from the table and tucks it back in her apron pocket.

"It's the smile," I add "It's clear you're her reason too."

She looks a little stunned by my answer. "Well," she says, dabbing at her eyes, "can I get you anything else?"

"No. Thank you," I say, raising my sub-par shake to her.

"Don't mention it. Like I said, keeps life interestin'." She winks at me and disappears through the wooden bi-fold doors into the kitchen.

I shuffle the food around my plate. Is that why I always chase the next best thing? Because it keeps life interesting? *No.* After this summer, I don't think it's the leaving that does that. It's not a place that I'm seeking anymore but a feeling. I think I could be anywhere in the world and feel it if I wasn't so scared of rejection.

I push a hand through my already rumpled hair. Or maybe it's my head that's scrambled from that all-nighter. I really need sleep.

I down the hamburger and fries and leave a twenty-dollar tip behind. Through drooping eyelids, I spot a little blue sign with a bed on it. It's not even ten in the morning but I've already lived the longest day of my life.

I park the truck at the Best Western and drag my duffel bag through the river rock entrance and into the low-lit lobby.

"How can I help you?" An attendant in a matching burgundy suit vest and business skirt ditches a book with a scantily clad couple on the cover.

"I'd like a room please."

"How many guests will be staying with you?" She scans the lobby.

"Just me."

A nervous laugh bubbles up from her chest. The sharp points of her black nails clack against the keyboard. "One guest, one bed. I'll need a form of ID and a credit card to put on file, please."

I fish my wallet from my pocket and pass the cards to her.

"Do you want to participate in our singles happy hour we're having tonight? It's free to all guests! You just have to RSVP."

What part of these dark circles say single and ready to mingle?

"No thank you," I say.

If this lady could hurry up and fork over my key I might actually make it to my room before passing out.

"Room 313. It's on the third floor," she clarifies.

"Thank you." I shuffle to the elevator.

With the press of a button the doors slide part way open and pause. They hang there for about ten seconds before closing.

Perfect.

I give it a good five seconds before trying again. Same thing.

I have two choices here: stuff myself through the slot or hike up the stairs. I'd rather not compete in an Olympic sport in the condition I'm in. Turn and slide, it is.

With a shove, my bag clears the gap and swings toward the buttons highlighting floors one, two, and three.

This is beginning to feel like a series of comedy scenes all smashed together.

Joey Tribbiani and Buddy the Elf would be so proud.

When the doors clamp shut, I slump against the back wall. Even the key card acts a little faulty the first two tries when I find room 313.

As they say, third time's the charm.

I'm greeted by a lovely shade of chocolate brown. Every-thing but the bedding on the king-sized mattress is that color. It's the last thing I remember before falling into a dreamless sleep.

When I wake next, a woodpecker pounds at the base of my skull. What time is it?

"No housekeeping, thank you," I yell.

A knock sounds again, and I groan. *This hotel.*

I peel myself off the comforter, trudge across the sea of dingy carpet, and yank on the door handle.

"I said, no—" The words die on my tongue as I stare into my father's eyes.

CHAPTER FORTY-THREE

HAILEY

A soft, golden light filters through the trees and spills over my slumped shoulders. Uncut grass grown wild and unruly hides the small stone I came to visit. I comb it back and press it down with my palms. *Josephine Hailey Hart, August 1977 – December 2002, beloved wife and mother.*

"I hope I'm not interrupting." A throat clears as my dad crouches beside me.

I wipe my eyes with the back of my hand before returning his reluctant smile.

"Do you come here often?" I ask him.

Whenever he wasn't working, I used to picture him visiting her. The thought made me sad, but I'm not surprised when he nods.

"She deserves flowers. I should bring them."

A tear splashes on the slate slab as I trace my fingertips over the floral petals engraved in a border around the edge. "You already did."

He squeezes my shoulder.

"Will it always feel like this?" I whisper, the weight of an elephant sitting on my chest. I want to retreat inside myself.

Hide in the dark cave at the back of my mind and take solace there.

The edges of his mouth wilt. It hurts me to see him this sad. How deeply he must miss her. Will that be my life now that I've lost Dean?

Honesty seeps through his answer. "Some days are worse; others are better."

I swallow, taking it in. "On the better days, what would you say to her?"

Do people do that? Do they talk to their loved ones after they're gone?

He releases a shaky breath. The strained muscles in his face slacken as if he sees her in the sky.

"Hi, Jo," he whispers. "It's me."

It's a little thing. Not monumental in the grand scheme of information I don't know about him. But to find out he calls her by a nickname feels like the most important thing to note. Like her first name wasn't intimate enough. Makes me think of Reed calling me Red.

"Our daughter came back home for the summer. You should see her." He smiles wistfully. "She has your eyes. She's kind and relentless." He chuckles softly to himself. "Both things she got from you. But she's also sensitive and strong, which, I'd like to think, she got from me. I don't want to let her down this time."

Tears slip from my eyes as he turns to face me.

"She'd be proud of you, you know," he says. "And not just because you share the same profession."

I wrap my arms around his neck and squeeze tightly. Dean and Reed are gone, but I'm grateful I still have him.

"I'm proud of *both* of you," a voice says from behind us.

I pull back from his arms.

"Aunt Karen!" I jump up.

"You didn't think you'd do this day without me, did you?" She squeezes around my neck.

"Hi, little sister." My dad approaches her slowly.

"You look good, big brother. Glad to see you're finally letting something penetrate your bomb shelter of an exterior. I mean, I always hoped it would be *me* who made you cry, but beggars can't be choosers." She winks at him as he rolls his eyes. Then she leans in and hugs him first.

Her face grows serious. "I'm sorry about Dean," she says to both of us.

"Thank you," we say in unison.

"It's a good thing I swing for the other team, because I was stuck for thirty minutes helping a room full of what can only be described as a firefighter calendar in that chapel, and I let my head spin up some wild ideas."

"Karen!" Dad barks. "That's my crew you're talking about."

"I know!" she squeals. "Which one of them are you planning on marrying off to your daughter?"

I scold her this time. "Karen!"

"The one who's not here yet," my dad fills in.

Aunt Karen's eyes bounce between us before she reads me in the way she's always been good at and changes the subject.

"Well, we better get back in there before one of them burns the place down. They know how to put out fires, but who the hell put them in charge of lighting candles with matches?"

"Dad? What are you doing here?"

Everything about him is all wrong, from his less-than-composed tear-soaked cheeks to his missing loafers.

"And what are you wearing?" I blurt out into the hallway.

He drops his chin to his pickle-colored tracksuit.

"The department store saleswoman said matching sets are really popular right now," he blubbers.

"From *where*? JCPenney? I don't think she meant—" I wave my hand in the air. "Never mind."

"As a matter of fact..."

My eyes widen. *My Rolex-wearing father was shopping at one of the last department stores left standing?*

"Who are you and what have you done with Emmett Morgan?"

He hiccups through his laugh. "Well, are you gonna invite this old track star in or not?"

I hold the door ajar and step out of the way. "Be my guest."

He strolls past the bathroom and mirrored closet and stops at the foot of the bed. "It's a single king," he comments.

Well, yeah. I wasn't expecting company, I think to myself. "How did you find me?" I ask instead.

He dries his eyes with his polyester sleeve and bulldozes over my question. "There's this Mexican restaurant down the street. You want to grab some food?"

I squint at him. Wait, *dinner?* That explains the raging headache. I must have only been asleep for a few hours. It's still the same day I left them, the same day we lost Dean...

"You haven't eaten yet, have you?" he asks.

I shake my head.

"Well, let's get out of this crappy hotel for some chips and salsa then." He strides out the door to the stairwell. Must know about the elevator situation.

We bat at Mardi Gras beads and streamers, elbowing our way through Singles Night to get to the lobby.

"How about I drive? You look like you could use the rest." He motions to the left side of the parking lot.

I gape at the familiar metallic-blue Ford F-150, calculating the distance in my head. "You *drove* here?" He had to have left at four in morning. Right about the time I got off the phone with Jack. "You never drive long distances," I whisper, feeling the weight behind that gesture.

"I needed to see my son," he says. "Am I allowed to ask if you're doing okay?"

It's my turn to blow past his question.

"Where's your Land Rover?" I pull on the passenger doorhandle.

He smirks as he pulls us onto the road. "In the shop. Ronny wrecked it. Right before he dropped out of school a month in and left on another European excursion with some gal he met on the internet."

A snicker tugs at the corner of my mouth. "Interesting," I say as he traverses the single city block to the Fiesta

Del Taco—a restaurant we could have walked to just as fast.

A draft of air blows out the front door of this place. It's movie theater cold inside. Something I missed while... *nope*. If I'm not going there with my dad, I'm certainly not going there inside my own head.

In a deserted corner booth, he orders two enchiladas with refried beans, and I get the burrito. The moment our waiter disappears, I ask him again: "What are you doing here?"

Tears leak from the corners of his eyes.

"I came to take my son to Silverwood."

"Did you feel that?" Dad gusts out an elated breath, and I have to keep pinching my arm to make sure that I'm awake. That I've not somehow slipped into a warped version of reality where my father's alter ego *enjoyed* an amusement park.

"I felt it," I say as the chest restraint and lap belt lift on our final roller-coaster of the day.

He steps onto the platform that leads riders in a single-file line through an exit gate. Ironically enough, it's not until we approach the parking lot that I feel *my* pulse pick up speed.

Don't be afraid. Be vulnerable.

"Thanks for coming," I say.

I know most people wouldn't understand that I needed to disappear at an amusement park at a time like this, but my dad of all people did.

He waits until we've both hopped in the front seat of the truck to respond. With his hands at ten and two and his eyes fixed on the windshield, he says, "You shouldn't have to thank your dad for being there for you."

I let his words sink in until they've settled into the pit of my stomach.

He clears his throat. "When you called a few weeks ago and asked me if I remembered that weekend we went camping... I never forgot it. Only because it wasn't my finest moment as a parent. I'm sorry for all the times I haven't been there for you in the ways you needed me to be."

"I just wanted you to see me," I admit. "And today you did that."

He sweeps a hand through his hair and blows out a shaky breath. "We've always been so different, you and me. I don't have to tell you that. Sometimes it scared the shit out of me just how little we could relate to each other. I never felt like I could give you the things you really needed until Jack called me about this job."

"You got it for me, didn't you?"

He jerks his gaze to me. "What? The *job*?"

"Yeah. I didn't want to get the spot because you pulled your strings or because you felt like I needed to amount to something."

"Reed... I promise you that's not what happened."

"Why did he say he owed you then?" I ask.

"Your mom and I represented him in a negligence lawsuit against the hospital. His compensation helped him pay for the delivery expenses of his daughter and the funeral for his wife. I'm sure that's all he meant. As far as your job, he called me after hearing from your recruiter. Jack always told me you'd be good at fire, but you got this job all on your own."

That should make me feel better than it does.

"But then I screwed it up," I add.

I'm waiting for the *I told you so* to follow that statement. The pretentious man married to the pursuit of hard work would harass me for fleeing the first chance I got. But that guy wouldn't be relaxed against his headrest. He also wouldn't be caught dead in those joggers and baseball cap either.

"Do you know why I flew with you to drop you off?" he asks.

"Because you didn't think I'd actually go."

He shakes his head. "I knew you would. I was afraid you wouldn't come back. Despite how much grief you give me on a daily basis, I knew I'd miss your zest for life."

I sigh. "You don't want to know my outlook on it anymore." The sadness I kept buried crawls its way back to the surface of my skin. I'd scratch it away if I thought it would get rid of it.

He reaches across the seat and places his hand on my forearm.

"I can't go back there," I whisper.

Just the thought of facing them all again... Looking Hailey in the eye after I left her like that.

"If you want to spend another week here, I'll ride every roller-coaster a hundred times in the front seat. If it's going back home for a while, your room is still waiting for you. But if deep down what you need is the family you made here, you better fight like hell against those feelings of inadequacy, because they miss you. You deserve to feel chosen not just by others but by yourself."

I feel them before he sees them. Hot tears prick my vision. For the first time in a long time, I let myself cry in front of him.

We share the crappy bed for another night before parting ways the next morning.

When he calls five minutes after I pull away from the hotel, I answer with, "Forget something?"

"Yeah. I forgot to ask you about your summer," he says.

And I spend the five-hour drive talking while my dad listens. He chuckles when I describe blisters and poison oak. He gasps over ants and spot fires. He cries when I tell him what happened to Dean and about my love for Hailey.

It feels like a new beginning.

CHAPTER FORTY-FIVE

HAILEY

Sometimes it takes figuratively weathering a size-twelve boot with worn treads and the laces too tight to understand someone. Navigating this loss, walking in my dad's shoes, I finally fathom it. Grief is claustrophobic and agonizing.

A soldier's coffin is draped in a flag while the elderly are decorated with flowers. Dean's is covered in pictures. I pick one up of him as a toddler. Chocolate smears his right cheek and mischief dances in his eyes. I set it back down next to the one of him with a cherry-red Strider bike, his helmet on too loose so it exposes his forehead. There are at least two dozen more painting his childhood memories... First steps, first tooth, first grade, first dance. Madison hangs on his arm for that one, and if it wasn't completely inappropriate for a church, I'd shred it until there were no remnants left of that two-timing...

"Are you thinking what I'm thinking?" Murphy's burly voice booms.

"If God himself wouldn't smite me for thinking it, then yes. That's what I'm thinking," I say.

"I think God has a sense of humor if you ask me. He was

perfectly fine letting farmer Dan over there believe he's going to get a woman looking the way that he does," Ramirez says.

Daniels threads his thumbs through the straps of his overalls and winks back at him. "You're lucky I wore a shirt under this."

"You boys are terrible," I say.

"You love us." Jackson carries a set of folding chairs down the aisle, passing them off to Marshal and Ramirez to build another row beyond the front pew. We're expecting a large turnout.

On his second trip, he hauls an easel up the altar steps and sets it up beside Dean's mahogany casket. I'm grateful his parents decided to keep it closed. I'd rather remember my friend's beautiful spirit than a waxy replica of his body.

Jackson places a framed portrait of the Iron Summit crew in the mount, and my eyes immediately find Reed. An ache spreads from my chest down my limbs until my whole body feels it.

"You miss him, don't you?" Marshall places a comforting hand on my arm. He's always been the sensitive one.

I clear my throat. "Of course I do. Dean was my best friend." A tear slips from my eye and I quickly wipe it with my sleeve.

"I meant Morgan," Marshall clarifies. "No offense, McCafferty." He taps the lid of Dean's casket.

"Well, Reed Morgan is a hard guy not to miss," I admit.

Murphy unfolds and straightens the last of the chairs. "Have you heard from him?"

I shake my head. I saw the look in his eyes when we got off that helicopter. It's the same look he gave me when I told him I couldn't leave town with him. He's not coming back.

"Don't count him out yet," my dad whispers, brushing past me and setting up a microphone on the opposite side of the easel.

"Does anyone know what's happening at this thing anyway? I've only ever been to old people's funerals," Daniels says.

"Expect a lot of *He died before his time* and *God takes the good ones too young*."

"Wow, Ramirez. I didn't know you were so religious," Daniels teases.

"My grandmother is Catholic."

"And I didn't know Catholics were so LGBTQ+ positive," Murphy mutters.

Ramirez rolls his eyes. "Well, you're not supposed to use birth control or get divorced either and she had one kid and three husbands. All religious people live their own version of the church they belong to."

"Let's maybe not do this in a place of worship," I say to them.

"Oh, I'm sorry, Hayes," Ramirez says. They've all taken to calling me that ever since they heard my dad do it. "Gentlemen" —he snaps his fingers—"let's give the lady some space so she can get her prayer on."

"It starts at five and there's an open mic," I remind them. "I better see all of you in one of those front-row seats and on your best behavior."

I can imagine it now. This is their first break since the season ended and most of them have already spent forty-eight hours at the local tavern. The last thing Dean's family needs is for the crew to show up to this thing plastered.

"Yes, Mother." Daniels salutes me.

They slowly filter out the back chapel door until I'm left in the room alone.

A picture of Dean and me eating pizza on my bed catches my eye. I run my fingers over the edges, wishing I could will that moment into existence one more time. It hurts not having him here.

I set it back down and swipe at the fresh stream of tears drifting down my cheeks. It's weird talking to a box, but it might be my only moment left alone with him. So, I sit down a little way away from his casket and close my eyes. If Dad can talk to Mom, I can do this too. I pretend Dean's standing in front me, listening to the goodbye I should have given him when I left McCall.

"Do you remember what you said to me the first time we met? *Is this seat taken?* It sat empty for years before you moved to town, and it never really bothered me all that much because I was used to the seats around me being empty.

"There was always one at my kitchen table and the rocking chair on our front porch. Our couch cushions didn't have any imprints until you came along and filled them. You took up space in my world, and it wasn't until that day on the bus that I started to notice when a chair next to me remained empty."

I peep around to the endless rows of vacant folding chairs stretching out on either side of me.

"Later this afternoon, these chairs will fill with people who love you. People whose lives you mattered in and ones who will feel the void you left behind. People like me. But I'm scared that without you, like the last four years of my life, the seat next to me will always feel empty."

I fall forward on my elbows and cover my face with my hands. The weight of all he left behind pulls at the roots that once made me feel deeply grounded. I know I can't fall apart at this funeral. I have people I need to be strong for, so I let myself do it now. I feel everything all at once, as if a wave came along and swept me under the current and out to sea. I'm drowning, silently drifting away, until a voice whispers, "Is this seat taken?"

CHAPTER FORTY-SIX

She's wearing a little black dress with long sleeves and straps that cross her upper back. Her hair falls in dark curls around her shoulders. Even from behind, she's beautiful.

I don't know how many minutes I stayed frozen in that doorway before approaching her. But it was long enough for my heart to break three times. Once at the sound of her voice in the otherwise silent room. The second, at the touch of her hand on an empty chair. And finally, at the sight of her sobbing into open hands. Whether I could've made different choices and changed Dean's fate is irrelevant. She doesn't deserve to know emptiness like this.

Her thick lashes drip blotches of ink down her cheeks like a midnight watercolor painting when she looks up at me.

"Reed?" She squints. I don't blame her for not believing it's me. In fact, I deserve a harsher reaction.

"I'd like to take this seat if that's okay with you," I say.

She nods, so I sit down beside her.

"It looks nice in here." The sun filters through stained-glass windows. I haven't spent much time in churches, but this is exactly how I pictured it: full of light.

"It feels like it's missing something," she says with a whimper. I reach over and brush away her tears with the pad of my thumb.

"Do you think it gets easier saying goodbye to someone you love if you do it enough times?" she asks.

"I'm not sure I'm the right person to ask. When I lose someone, I go too. I find somewhere else where I'm not reminded of their loss at every turn. If I'm somewhere new, I convince myself I don't have to feel the gaping hole in my life."

She reaches over and touches my chest. It's comforting, her touch. So comforting that I could let myself get lost in it. I could close my eyes and let her hands ghost over my skin. Every part of me would feel safe in that sensation. And while it would be just as easy to run away, I promised Dean I would make the hard choice. I'm going to finally live up to that for once.

So I don't touch her back. Not yet.

"I'm so sorry I left without saying anything. I'd convinced myself it would be better for the both of us if I went somewhere else. But nothing's right without you. I want to fill all the empty seats in your life. The one at your kitchen table and on your front porch. Especially this one today."

She hesitates, studying her clasped hands in her lap. "Does this mean you're staying?" Her eyes drag a path up my chest to my face. "I've never asked you that. It seemed selfish, expecting you to choose my hometown. But I just don't see myself leaving here now that I'm finally getting to know my dad."

I pull away so I can look into her beautiful brown eyes and she'll see that I mean it. "It's the people, not the place for me."

I think of that waitress from the diner. Hailey's my *Someone I love*, my *Reason for everything*.

"And your dad is a great guy, Red. You deserve to know him."

I didn't think I'd be able to keep Jack's promise. That it

would feel like I was hiding something from her. But I see now that they need this clean slate. There's nothing notable anymore about the one night we spent together way back when. For so long that camping trip seemed like a thorn in my life. But with forgiveness, I've finally let it go. I'll let Jack tell her in his own time if he ever wants to.

"And I promised to take my time with you, remember? I haven't gotten to do that yet. I'm staying if you'll let me."

"I love you," she says as she melts against my chest, her palm falling forward to catch herself. It rests on my seat. The one I plan to fill for the rest of her life.

CHAPTER FORTY-SEVEN

"Rookie! You came back," a sloshed Daniels says. He has to stand on his tiptoes to shake Reed by the shoulder, and he sways forward a bit when he does it.

"You shaved your mustache," Reed comments.

"I told you guys not to go to the pub," I whine. They smell worse than they look.

"There's not a lot to do around here," Evans drawls next to him.

"You guys spent an entire summer in the woods and you're telling me there's nothing better you could have come up with than this?" I ask.

"We'll be on our best behavior," Marshall breathes out, bending his right arm at a ninety-degree angle and holding up three fingers. "Scouts honor."

"We promise." Murphy winks at me as he scrapes his fingers down his beard.

"I'm holding you to it!" I warn them all with a finger while my attention lasers in on the stream of Dean's relatives trickling in and filling the chapel pews. As the line starts to slow, a woman in black stiletto heels and a pair of sunglasses scans the crowd while hugging the door frame. Just like every other guy at my high school, including Dean, I can pick her out in a crowd. I keep my posture poised as I approach her rather than becoming the barreling ball of furry I want to be.

"What the hell are you doing here?" I whisper-shout, backing her into the foyer and out of the chapel entrance.

Madison lowers her glasses down the bridge of her nose, revealing puffy red rings around her blue eyes.

Good, she's been crying. She should feel guilty.

"I... didn't get to say goodbye." Her bottom lip wobbles, and if it were any other person in this church right now, I'd lean in, wrap my arms around them, and comfort them through their pain. But it's the girl who let him die with a broken heart. That lip could fall off from all of its quivering for all I care.

"You said goodbye to him the moment you slipped into someone else's arms," I remind her.

A rush of energy jolts through my body. It feels good, liberating even, to stand up to her for the first time.

"Hailey... I..." She tries to touch my arm, like that gesture alone will make me forget her actions. Not just her infidelity but the way she's dismissed *me* for years, pretending I never really existed unless it was important for appearances' sake to make it known.

"You know, you're right." I stop her from finishing whatever pathetic excuse she was about to come up with. "You should be here."

"Oh, thank you!" She gasps and grins like I just granted her access to Coachella without a pass.

"You should be in a church," I continue, "asking God for forgiveness."

I leave her in the foyer. I imagine a pair of glassy eyes watching the back of my head as I sit down next to the crew of guys who she could have gotten to know if she hadn't screwed things up with Dean. At least she didn't come with Ben. I've seen him once since we got back. Long enough for him to put in his notice and transfer back home to Arizona. It's probably for the best.

I hope she's surprised by me. When someone breaks your best friend's heart, you remind them of all the reasons why they never deserved a spot in their world in the first place.

The congregation now looks like a sea of black, something I hate the most about funerals.

The only discernible difference in the men sitting in the front row is their hair. Red, black, long, bald. Their shoulders are touching, and they've all found what looks to be matching suit jackets, probably from Pinned and Perfect on Third Street —the only place in this small town that rents any kind of formal wear. They look like a brotherhood. One I ran from for a very long time until I lived it for myself this summer. One I'm glad I belong to now.

I slip into the empty seat between my dad and Reed.

Reed places his warm palm on my knee. "Everything okay?"

"Yeah, just finding my voice," I say.

The small cleft that I've come to love brackets one side of his grin. Then he leans in until his lips are touching the shell of my ear, and he whispers, "You're really sexy when you're bossy."

A man older than the hills in a white dress shirt approaches the podium.

I blush and swat Reed's knee. "Pay attention." As I pull away, I lock eyes with the man sitting beside Reed. He's formally dressed like the last time I saw him, but there's no phone in sight.

"This is my dad, Emmett Morgan," he whispers. "Dad, this is Hailey Hart."

He extends his palm and shakes my hand.

"It's a pleasure to meet you, Hailey."

It's not until Reed smiles at his dad that I see it: warmth and vulnerability in his expression. A silent truce living between them, one that feels a lot like forgiveness.

"The pleasure is mine, Mr. Morgan," I say as the soft instrumental music quiets and the reverend begins to speak.

"The McCafferty family has been coming to my congregation since the day they moved to town." He fumbles in the chest pocket of his suit, pulling out a white handkerchief, and barks a gravelly cough into it.

"With five kids, they've always sat in the back. As the oldest child in the family, Dean was responsible for making sure his siblings stayed entertained during the service. He'd color with them, fold them paper airplanes they'd launch toward the congregation, and he'd let the littlest one sit on his lap so she could see over old Gladys's bouncy perm.

"He was a wonderful brother, but he also cared a lot about the world. Four years ago, he came to me with a decision he was deliberating on for his future. He started our conversation with a hundred questions that all asked the same thing: 'Reverend Michaels, will you please tell me what to do.' I never said much, I just let him do the talking. And by the time he was finished, Dean had made the decision to become the next wildland firefighter for the United States Forest Service.

"I didn't have to be a part of his crew"—he looks over at our row—"to know he made a difference in the world. He was loved enough to make an entire row of brawny men cry."

I look to my right and sure enough, Murphy is weeping into a black cloth and Ramirez is pursing his lips and dabbing at the corners of his eyes with his pinkies.

"He was a devoted son, a loyal friend, a gifted firefighter, and a remarkable son of God. At the gates of heaven, he is being welcomed home today. I'd like to invite those who wish to pay their respects to please come forward."

He descends the stage on wobbly legs and perches on the empty end of a bench to listen.

Dean's mom gets up first. She's calm and centered, something I've always admired about her, but also something I imagine a mother of five has to be. My eyes glass over as she relays all the ways in which she's grateful that Dean made her a mom. She thanks everyone for coming and glides gracefully back to her children.

Murphy gets the crowd belly-laughing with a story of Dean mistaking a mountain goat for a bear, and Ramirez recounts the time Dean got the entire crew to perform "Single Ladies" for him when his grandmother was diagnosed with cancer last fall.

When there's a quiet lull, I consider getting up there too, but decide against it. It felt more personal, keeping my thoughts to him private.

As the reverend braces to stand, I feel a soft squeeze on my knee. The seat next to me empties as Reed stands up.

CHAPTER FORTY-EIGHT

REED

If you're called something enough times, you start to believe it. For me, that's confident. Growing up as a middle child it was the only way I could ever be seen or heard, so I embodied it. It didn't matter if I felt like I was failing or falling apart on the inside, on the outside I was a cheetah, bold and brave. But right now, my hands are shaking against the top of a wooden podium, and my breath is seeping out of me in quivering pants. I don't know what compelled me to step up to this microphone, but I think it might have been a mistake.

It was obvious that the people who came up here before me are good with words and feelings. Take Dean's mom, for example. Her speech poured out of her like a cup of hot cocoa, warm and comforting. She didn't clear her throat and send a shower of static through a speaker from standing too close like me. She also spoke from the heart. Something that feels impossible for a guy who refuses to face his feelings. I would have been better off preparing something to say. But I didn't know I'd be getting up here.

There are sixteen rows of people watching me, and had this been tenth grade debate class when I delivered an epic George

Washington rebuttal, I'd have nailed it. My goal would be to make people laugh, not help people who are crying. What am I supposed to do now that I'm up here?

I have no choice but to open my mouth and speak.

"Since the day I met Dean McCafferty, he's been a royal pain in my ass. Sorry for the language, Reverend," I add as the man's cheeks turn bright pink.

A collective laugh bursts in the crowd, and the built-up tension in my body relaxes.

"He was ruthless when it came to doing the right thing, cocky as hell, and a total hardball in the face of a challenge," I continue.

More laughter, and this time, my mouth screws up into a smile. Without knowing it, these people are the ones comforting *me*.

"When I joined Iron Summit mid-season, I got stuck training with him on my first day. I remember thinking there's no *way* this lazy noodle makes a good squad leader. He was flopped on a stump eating a turkey sandwich, watching me sweat through every layer of clothes I had on."

Tears turn into smiles, laughter into medicine. Nerves still bounce around in my abdomen, but I stay put because there's something I really need to say and I can't leave this stage until I do.

"I judged him on the spot the same way a lot of people do with me. They think I'm the conceited jock or a player with women. They believe I'm Rex's attention-seeking younger brother or Ronny's cocky older one. They label me confident, reluctant to settle down, always chasing the next best thing. What they don't see is the guy who wants to work hard and to be understood. The one who longs for validation from his parents, his peers, and in his love life."

Gosh, this is getting embarrassing, but it also feels wildly freeing to admit, so I keep going.

"Dean saw those things in me. He may not have chosen me to be on the crew initially, but he chose to mentor me once I was. He taught me how to dig a cup trench... and fell a tree." My voice cracks as I try and fail to block the memory of him trapped beneath one. I haven't allowed myself to picture it until now. But I need to. This is the only way forward, letting it all in.

"Most of all, he taught me how to be vulnerable."

My lip quivers, and I swipe at a tear.

"It was the greatest gift I've ever been given getting to be his friend."

I don't know how people do this, face the onslaught of emotion. Luckily, I don't have to do it alone. There's a line of people I love ready to hug me as I descend the stage steps. Hailey's first, and then my dad. Jack leans in and tells me it's going to be okay. Coming from him, I know that has to be possible. We may not get to choose who we love and lose, but there's no greater way forward than with these people by my side.

When the service ends, we circle his casket. It's hard to believe it holds anything more than Kleenex with seventeen pallbearers carrying it. We transport him out of that chapel and to a shady grove of trees. It's there, surrounded by my new family, I finally admit to myself... *the fire changed me.*

It was because of Dean that I let it.

CHAPTER FORTY-NINE

The Hopper is empty for seven o'clock on a Friday night, but it's perfect. It feels like we have the place all to ourselves.

"Now this is my kind of celebration of life," Daniels says, back in his pair of overalls.

When the bartender slides a tray of tequila shots to the edge of the oak countertop, he picks the first one up, holding it high in the air.

"To White Horse." He toasts over the end of a newscast report on the tavern's TV updating the full containment of the fire.

Every member of the crew clinks their glass together before downing their drink.

"To Dean," Jackson toasts next, and this time I step in.

"Greatest friend we've ever known," I add.

"Cheers," they all say as we tip the alcohol down our throats. It's been a minute since I've shot straight tequila and I cough as it goes down.

"To Murphy," my dad says next, and everyone flashes him a confused look.

Murphy's burly beard drops in a larger-than-life smile.

He's in on this. I don't have the faintest idea what my dad's going to say.

My dad catches my eye and shocks the room with, "Your new superintendent."

Everyone but me peers in Murphy's direction.

"Did you know about this?" I hear Ramirez ask Murphy as I silently question my dad: *How long have* you *known about this?*

"This old body needs to work eight to five, no weekends. I'm the new Forest Service Commander. Just got the job this morning. And I'm going to get to know my daughter."

Keep it together, Hailey. I've cried enough today to fill an ocean. But *this.* This is what starting over looks like.

He grips both of my shoulders with his palms. "Hayes, I wasn't around like I should have been. I'm hoping you meant it when you said I wasn't too late."

I wrap my arms around his middle, and the entire crew chants with boisterous applause. "Hart, Hart, Hart, Hart."

"One more thing," he whispers in my ear before he pulls back and reaches for another shot glass.

"To Morgan."

Reed's smile slips as he tries to read my dad's face.

"I was right about you," he says, stepping toward him. "Dean was too. You started as a rookie on this crew, but now"—he holds his hand out to shake Reed's—"you're the Alpha Squad Leader of Iron Summit."

Reed stares at him with a dumbfounded look. I can tell he's questioning if he heard him correctly.

"With all due respect, Supt, there are guys who've been on this crew—"

He stops him with a hand to the chest.

"We took a vote, Reed. It was unanimous."

Murphy places a hand on Reed's shoulder. "Congratulations, rookie. You graduated from kindergarten."

There's an old wooden jukebox in the corner of The Hopper. Ramirez has hand-selected "The Best" by Tina Turner to blast through the speakers. One by one, he pulls each member of the crew onto the dance floor.

"What do you say, Red. You want to dance with me?"

"I don't know, does an alpha squad leader have two left feet?" I ask.

He scrunches up his nose, shaking his head. "I have two right ones."

He yanks me by the arm beneath the dim lights and the room spins. I don't know if it's the circles he's twirling me in that's making me dizzy or just him. Being with him is a rollercoaster ride. You never get the chance to catch your breath.

"So, what now?" he asks, pressing his hips against mine and swaying in time with the music. "Do we start over too?"

I'd like to tell him to get me out of here and take me home. Instead, I shake my head and say, "No." I don't want to start over when our beginning has been my favorite part. "We pick up right where we left—"

He dips me backward, cutting off my answer, and I squeal. When he rights me, his hand splays across my lower back, pressing me into his chest.

"Which was where, exactly?" he whispers against my lips.

"Which was right"—I lean in closer—"about"—graze our noses together—"here."

When our lips finally touch, I don't feel alone anymore.

EPILOGUE

Reed
6 years later...

My beautiful wife presses her side against the living room windowpane. A fresh coat of hunter-green paint frames the glass overlooking the side of the yard closest to the lake. Her jeans hug her thighs, and her hair is woven into a tight braid just how I like it. I sneak up behind her, gripping her hips and nuzzling my nose into the spot behind her ear that makes her hum. She snakes her arm around my neck and I wrap mine around her waist.

"What are we watching?" I draw my attention to the overgrown pine tree a few yards from the edge of the water. Two little sundrenched feet sail toward the sky.

"He's so good with her, isn't he?" she croons.

I can see the faint reflection of Hailey's wistful smile through the window as a happy little sigh escapes her lips—a sound I bottled up and tucked away in my heart a long time ago.

"He is," I agree.

The tiny squeak of a voice melts its way through the glass. "Papa, push me higher! You're going too soft."

Our daughter's long chestnut hair fans against layers of lime green sparkly tulle.

"It's my job to keep you safe, Jo," Jack reminds her.

"But *Paaapaa*," she whines, "I'm not Jo today, remember? You're supposed to call me Tinkerbell, because look at me... I can fly!" She stretches her arms out wide, my brave girl. I'd like to think she gets that from me.

"Oh shoot, you're right. How could I forget," he says in an exasperated voice, smacking his forehead.

She giggles and turns around to look at him.

"That's what old people do. They forget sometimes."

"Hey, you take that back, young lady." He tickles her gently under her armpits, and she squirms against the rope.

"Never!" She giggles again.

Hailey sighs.

"What's on your mind, Red?" I tuck my chin on top of her head.

"I was just thinking how far we've come."

She stares at Jack as he slows the swing and lifts Jo down, holding her hand as she skips across the yard toward the cabin.

"Do you still wish you'd had moments like that with him?" I ask.

It comes from a place of knowing that once upon a time she didn't always feel okay. A time when he made her feel anxious instead of safe like he does now.

Hailey shakes her head. "Why would I when I have something"—she squats down and swings her arms wide as Jo barrels through the front door—"even better." She winds our four-year-old's hair around her hand and wraps her up in her arms.

"Are you guys talking about my birfday?" Jo gasps.

We're still working on that "th" sound because I don't correct her when she says it wrong. I want to pretend those two letters never existed.

"Why do you ask?"

"Because it's in two weeks," she reminds us.

"No." I shake my head. "There's no way. Tinkerbell never gets older. She has to stay four forever."

Jo frowns. "I don't fink I like that part about being Tinkerbell very much."

"Good thing you can be whatever you want to be, Josephine McCafferty Morgan," Jack says.

"Daddy, do you promise you'll be back for birfday cake?"

Jack rests a palm on my back. "He wouldn't miss it, right, rookie?"

He gives me a fatherly look of pride.

I crouch down low so I can look Jo in the eyes as I say it. "Not for the world." She wraps her little arms around my neck and squeezes. I fake wheeze for air because it makes her laugh.

Hailey leans in and kisses me. Then she says my three favorite words: "I love you."

"Remember me, Red." I swat her butt then tip my helmet to Jack. "Superintendent."

"Make us proud out there."

Whenever he says "us," I know it means more than just the people in this room. I did three more years with Iron Summit before I got a spot as a smokejumper. I promised Hailey the day we got married beneath the pine trees on the shore of Payette Lake that I'd be around, for her, for our daughter. So, I go and do what I love, but then I come back to this cabin, Hailey's childhood home, to be with the people that I love.

"I'll be back by the time everyone arrives," I tell Jo. She's the one who has the hardest time with me being gone.

"Yay! Mo and Bo will be here! And Aunt Karen, too," Jo says, bouncing up and down.

"Yes, they will!" I say confidently.

Both of our parents show up now for Jo in a way they never really did for us. But that's the beauty of second chances.

"See you all soon," I say, before slipping out the front door.

It's harder now to do the daredevil things I once loved. There are two beautiful girls on the other side of every decision I make—a constant voice in the back of my mind reminding me to stay safe for them, to come home to them.

Two posts with a pavilion roof welcome me to the McCall Smokejumper Base, and just as I do every time I come to work, I haul my gear slung over my shoulder to the locker room.

"What are you doing?" Murphy asks to the rectangular door next to mine. His phone is pressed to his ear as he unloads his gear inside of it.

He's the only one from our original crew who stuck with fire. I think of the guys, and while I miss them, we still get together from time to time.

We've watched Daniels purchase land like he always said he would. He grew his mustache back and gets to wear those damn overalls he loves every day. It turns out they look pretty good on a potato farmer.

We've gotten the privilege of seeing Evans model for *GQ* and give him crap all the time for it. Except for Christmas, when he gifts us all a generous supply of Hanes briefs.

We sat in the audience of Marshall's graduation from Harvard. He works for NASA now as a mechanical engineer.

And we all showed up with "It's a boy!" balloons the day Jackson became a dad.

I'm proud of how far we've come. Especially Murphy. Coming out couldn't have been easy, but he did it for Ramirez.

"We're not getting a damn cat! Drop it," he barks into the speaker. He gives me a disgruntled nod before closing his locker door. "I love you too, baby," he coos, and ends the call.

"Trouble in paradise?" I tease him.

"That man thinks we need something to nurture. I told him to go get himself a house plant."

"Happy wife, happy life is my motto," I say.

"And what should that make mine? Happy spouse, happy house?"

I snicker. "It makes you the happy owner of a cat."

There's a moment of this job I like the most: right after I jump. For a minute and thirty seconds I'm suspended in the air, floating in the sky. It's silent when I think of them.

I've learned some people come into your life for a season, filling your world with change you hardly notice until it's slipping through your fingers like the last days of the summer sun. There will always be a part of me that sees Teddy and Miles in the glimmer of lake water. They shaped my earliest experiences of life and friendship, and saying goodbye to them was devastating. But now I look back with such fondness. A season that taught me how to love and let go.

Other people come into your life for a reason, teaching you things you'd never learn on your own. I'll never not see Dean McCafferty's face in the backcountry fire that sweeps across the ground. He lives and breathes out here, my constant companion in the trees.

And sometimes, with a stroke of luck or fate or however you'd describe the magic of serendipity when someone steps into your world at the exact turning point you need them to, you find the people who are there for a lifetime. They're your parachute. The ones you hang on to in good times and bad. Because, like a wildfire, *life* can change in a second. And they'll be the ones who carry you home.

THE END

ALSO BY MEAGAN WILLIAMSON

If I Never Remember

I Don't Want to Be – Gavin Degraw
In the Stars – Benson Boone
Bennie and the Jets – Elton John
Starting Over – Chris Stapleton
White Horse – Chris Stapleton
Born for This - The Score
Sunshine – One Republic
You Should Probably Leave – Chris Stapleton
Lose Control - Teddy Swims
Play with Fire – Sam Tinnesz
Beautiful Disaster – Jon McLaughlin
Never Let Me Go – Florence & the Machine
Something in the Orange – Zach Bryan
Love the Hell Out of You – Lewis Capaldi
Dare you to Move – Switchfoot
Save You a Seat – Alex Warren
A Drop in the Ocean – Ron Pope
Forever and a Day – Benson Boone

- Listen on Spotify -

ACKNOWLEDGMENTS

If I thought it was surreal writing a love letter to all the people that made publishing my first book possible, doing it a second time is even more so. Somehow I've swindled an amazing team into believing in my work enough to come back again. Old and new, I couldn't have done it without the following incredible people:

Shayne, when I first dove into the research for this book, I was drowning in jargon. I couldn't figure out how the hell I'd ever be able to do this industry justice without actually living it. It was intimidating and daunting until I reached out to you. You brought wildland firefighting to life in a way Google never could. I admire the many years you dedicated in service to this career. I'm in awe of your bravery and strength and appreciate every piece of insider knowledge you shared with me. Learning from you became my favorite part. And if there happens to be a mistake anywhere in these pages, I take full responsibility!!!

Britt, somehow you take the words I send you and fairy-godmother them into nothing short of magic. I admire your attention to detail and your willingness to keep my voice woven in my words while also making them the best version they can be. Let's do this again, yeah?

Nysha, I send you an idea and you turn it into a work of art. They say don't judge a book by its cover... well, not unless it's been done by the queen herself! Thank you for sharing your talent in this book series.

Mom, Abigail, Kiersten, and Alli, your honest beta reader

feedback evolved this story into what it is today. I'm grateful for your advice and the unique talents that each one of you brought to the table. Your unhinged comments and gushing excitement made me smile my way through the editing trenches. I love you all!

To my extended family and friends, in small and mighty ways, you showed up for me when I needed it most. It's not always easy being a work-from-home mom, but it's possible because of your meals, childcare, words of wisdom, and loving support.

To the first person who reads everything that I write. The one who recognizes my beige flags I unintentionally weave into characters and finds it endearing. To the guy who lies awake with me at night and dreams of the places this career could take us. I owe it all to you. With you is my favorite place to be. And to our children... there's no role I cherish more than being your mom. I love you more than all the words could ever say.

To the local and online bookshops, book clubs, bookstagrammers, and readers who have taken a chance on my books, THANK YOU! You are the wings beneath my words, taking them to new places I couldn't reach on my own. In a world where we often feel more different than the same, together we're finding common ground in stories. We're making books a love language. And I'm not sure there's anything more beautiful than that.

ABOUT THE AUTHOR

MEAGAN WILLIAMSON lives in Meridian, Idaho with her husband and three children. As a former teacher turned romance author, she spends her days writing and dreaming of sharing the kind of love stories that stay with you long after the last page. She loves spending time outside, celebrating holidays, and country music turned way up.

https://www.authormeaganwilliamson.com/

www.ingramcontent.com/pod-product-compliance
Lightning Source LLC
Chambersburg PA
CBHW022017310726
48972CB00006B/1694